"Hey, t
you?"

He spoke with such affected nonchalance, the nape hairs of both Grant and Brigid instantly tingled. They knew from years of experience that the stranger the circumstances, the more casual Kane pretended to be.

A huge round pit occupied most of the floor space, but it wasn't very deep, perhaps only six feet. When the outlanders saw what lay at the bottom, they experienced shuddery sensations of dread, realizing that the cavern contained far darker secrets than failed time-manipulation experiments from the twentieth century.

Deeply engraved into the rock floor was a vast geometric design, a complex series of interlocking cuneiform glyphs that formed a dizzying spiral of concentric rings a hundred meters or more in diameter.

For a second time, Kane murmured softly, blandly, "Huh."

Other titles in this series:

James Axler
Outlanders®

SATAN'S SEED

A GOLD EAGLE BOOK FROM
WORLDWIDE.®

TORONTO • NEW YORK • LONDON
AMSTERDAM • PARIS • SYDNEY • HAMBURG
STOCKHOLM • ATHENS • TOKYO • MILAN
MADRID • WARSAW • BUDAPEST • AUCKLAND

First edition August 2007

ISBN-13: 978-0-373-63855-0
ISBN-10: 0-373-63855-8

SATAN'S SEED

Copyright © 2007 by Worldwide Library.

Special thanks to Mark Ellis for his contribution to
the Outlanders concept, developed for Gold Eagle.

Printed in U.S.A.

We have nothing with the outcast and the unfit:
let them die in their misery. For they feel not.
Compassion is the vice of kings: stamp down
the wretched and the weak: this is the law of the
strong: this is our law and the joy of the world.
　　—Aleister Crowley, 1904

The Road to Outlands—
From Secret Government Files to the Future

Almost two hundred years after the global holocaust, Kane, a former Magistrate of Cobaltville, often thought the world had been lucky to survive at all after a nuclear device detonated in the Russian embassy in Washington, D.C. The aftermath— forever known as skydark—reshaped continents and turned civilization into ashes.

Nearly depopulated, America became the Deathlands— poisoned by radiation, home to chaos and mutated life forms. Feudal rule reappeared in the form of baronies, while remote outposts clung to a brutish existence.

What eventually helped shape this wasteland were the redoubts, the secret preholocaust military installations with stores of weapons, and the home of gateways, the locational matter-transfer facilities. Some of the redoubts hid clues that had once fed wild theories of government cover-ups and alien visitations.

Rearmed from redoubt stockpiles, the barons consolidated their power and reclaimed technology for the villes. Their power, supported by some invisible authority, extended beyond their fortified walls to what was now called the Outlands. It was here that the rootstock of humanity survived, living with hellzones and chemical storms, hounded by Magistrates.

In the villes, rigid laws were enforced—to atone for the sins of the past and prepare the way for a better future. That was the barons' public credo and their right-to-rule.

Kane, along with friend and fellow Magistrate Grant, had upheld that claim until a fateful Outlands expedition. A displaced piece of technology…a question to a keeper of the archives…a vague clue about alien masters—and their world shifted radically. Suddenly, Brigid Baptiste, the archivist, faced summary execution, and Grant a quick termination. For

Kane there was forgiveness if he pledged his unquestioning allegiance to Baron Cobalt and his unknown masters and abandoned his friends.

But that allegiance would make him support a mysterious and alien power and deny loyalty and friends. Then what else was there?

Kane had been brought up solely to serve the ville. Brigid's only link with her family was her mother's red-gold hair, green eyes and supple form. Grant's clues to his lineage were his ebony skin and powerful physique. But Domi, she of the white hair, was an Outlander pressed into sexual servitude in Cobaltville. She at least knew her roots and was a reminder to the exiles that the outcasts belonged in the human family.

Parents, friends, community—the very rootedness of humanity was denied. With no continuity, there was no forward momentum to the future. And that was the crux— when Kane began to wonder if there *was* a future.

For Kane, it wouldn't do. So the only way was out— way, way out.

After their escape, they found shelter at the forgotten Cerberus redoubt headed by Lakesh, a scientist, Cobaltville's head archivist, and secret opponent of the barons.

With their past turned into a lie, their future threatened, only one thing was left to give meaning to the outcasts. The hunger for freedom, the will to resist the hostile influences. And perhaps, by opposing, end them.

Prologue

Gerlachov Peak, Slovakia, 1946

Aleister Crowley waited for the end of his last day in the twentieth century. He hoped he would not live to see the sun set behind the Carpathians again.

He struggled across the wooden ramp to the mouth of the cave and stood on the ledge, shivering in the frigid wind. The thermometer attached to the rock wall showed the temperature as very close to zero—cold for this time of year, even at such an altitude.

The terrain spreading beneath and beyond the wide shelf of rock was a stunning sight. The snow-covered slopes, hell-deep passes and rocky ramparts stretched almost to the limit of Crowley's vision, then dropped away at the border of Moldavia.

The land surrounding the highest mountain peak in the Tatra Range was almost always locked in the embrace of ice and snow. Not even the whalebone-tough Szganys braved the mountain crests, and so Gerlachov Peak made a perfect staging area.

Crowley refused to refer to the cave as a refuge or a hideout or even a sanctuary. Those weak words led to defeatist thoughts, which he did not permit, not in himself nor in any member of the Brotherhood of the Black Sun.

Shielding his eyes with a gloved hand, he scanned the darkening sky. The setting sun peered out from behind the thick fleece of cloud cover, painting a brilliant scarlet streak over the distant thunderheads. Within half an hour, full night would settle over the mountain passes, and the procedure, the ritual, could not be initiated without the presence of Countess Paula von Schiksel and her package.

In the sky he glimpsed the dark dragonfly shape of an autogyro, lancing swiftly toward the broad ledge projecting from the mouth of the cave. Crowley figured the countess was even now radioing in her arrival instructions.

Almost as soon as the thought registered, a contingent of troopers marched up the ramp, passing him without a word as they assumed positions around the edges of the concrete landing pad. The men wore modified SS officers' uniforms, and beneath the peaked caps their faces were completely concealed by tight black balaclavas, their eyes covered by goggles with tinted lenses. Insignia patches sewn on the right sleeves of their jackets displayed a jet-black disk against a bloodred background. Nine thin lines, stylized representations of sun beams, radiated from equidistant points around the disk.

Crowley, resplendent in his voluminous uniform of indigo, bright red and orange silks and a high-crested headpiece, scowled resentfully at the reception committee. He felt the high altitude pulling at his ponderous flesh, exaggerating his massive weight, adding to his many physical woes, not least of which was his gnawing need for another four percent solution of sugar water and heroin.

Seeing the men in the full dress uniform of Black Sun troopers brought to mind a swarm of midnight-colored praying mantises, poised to pounce on any prey that might come flitting by.

Swallowing a curse, Crowley stamped on the ground, feeling the cold seep into the marrow of his bones and settle in his arthritic joints. Rolls of fat jiggled beneath his tunic. Heavy pendants of flesh drooped on either side of his pockmarked nose. His obsidian eyes, the irises completely surrounded by the red-netted whites, glittered with impatience.

Engine growling, the autogyro hovered over the concrete slab, listing from side to side. The rotor wash churned up snowflakes that eddied in loose, detached clouds. Crowley winced when tiny splinters of ice stung his face. The aircraft slowly settled on the pad, and troopers hurried out to secure the wheels to eyebolts sunk deep into the concrete.

The propeller and the overhead rotor blades stopped spinning. The canopy of the autogyro slid back and the delegation of troopers scurried to arrange themselves in stiff, formal postures. It was obvious from their manner that if a brass band had been present, it would have been playing "God Save the Queen," or more appropriately, *Deustchland Uber Alles*.

Crowley tried to appear properly respectful despite his physical misery. As the liaison between the Ordo Templi Orientis and the Brotherhood of the Black Sun, he preferred to have other people come to him, letting intermediaries handle menial tasks such as meeting dignitaries. But the intermingled affairs of the OTO and the brotherhood had reached a stage too crucial for the delegating of authority.

If the chronoscopic transtemporal dilator actually accomplished what both Lam and the Third Reich's scientists claimed, then it was worth losing a few extremities to frostbite to ensure continued cooperation.

Before climbing out of the autogyro, Countess Paula von Schiksel handed down a blanket-wrapped bundle to one of the black-visaged troopers. Cradling it in his arms, the soldier hurried past Crowley into the cave. He heard a faint whimper from beneath the folds of fabric and caught an errant whiff of chloroform. The other troopers thrust out their stiff right arms in the old Nazi salute.

The countess stood upon the wing, deliberately striking a pose with one hand planted against an ample hip as if she were the subject of a cover story for *Look* magazine.

She wore a leather aviator's cap, the smoke-gray lenses of the goggles concealing her hard blue eyes. She was tall, at least five feet ten inches, and the fur-collared flight jacket did little to conceal her voluptuous figure, nor did the tight red slacks tucked into calf-high boots.

Lithely, she leaped down from the wing and strode across the landing pad, walking with a she-tiger's arrogance that stopped just short of being a swagger. She was the kind of woman whose every movement evoked male fascination.

As the countess approached Crowley, she stripped off the aviator's cap, shaking loose her heavy, wheat-white hair. From her belt she removed a two-foot-long riding crop, which she tapped against her right leg as she walked. The small whip should have looked like a ridiculously superfluous accessory, but it didn't and Crowley wasn't sure why. Perhaps the confidence, the complete self-assurance the countess exuded as she walked across the landing pad had something to do with it.

Crowley felt a tiny quiver in his throat and elsewhere

at her proximity. Rarely had he seen a woman more beautiful, yet he knew she was untouchable, a creature of great power, remote from the touch of men.

Crowley inclined his head toward her. "Countess. You're late."

A darkness clouded the woman's Viking eyes, her bright red lips pursing in disapproval. Crowley had spoken in English, and she replied in the same language, made harsh and metallic by her Teutonic pronunciation. "Have you never traveled with a child, even one who is drugged? It is no pleasure cruise along the Danube, let me assure you."

Recalling the cross-country trips taken with his own children, Crowley declined to address her comment. "The power reserves are down by eight percent. If they drop by twelve—"

"Then we recharge the batteries," she interrupted sharply, stalking past him into the cave.

"According to Rukh, that would take three months."

The countess snorted. "He is a nervous old biddy."

As she passed a trooper, she took from him an offered Gestapo cap with silver officer's braid and a skull-and-crossbones insignia positioned over the hard black visor. She paused to settle it on her head at a rakish angle, then shrugged out of her leather jacket, handing it to the soldier. Beneath it she wore a tight tunic of bloodred satin tailored to conform to the thrust of her full breasts. It was cinched tight at the waist by a knotted black sash.

The countess continued walking and Crowley hurried to catch up to her, grimacing at the needles of pain stabbing through his arthritic ankles.

"He has every reason to be nervous," he declared angrily. "This is a totally new kind of technology we're dealing with."

"*Ja, ja,*" she said dismissively. "A mixture of science and your so-called magic. I've heard it all before, Herr Crowley, back when you were working for both the Allies and the reich, hoping to arrange world affairs so they would destroy each other, leaving you sitting in, as the Americans say, the fabled catbird seat."

Crowley decided to drop the subject. Just being in such close proximity to the Scarlet Queen caused him to shake with a tremor. She was radiantly, exquisitely beautiful. Looking at her, he found it hard to believe she was capable of the most inhuman, cold-blooded acts.

But he knew from experience that her capacity for cruelty was beyond all dimension. A lust for power ruled Countess Paula von Schiksel, a lust she had satiated all during the war with her personal information network, gaining information by torture, blackmail and murder. Crowley worshiped her.

A low-ceiling stone passageway stretched out before them. Naked lightbulbs inset into the roof shed a cold illumination that glinted off frost-coated mineral deposits imbedded in the rough walls. Broken chunks of ice littered the path and proved hazardous to walking.

The tunnel did not feel appreciably warmer than the ledge, but once away from the frigid bite of the wind, the pain in Crowley's joints began to ease.

Countess von Schiksel halted before a heavy metal slab of a door. She rapped on it sharply and the panel quivered, then slid aside with a prolonged squeal. Beyond it, over the threshold, stretched a long white corridor bathed in pale blue light. A faint resonance, a thready pulse of vibration tickled Crowley's eardrums.

A steady, high-pitched drone underscored the heavy throb of machinery and the roar of turbines. They smelled the astringent odor of hot metal and the nostril-stinging reek of burning oil. A cadaverous man stood in the doorway. An upstanding shock of stiff gray hair rose above his gaunt face. He wore a white laboratory smock, the collar buttoned high on his wattled neck. His rheumy blue eyes appeared huge, magnified behind the thick lenses of round-rimmed spectacles. Crowley thought the man looked absurd, like Boris Karloff from *The Invisible Ray*.

In his hands, thick knuckled and gnarled like old tree roots, he held a clipboard. "Good evening," Janos Rukh said in sarcastic but heavily accented English. "I'm glad you could make it."

The countess ignored him, sweeping past the man into the corridor. Crowley followed, squeezing his bulk through the narrow doorway. Apparently not offended by the woman's show of contempt, Rukh addressed Crowley.

"You realize, of course," the scientist said, "that once we open the portal, there can be no delay. We have no idea how long the power grid can maintain the event horizon, so we must be prepared to move swiftly and decisively. The troops must be ready."

Countess von Schiksel cast a scornful glance over her shoulder. "My troops are not the ones who will have problems moving swiftly. They are not arthritic *or* fat old drug addicts."

"I'm thinking of the girl," Rukh snapped.

The countess kept striding along the corridor, her boot heels clacking loudly against the concrete floor. "I will make sure Tshaya moves with the proper alacrity at the proper time, Dr. Rukh. Make no mistake about that."

The corridor ended in a vast space, but it seemed small because it was filled with the dark bulk of huge machines, every piece of which seemed to rattle, clank and roar—grinding gear wheels, arcs of electricity and whistling jets of steam. Convection currents danced like translucent, crackling veils from the forks of tall, Y-shaped induction pylons.

The mechanical cacophony assaulted their ears, and the stench of hot diesel fuel was cloying. Even over the deafening racket and machine rumble, they felt rather than heard a rhythmic wave of invisible energy, like a subsonic drumbeat throbbing to the marrow of their bones.

Positioned between two of the machines was a massive generator. More than twelve feet tall, it resembled two solid black cubes, a slightly smaller one balanced atop the other. The top cube rotated slowly, producing a steady drone.

A dozen yards opposite the generator, the floor dropped away, forming a vast pit of absolute, impenetrable blackness. The pool of darkness stretched from wall to wall, measuring at least a hundred yards in diameter. The domed roof formed a cap over the perfectly round hole that fell away to unguessable depths. The pit looked like a disk of solid obsidian, reflecting no light whatsoever cast by the bright halogen tripod-mounted spotlights around the rim.

The pit was blacker than anything in Crowley's experience, so black that his eyes refused to encompass it except as an utter emptiness.

Gazing at the yawning black abyss, Crowley quoted Friedrich Nietzsche under his breath: "'When you look into an abyss, the abyss also looks into you.'"

The abyss and the double-tiered generator had been

inside the mountain for many thousands of years, the source of legends and myths among the Slovaks, the Roma and the local Szganys. Their purpose had remained a mystery until a year ago, shortly after Germany's surrender.

Lam had imparted the true nature of the *Schwarze Sonne* to Crowley, but only a handful of the reich's scientists understood the basic principles of the generator, much less the operating mechanics of the power systems. Janos Rukh was one of the few, a fact he had no reservations about flaunting.

Rukh strode toward the control console chairs. Tshaya and her brother, Heranda, reclined in them. Even if Crowley hadn't known the pair of eight-year-old children were twins, their jet-black hair and bold-nosed features were almost identical.

A metal cagelike framework enclosed Heranda's head, needle-pointed electrodes piercing his skull to stimulate different areas of his brain. His face was completely blank, eyes taped shut, mouth slightly open.

Tshaya lay in the chair beside him, clasping his right hand. Her eyes were open, although Crowley wished they weren't. They were the most disquieting pair of eyes he had ever looked into, colored like moonstone, milkily translucent. They were blind eyes, but their magnetic stare held him nonetheless. Both children wore simple sleeveless shifts of white fabric and slippers.

Rukh glanced toward a machine behind the boy's chair, squinted at the lines inscribed on graph paper and grunted. "Good. His sister's presence seems to have calmed him. He is entering an alpha state. We can begin."

The countess eyed Crowley haughtily. "I have little faith in this procedure…but I trust you are aware of the price of failure?"

"Tshaya and Heranda were the best candidates Mengele and the Abnenurbe Foundation could find in the camps," Crowley retorted defiantly. "They are descended from a long line of mystics and seers."

Countess von Schiksel's lips worked as if she were on the verge of spitting. "Gypsy trash, that's all they are."

"Perhaps so," Crowley conceded. "But among their own tribe, their pedigree is impeccable, despite their physical disabilities."

"The tests were inconclusive," the countess argued, her voice rising. "We're operating strictly on guesswork, everything based on simulations."

Rukh said defensively, "We can't risk the children, the entire activation process, in another test. The part of their brains that act as interfaces with the chronoscope's focus conformals could be damaged."

He waved toward the generator. "That's why it is so important to act now, while the power reserves are at optimum."

The tall woman heaved a sigh seasoned with a German obscenity. From a jacket pocket she withdrew a silver whistle attached to a tiny chain. Placing it between her lips, she blew a long, shrill note that cut through even the mechanical racket.

With a loud tramping of boots and clinking of metal, four dozen Black Sun troopers jogged up the aisle between two machines. They arranged themselves in a semicircle at the rim of the pit. Unlike the soldiers who had met the countess outside, these troopers wore coal-scuttle helmets atop their masked, goggled heads.

They wore black jumpsuits, and thick flak vests encased their upper bodies. All of them carried long-barreled Schmeisser submachine guns at twenty-five-degree angles across their chests. Walther P-39 pistols were snugged into flapped holsters on their hips, and grenades hung from wide Sam Browne belts that crossed their torsos.

Hard blue eyes shining like those of a raptorial bird, Countess von Schiksel turned toward Rukh. "Begin!"

The white-haired scientist stepped to the control console and flipped a pair of toggle switches. Heranda stiffened in his chair as if he had received a jolt of electrical current. Tiny skeins of blue lightning played over the metal framework encasing his head.

The droning whine of the generator changed in pitch. Crowley felt his heart begin to pound painfully within his chest and for a wild instant he feared he was suffer-

ing another infarction. Resisting the impulse to grope
for his nitroglycerin pills in his pocket, he turned his
face to the pit of darkness. A tingling sensation began
at the base of his spine and he realized his increased
heart rate was due to the energy field spreading up from
the black pool. Two of the tripod-mounted spotlights exploded in a blaze of blue sparks.

The impenetrable surface of the pit seemed to shift
and swirl. It suddenly formed an elaborate mosaic pattern of black and white. Eyes wide and mouth dry, he
watched as a grid tracing, like white shadows against a
black background, stretched from edge to edge.

"Prima Materia," Crowley husked out hoarsely. "It
does exist."

Rukh shouted jubilantly, "Interface established! We
must act now! Crowley, get the girl! Crowley!"

With great effort, Crowley tore his gaze away from
the pool and strode quickly to the chair in which Tshaya
reclined. Carefully, he pried her small fingers away
from the hand of her brother and tugged her to her feet.
The girl did not resist, although she uttered a faint
whimper when separated from Heranda.

Holding her by the wrist, Crowley led Tshaya to the
rim of the pit and halted. He bent down and whispered
in her ear, even though he knew she was deaf, "Let
your instincts guide you on this journey, sweetness. Do
what thou wilt."

For a long moment, Tshaya did not move. Then, tentatively, as if she were testing the temperature of bath water, she extended one foot and touched a glowing white square with her toes.

A stream of fierce energy poured into Crowley's body through the child's hand. Crying out in alarm and pain, he released her, stumbling back a pace. Once free of his grasp, Tshaya did not hesitate. She stepped forward and down, crossing the white tracery of the pattern, walking with a graceful, single-minded deliberation to the center of the swirling mosaic.

Shaking his stinging fingers, Crowley stared as the undulating pattern seeped up over the little girl, adhering to the shape of her body like a layer of thin fabric. She stood motionless, laced with alternating stripes of deep black and coruscating white. The entire center of the grid bulged up and swirled around her. When it receded, Tshaya was gone; as if with the movement of the mosaic, she had shifted out of one world and into another.

Without looking behind him, eyes still fixed on the point of the pattern where the girl had vanished, Crowley shouted, "Countess! It is time! Order your men forward!"

When he heard no reply, Crowley glanced over his shoulder to see Countess Paula von Schiksel staring with eyes wide with shock. He shouted again, impatiently, "Countess! Do you hear me?"

The woman blinked, as if rousing herself from a deep slumber. In an unsteady voice, she announced loudly, "March forward!"

Aleister Crowley permitted himself a small smile of equal parts satisfaction, relief and anticipation. He did not know where his final day in the twentieth century would end, but at least he was on his way. Steepling his fingers beneath his chin, he whispered to the black pit, "Do as thou wilt."

Chapter 1

The Tatra Range, Slovakia, 2203

Kane watched the line of distant round lights gently bobbing. Despite the fur lining of his parka's hood, he heard the steady rumble of powerful engines.

Pushing the goggles up on his forehead, Kane raised a compact set of binoculars and peered through the eyepieces, sweeping them over the bleak, almost monochromatic terrain. The sky to the east showed the pastel colors of dawn. Shadows of the Carpathians and the pinnacle of the Gerlachov Peak acquired sharp outlines against the swiftly growing brightness.

Flurries blew in from the north, a melange of snow, ice and sleet flung by a polar wind across the rocky wilderness. Kane cursed through clenched teeth as the sharp-edged ice particles stung his exposed face. The wind fell as suddenly and as dramatically as it had risen, leaving a feathery swirl of wet snowflakes eddying through the air.

The weather for the past two centuries had always

been unpredictable, but usually summers even in the high altitudes eased into a few weeks of autumn. Here in mountainous Eastern Europe, summer plunged straight into winter without a pause, but at least he felt appropriately dressed. He wore several layers of clothing—thermal underwear, a sweater, a fur-lined parka and heavy Thermax pants. Specially designed snow boots encased his feet, and chemically warmed protective gauntlets covered his hands.

Beneath the outer layers he was clad in a one-piece black garment that fitted as tightly as doeskin gloves. The coverall was known as a shadow suit.

Although the suit did not appear as if it could offer protection from a mosquito bite, it was climate controlled for environments that reached highs of one hundred and fifty degrees and as cold as minus ten degrees Fahrenheit. Microfilaments controlled the internal temperature. Kane guessed the current, predawn temperature hovered around minus five.

Kane scraped frost from the ruby-coated lenses of his binoculars with a gloved forefinger, but the curtains of snow prevented a clear view of the convoy of vehicles. He knew they chugged overland from the direction of Gerlachov Peak, but the District Twelve intel provided by Major Zuryakin had informed him of that two days ago.

The transcomm in Kane's inner breast pocket

chirped. He reached inside his parka, twisting a knob on its surface. "Go ahead."

"We count five," said Major Illyana Zuryakin. "Five heavy-duty mil-spec vehicles. They appear to be armored and armed."

Kane grunted noncommittally, squinting toward the bobbing headlights.

"Does that trouble you, Kane?" Illyana Zuryakin spoke impeccable English and her mastery of subtle nuances, like sarcasm, was pitch-perfect, as well.

"Hell yes, it troubles me," Kane snapped. "The only reason I'm standing out here freezing my ass in the first place is because it troubles me. Any sign of personnel?"

"*Nyet*, but our intelligence indicated there are over a dozen well-armed men in the party, possibly more."

Kane refrained from commenting sourly on the relative trustworthiness of District Twelve intel. Instead, he said, "The Cerberus sat photo sweep picked up at least *two* dozen well-armed men."

"So?" The major's one-word retort was both a dismissal and a challenge.

"So," Kane replied inanely, "I'm just saying."

The trans-comm accurately conveyed the woman's sigh of exasperation. "Your liaison, Brigid Baptiste, was right."

Kane stiffened reflexively. "About what?"

"About what it was like working with you."

Kane didn't even bother to repress the irritation in his tone. "What's that supposed to mean?"

"You can ask herself when we rendezvous." Major Zuryakin's voice held a flinty edge. "Get the rest of your team together and meet us at the strike point. We haven't much time. Understood?"

Kane bit back a profane reply. "Understood."

Venting an impatient sigh, he peered through the binoculars again. Despite the fact that the snowfall was thinning, he still couldn't make out much of the convoy except shapes.

Tall and lean, long and rangy of limb, Kane resembled a wolf in the way he carried most of his muscle mass in his upper body. His thick dark hair, showing just enough chestnut highlights to keep it from being a true black, stirred in the chill breeze. A faint hairline scar stretched like a piece of white thread against the sun-bronzed, clean-shaved skin of his left cheek. His pale blue-gray eyes held the color of the cold dawn light on a sharp steel blade.

He gave the three-pound block of C-4 a final visual inspection, made sure the detonation cap was secure and glanced around at the tumbles of snow-layered stone. After reassuring himself for the third time that the demolition charge was planted in the right place, Kane turned away.

Below him, in an overhung niche, rose a copse of

snow-dusted pines. He picked his way down a steep, treacherous path toward the niche, avoiding thorn-bushes to the right and frost-sheathed outcroppings of granite on his left.

When he reached the tree line, he heard a faint rustle, and from the corner of his eye he glimpsed the snow-plastered bark of a pine shedding a white flurry. Automatically Kane fell into a crouch, stiffening his right wrist tendons. Sensitive actuators clicked and with a faint, brief drone of a tiny electric motor, the butt of his Sin Eater slapped into his hand.

The official side arm of the defunct Magistrate Divisions, the Sin Eater was strapped to a holster on his right forearm. The 9 mm autopistol had no safety or trigger guard, so when the firing stud came in contact with a crooked index finger, it fired immediately. However, Kane kept his finger extended and out of contact with the trigger stud.

For a crazed instant, he thought the tree was uprooting itself, tearing itself free of the frozen ground to clutch at him with skeletal branches. He sprang to one side, barely able to bite back a cry of alarm, raising the Sin Eater.

Gusting out a profanity, he lowered it almost immediately when he realized Domi, her white face and white parka forming a perfect camouflage, had stepped out from the hollow of the tree to meet him.

"For God's sake," he blurted, embarrassed and angry because of it. His breath formed a cloud of steam before his eyes. "Why didn't you say something?"

Her angular, hollow-cheeked face twisted in annoyed puzzlement. "Like what? You knew this was my position."

Domi's skin was as smoothly pale as porcelain. An albino by birth, the girl's bone-white hair was cropped short and spiky, her eyes the bright color of polished rubies.

Every inch of five feet tall, Domi barely weighed one hundred pounds, and at first glance she gave the impression of being waiflike. But there wasn't much of the waif about her compactly lithe body, what little of it could be discerned beneath her bulky cold-weather gear.

"Never mind," he snapped.

"You sure are getting jumpy in your old age," Domi observed cheerfully. "*And* grumpy."

Shoving the Sin Eater back into its holster, he retorted sarcastically, "With the kind of coworkers I have, I can't imagine why. Let's go."

The two people sidled through the close-growing trees to the edge of the road. Little more than a trench gouged through the snowfield, it tracked up and over a rise a quarter of a mile to the east. The sound of multiple engines steadily increased in volume.

"Still think this was a mistake," Domi declared, her

childlike voice sharp and petulant. "Letting Russkies run this op 'stead of our own people."

"Yeah, so you've said," Kane replied casually. "About twenty times since yesterday and thirty times the day before yesterday."

"Got our own specialists now," Domi said doggedly. "Don't need no stinkin' Russkies."

Kane blew out a steamy plume of breath in an exasperated sigh. "This is their territory, and they were already onto the Millennial Consortium before we arrived. So, yes, we *do* need those stinkin' Russkies."

"And they need us," interjected a deep, rumbling voice from behind them. "Just as much if not more."

Domi and Kane turned to see a big figure looming in the shadowy lee of a craggy overhang. Grant stood six-feet-five-inches tall in his thick-soled jump boots, and like Kane and Domi he wore a hooded white parka. The spread of his shoulders on either side of his thickly corded neck was very broad. Because his body was all knotted sinew and muscle covered by deep brown flesh, he did not look his weight of 250 pounds.

His short-cropped hair was touched with gray at the temples, but it did not show in the gunfighter's mustache that swept out fiercely around both sides of his tight-lipped mouth. He held a Copperhead close-assault subgun in his hands. Under two feet long, it looked like a toy within his grasp. Equipped with an extended magazine holding thirty-five 4.85 mm steel-jacketed rounds, the weapon possessed a 700-round-per-minute rate of fire. The grip and trigger unit were placed in front of the breech in the bullpup design, allowing for one-handed use.

An optical image intensifier scope and laser autotargeter were mounted on the top of the frame. Low recoil allowed the Copperhead to be fired in a long, devastating, full-auto burst that could empty the magazine in seconds.

As Grant stepped out from beneath the overhang, he said, "I'm not forgetting the way we were double-crossed the last time we worked with the Russians."

Grant's oblique reminders to events nearly five years before hadn't become as repetitious as Domi's complaints, but the big man's objections to teaming up with Major Zuryakin were hardly new.

"Sverdlovosk was a rogue District Twelve agent," Kane said. "We can't judge the entire organization by that bastard."

"Why not?" Grant challenged.

"It's too damn late for one thing," Kane shot back. "Besides, could you judge all of the Magistrate Divisions by me and you?"

When no response was forthcoming, Kane continued. "We've already agreed to let Zuryakin and her D-12 troops run the show. We pull out now, it's a shit-serious diplomatic screwup we'll never recover from. We're going to need their resources against the overlords."

Both Domi and Grant scowled at him but said nothing. They knew Kane spoke the truth, even if they didn't like it. Diplomacy, turning potential enemies into allies against the spreading reign of the overlords, had become the paramount tactic of Cerberus over the past couple of years.

Lessons in how to deal with foreign cultures and religions took the place of weapons instruction and other training. Over the past several years, Domi, Brigid Baptiste and former Cobaltville Magistrates Grant and Kane had tramped through jungles, ruined cities, over mountains, across deserts and they found strange cultures everywhere, often bizarre recreations of societies that had vanished long before the nuclear holocaust.

All the personnel of Cerberus, nearly half a world away atop a mountain peak in Montana, had devoted themselves to changing the nuke-scarred planet into something better. At least that was their earnest hope. To turn hope into reality meant respecting the often alien behavior patterns of a vast number of ancient religions, legends, myths and taboos.

With a resigned grunt, Grant said, "Let's get going. The trigger is set."

As he stepped away from the overhang, a pale thread

of violet light bisected a drift of powdery snow. The photoelectric cell affixed to a shelf of stone served as the trigger for a proximity detonator. An explosive charge had been planted high on the roadside as an insurance policy in case any of the convoy broke through the ambush.

As the three people slogged through the packed snow banked up on the side of the channel, Grant muttered sullenly, "You know, it was a lot easier when we shot whoever gave us the stink-eye without worrying about diplomacy."

"Yeah," Domi chirped with a crooked grin. "The good old days."

Kane understood and sympathized with his partner's discomfort even though the man was exaggerating their former methods of operation. He didn't trust the Russians, either. Until he, Grant and Brigid visited the country on their first official op for Cerberus, no one knew if the place even existed as a cohesive culture and nation.

Like most intercontinental locations, Russia was a big mystery—except to the Russians, who weren't providing information. The few scraps of intel that had leaked out since the atomic megacull of 2001 had to be assembled like a jigsaw puzzle with most of the pieces missing.

Moscow had been hit very hard, as had most of the

other Russian industrial cities. The entire country had suffered through skydark, the nuclear winter, like the rest of the nuke-ravaged planet, but because of its extreme northern latitudes, it was believed that for more than thirty years, temperatures rarely rose above ten degrees Fahrenheit. Speculation had it that more Russians died during skydark than during the actual holocaust.

When the Cerberus team arrived in the country nearly five years before, they learned the massive loss of life that came as an aftermath of the day-long war two centuries before was not a speculative matter. They had also been introduced, very unpleasantly, to District Twelve, the ultrasecret arm of Russia's internal security network.

Coming to a halt at the base of a snow-covered outcropping, Kane looked around, very aware of the growl of multiple engines floating above the crest of the rise. "Where the hell is everybody?" he muttered.

"Here."

Kane turned in the direction of Major Zuryakin's voice. The snow banked high on both sides of the road dislodged a dozen figures. The District Twelve operatives were attired in identical white snowsuits that covered them from head to toe, their faces concealed by white knit balaclavas. Their zippered pockets bulged with equipment, giving them a distinct resemblance to albino walruses.

Zuryakin had mentioned that all D-12 field troopers were trained to live rough—they carried no sleeping bags, and anything pertaining to their survival that couldn't be jammed into a pocket or a small haversack was abandoned. Each operative carried a black, very utilitarian AKSU subgun.

Major Zuryakin herself wasn't a particularly tall woman, but she was broadly built with chunky hips and thick thighs. Unmistakably unfeminine, her hair was cropped to little more than a skullcap of silvery bristles. A white leather patch covered her left eye, and her right gleamed with the pale gray hue of Arctic ice.

"Took you long enough," she said reprovingly.

Grant frowned. "How do you figure that?"

From a pocket, the major fished out a silver flask. She stepped toward them, uncapping it. "Because the vodka is almost boiling from being so close to my *pizda* for so long. Have a breakfast drink, *tovarisches*…it might be your last opportunity."

Chapter 2

"Can't turn down a high-class invitation like that." Kane accepted the flask, took a long swallow from it and struggled to keep his expression neutral as the liquor scorched a path down his esophagus and into his stomach. He passed it to Domi.

"We've faced the Millennial Consortium before, Major," he said. "They're fairly predictable."

"As are we of District Twelve," Illyana Zuryakin replied smoothly. "Or so some people say."

"I didn't think your organization officially existed," Grant commented.

The woman shrugged negligently. "*Da,* even mention of it to those who are not themselves members is a capital offense. But our mission statement is known to all—to find predark secrets, predark tech. To *keep* predark secrets, predark tech. Specifically, to secure any and everything related to the Totality Concept researches, and that is why we are on a collision course with this Millennial Consortium of yours."

"They're not ours," Kane said.

Zuryakin angled a questioning eyebrow. "No? They come from your country, do they not?"

"Got us there." Domi sipped at the vodka, shuddered and passed the flask to Grant.

Kane did not dispute the girl's admission, although he wished he could.

The Millennial Consortium was, on the surface, a group of organized traders who spent their lives selling predark relics to the various villes. In the Outlands, it was actually the oldest profession.

Since first hearing of the Millennial Consortium a couple of years before, the Cerberus warriors had learned firsthand that the organization was deeply involved in activities other than seeking out stockpiles, salvaging and trading. The group's ultimate goal was to rebuild America along the tenets of technocracy, with a board of scientists and scholars governing the country.

Although the consortium's goals seemed utopian, the organization's overall policy was cold-bloodedly pragmatic. Their influence was widespread, very well managed and they were completely ruthless when it came to the furtherance of their agenda, which when distilled down to its basic components, was nothing more than the totalitarianism of a techno-tyranny.

Nor were their movements restricted to the continental United States. Not too long before, Cerberus had thwarted a joint consortium-overlord operation in China.

"This part of Slovakia is a very long way from America," Major Zuryakin pointed out, receiving the flask back from Grant, who had declined to partake of its contents.

"Hell, Slovakia is a very long way from anywhere," Grant retorted. "Who lives around this place, anyway?"

The major recapped the flask. "Slovaks, mainly."

Kane rolled his eyes. "Big surprise. The point is, there doesn't seem to be anything in the Tatras that even Slovaks would want, much less an outfit like the consortium."

The comm clipped to Zuryakin's breast pocket suddenly crackled. A male voice speaking in agitated Russian filtered out. The major responded tersely, with a note of impatience underscoring her tone.

Addressing the Cerberus team, she said flatly, "Corporal Petrovich reports the convoy has stopped."

"Why?" Grant demanded.

"He doesn't know, but he suspects your scouting party might have been sighted."

"Scouting party?" Kane echoed. "We don't have a scouting party. It's just the four of us."

"Um…" Domi began. When Kane and Grant glanced toward her, the girl asked, in a tone full of exaggerated innocence, "Where's Brigid?"

Repressing a curse, Kane reached up behind his right ear and activated the Commtact attached to the mastoid bone. "Baptiste, where are you?"

LYING NEARLY FACEDOWN on the roadside, Brigid Baptiste found breathing difficult, since the cold seared the moist, soft tissues of her mouth and sinus passages like razor-edged ice blades. Snow flurries danced across her eyes, flakes clinging to the lashes.

Through slitted eyes, Brigid scrutinized the big machine idling almost directly opposite her position. Diesel fumes tickled her nostrils, making her want to sneeze, but she feared to move even her hand to cover her nose and mouth.

With the lower half of her body burrowed into a snowdrift, she counted on her white parka to render the rest of her nearly invisible, or at best, help her blend in with her surroundings. She didn't even dare draw the Iver Johnson TP-9 autopistol. Its blued stainless-steel frame would draw attention like a drop of India ink spilled on a white linen tablecloth.

A slender woman with a fair complexion and big eyes the color of emerald, Brigid's high forehead gave the impression of a probing intellect, whereas her full underlip hinted at an appreciation of the sensual. Her delicate features had a set, almost feline cast to them.

The glaring headlights of the lead vehicles weren't

aimed directly at her, but she kept her eyes narrowed so they wouldn't glint with a reflection. The thudding rhythm of the engines was so loud she fancied she could feel the vibrations in her bones.

Despite her situation, Brigid took a small comfort in recognizing the low-slung, boxlike vehicles as Scorpinauts. Propelled by eight massively treaded wheels, four to each side, the machines were sheathed in armor plate studded with rocket pods and sealed weapons ports. At the end, jointed armatures sprouted two swivel-mounted .50-caliber machine guns, looking like a pair of foreclaws.

Brigid, Grant and Kane had first encountered the Scorpinauts nearly a year before in China. They had been described as omni-purpose Future Combat System vehicles designed to replace tanks in a variety of ground wartime situations.

From rectangular turrets protruded the tapered, ten-foot-long snouts of 40 mm cannons. The barrels were locked in a backward position, giving the FCS vehicles the aspects of mechanical scorpions, with the fore-mounted machine guns representing claws and the cannon barrels the stinger-tipped tails.

The Millennial Consortium had supplied the Scorpinauts to the warlord Wei Qiang to bolster his bid to conquer China. Apparently, the consortium had found the vehicles in a Continuity of Government—COG—vault.

Static hissed into her head, followed by Kane's voice. "Baptiste, where are you?"

Brigid winced and by moving very carefully, reached up to make an adjustment on the Commtact's volume control. The little comm unit fit tightly against the mastoid bone, attached to implanted steel pintels. The unit slid through the flesh and made contact with tiny input ports. Its sensor circuitry incorporated an analog-to-digital voice encoder embedded in the bone.

Once the device made full cranial contact, the auditory canal picked up the transmissions. The dermal sensors transmitted the electronic signals directly through the skull casing. Even if someone went deaf, as long as he or she wore a Commtact, the person would still have a form of hearing, but if the volume was not properly adjusted, the radio signals caused vibrations in the skull bones that resulted in vicious headaches.

"Go ahead," she replied, subvocalizing so her voice was barely above a whisper.

"Report."

"The convoy has come to a halt—"

"So we've been told," Kane broke in. "Why?"

Brigid tamped down her rising irritation. "I have no idea. All I know is that I'm lying facedown in the snow and the lead transport is about fifteen feet away from me."

She paused and added, "It's a Scorpinaut in case you

had any doubts that we're up against the Millennial Consortium."

"Do you want me to come to you?"

"Negative," Brigid answered. "I can find my way back…I just won't be doing so until I get an idea of what's going on—"

A new sound commanded Brigid's attention, a metallic clanking and clinking. A side hatch on the nearest Scorpinaut popped open, pushed from the inside. A ragged human shape half fell, half leaped out, landing clumsily on one knee.

Clothed in a collection of multicolored tatters, the figure could have been a man or a woman, old or young or in between. Then a scrap of headcloth slipped away, revealing a seamed, bewhiskered face. The man was most probably one of the Roma, a Szgany member of a local Gypsy tribe who lived in the sparsely populated mountainous regions.

"Brigid," came Kane's curt voice. "Do you read me?"

Absently, Brigid noted that Kane rarely addressed her by her first name unless he was agitated. She watched the ragged man rise and begin a shambling run, slogging through the snow. He sprinted in a raw panic, a gibbering torrent of mindless terror erupting from his mouth.

He ran less than twenty feet before the right-hand

machine gun swiveled toward him, flame flickering from the bore. A loud rattling roar overwhelmed the muted rumbling of idling engines.

A storm of .50-caliber bullets pounded into the man's back, punching entirely through his body, breaking his chest open amid flying ribbons of blood. He hit the ground gracelessly on his face and slid forward, leaving a crimson smear on the hard-packed snow.

The machine gun burst was short, barely two seconds in duration, but every round found a target.

Throat constricting, Brigid whispered, "*Now* I have an idea of what's going on."

"Are you all right?" Kane demanded.

"Except for a very cold nose, yes. The shooting wasn't due to me, but to a poor Gypsy. He either escaped from a Scorpinaut or was pushed out. Either way, he's very dead. I have a feeling the convoy will start moving again."

Almost as soon as she finished speaking, she heard a clashing of gears and the two lead machines lurched forward. Snow spumed from behind the heavy tires in double rooster tails. Brigid lowered her head, feeling the frozen rain patter and pelt her. She dimly heard a mushy crunch when the wheels of a Scorpinaut rolled over the body of the Gypsy.

"They're on their way to you," she said. "Tell Zuryakin to put the ambush back on the schedule."

"Will do. What about you?"

"If I can move without being spotted, I'll join you shortly. If not—"

"If not," Kane broke in, "maintain your position."

Brigid bristled at his stern tone, what she called his command mode, but she didn't allow herself to express her automatic irritation. "Acknowledged."

Remaining prone, Brigid tried very hard to look like a slush-covered bump in the ground as the convoy rumbled past her, the creak of suspensions filling her ears and exhaust fumes stinging her eyes. Not for the first time that morning, she wondered what the Millennial Consortium considered so valuable in such an isolated region that they had diverted so many of their resources to gain it.

When the fifth and last Scorpinaut in the convoy came abreast of her, Brigid nibbled at her full underlip, then reached a decision. Swiftly she rose, shaking free of the crusted layer of snow blanketing her and lunged toward the rear of the big vehicle.

Her boots skidding in the slippery slush, she raced across the open ground, the clank and wheezing of the machine completely muffling the pounding of her feet. Legs pumping, she jumped across the shallow channels dug by the Scorpinaut's wheels and sprinted behind it for a few seconds, looking for handholds.

Brigid bounded nimbly onto the back of the vehicle,

feet braced on the bumper, hands wrapped around the cannon barrel. She struggled to keep her balance as the Scorpinaut bounced and rocked across the terrain. The vibrations of the chassis blurred her vision and rattled her teeth.

Brigid Baptiste was not impulsive or reckless by nature. Having spent almost half of her life as an archivist in Cobaltville's Historical Division, she had been trained to be methodical and analytical, reason always winning out over emotion. But she had learned over the past few years that making snap decisions was sometimes a prerequisite for survival in her work with Cerberus.

Squirming her way upward, Brigid felt the cold radiating from the frigid metal even through her gloves. She noted that that vehicle was plated with a lightweight ceramic composite armor. The long-dead FCS designers had exchanged protection for speed and mobility.

Using her elbows and toes, Brigid crawled atop the machine's smooth dorsal surface just as the gears downshifted. The sudden, rough surge in forward motion caused her to slip backward, and she clutched at the rim of the topside turret hatch. She hooked her fingers over the raised collar of steel surrounding it, clinging tightly as the vehicle swayed from side to side.

Brigid was still clinging to it when the hatch swung open.

Chapter 3

Engine laboring, the first of the vehicles crept up the crest of the grade, spumes of frozen powder arcing from beneath its huge knobby tires. Suspensions creaked loudly and the axles groaned as four Scorpinauts rolled one by the one over the ridgeline.

On one knee behind a bulwark of stone, Kane grudgingly but silently admitted that the District Twelve operatives knew what they were doing. They had seemingly melted into the snowbanks bordering both sides of the road and could not be seen although he knew where to look. To the crew of the Scorpinauts, they would be completely invisible.

Domi craned her neck to peer down the roadway and Kane started to admonish her, but ruefully realized her own natural camouflage was superior to that of the Russians. Softly, she said, "First wag ought to get to the mine any second now. Ought to be something to see."

"Yeah," Grant grunted, kneeling on Kane's right side. "Assuming it's not an antiquated piece of shit like most of their ordnance."

Annoyed by Grant's characteristic pessimism, Kane snapped impatiently, "That's why we brought our own insurance policy, remember."

Grant snorted. "I think it'll be a necessity. The mines they planted are based on the old Tellermine 35 design—pressure triggers alone. If the millennialists don't drive right over one, but straddle it instead—"

"Like I said," Kane broke in, "that's why we have an insurance policy. Stop harping on it, will you?"

Grant regarded him bleakly. "You're goddamn bad-tempered this morning."

"Old age," Domi interjected. "Told him already."

"Yeah, you'd be the one to know about that," Kane retorted.

Domi's eyes flashed like rubies catching an errant sunbeam. "What's that supposed to mean?"

"You're the one sleeping with a man old enough to be your great-great-great-*great*-grandfather—that's what I mean."

Domi's lips peeled back over her teeth in a silent snarl. "And *you're* the one who—"

"Girls, girls," Grant rumbled reprovingly. "Let's keep our minds on the job."

Both Kane and Domi turned angry eyes toward him. Those eyes widened when a tremendous explosion pressed against their eardrums. They whirled around just in time to see the lead Scorpinaut vanish in a billowing fireball.

"Didn't straddle that one, by God," Domi said in a small, hushed voice.

The other vehicles applied their brakes, slewing clumsily, trying to avoid the Scorpinaut that lay at an angle in the middle of a steaming crater. Black smoke poured from the splits in the hull. Kane gazed at it, searching for movement behind the ob slits and ports. Only streamers of dark, spark-shot vapor curled out of them.

Emitting electronic whines, the topside turrets of the other machines rotated on smooth gimbels, the tapered, ten-foot-long snouts of the 40 mm cannons swinging around and locking in a forward position. They chugged around the wrecked Scorpinaut and halted again, engines idling.

"Looking for us," Grant muttered. "Trying to find targets."

"They could just open up with everything they got," Domi pointed out. "Hose their ammo around."

Kane shook his head. "The consortium doesn't do anything wasteful or indiscriminate that I've seen. They probably have to fill out requisition forms in triplicate for every bullet they fire."

"I hate those guys," Grant said.

"Yeah, so you've said," Kane replied distractedly,

noting that the fifth Scorpinaut remained on the crest of the rise. "That's why we're here, I thought."

A FCS vehicle began rolling forward slowly, the jointed armatures rising from the hulls, and the swivel-mounted machine guns spit tongues of flame in stuttering rhythms. The barrels were directed downward and lines of impact scampered across the ground in a criss-cross pattern, flinging up geysers of dirt and snow in all directions.

"Using that one as a minesweeper," Grant declared. "Smart."

"They're cheap, not stupid," Kane said.

Grant turned around, digging into the snow behind him. "Yeah, I know, that's why I hate them."

He dragged out a long vinyl case and popped open the lid, lifting out a four-foot-long hollow tube, six inches in diameter. One end of it flared out like the mouth of an ancient blunderbuss. A smaller cylinder was attached to the side of the Dragon M-47 rocket launcher.

The comm in Kane's breast pocket crackled and Zuryakin's voice demanded, "Kane, do you see what I'm seeing?"

"Very clearly, but we're taking countermeasures."

A thunderclap detonation swallowed up the Major's response. The explosion of the mine stunned their ears and briefly blinded them with a layer of snow and grit.

Fanning the air in front of his face, Kane tried to fix the Scorpinaut's position in the cloud of haze. "Major, how many mines did your people plant?"

"Three," she answered. "We didn't want the entire convoy destroyed, just disabled."

"We may not have much option about that," Kane replied, turning toward Grant.

The big man held a flowerpot-shaped object in his left hand. Moving with expert ease, he plucked a two-foot-long finned missile from the carrying case and fitted its tapered end into a socket within the cup, giving it a half twist. The projectile clicked solidly into place.

Suddenly, Domi cried, "Look!"

Kane whipped his head around so sharply his neck tendons twinged in protest. He followed the girl's pointing finger to the ridgeline and saw the fifth Scorpinaut coasting down the face of the grade, gaining speed perilously as the front end skewed around at an angle.

A figure half stood atop the turret, parka hood thrown back revealing sunset-colored hair.

Between clenched teeth, Kane growled, "So much for maintaining her position."

THE HEAD AND DUN-COLORED shoulders of a man emerged through the open turret. He struggled up, his bulky cold-weather gear bunching at the shoulders and impeding his movements. He faced forward, a black woolen knit cap covering the top of his head and his ears.

Brigid continued to cling to the lip of the hatch, her hands barely an inch from the man's back as he stared ahead. The FCS vehicle rocked and swayed as it slowly climbed the grade. Pulverized snow flying from beneath the wheels of the Scorpinaut preceding them made for a ghostly visibility. The snow was mixed with ice pellets that stung her cheeks.

Fingers cramping, Brigid prayed the man would tire of being pelted and drop back down into the interior of the machine. At least then she could pull herself into a sitting position and relax her tense muscles. As it was, she could not remember when she'd last had any decent sleep. She ached in every bone and felt as if she would never be warm again.

Her thoughts flew back ninety hours earlier, when she sat sipping coffee in the cozy cafeteria of the Cerberus redoubt and examined the latest satellite imagery downloaded into the installation's computer systems.

Although most satellites had been little more than free-floating scrap metal for nearly two centuries, Cerberus had always possessed the proper electronic ears and eyes to receive the transmissions from at least two satellites.

One was of the Vela reconnaissance class, which carried narrow-band multispectral scanners. It could detect the electromagnetic radiation reflected by every object on Earth, including subsurface geomagnetic waves. The scanner was tied into an extremely high-resolution photographic relay system.

A year's worth of hard work on the part of resident techsmith Donald Bry had at long last allowed Cerberus to gain control of the Vela and the Comsat. He had programmed the Vela to transmit any imagery to fit a set of preselected parameters. Only five days before, Cerberus downloaded a telemetric sequence that showed a great deal of unusual activity in a very remote region of Slovakia.

Although the overlords didn't seem to be culprits, enhancements of the images indicated that another set of adversaries were very busy in the vicinity of Gerlachov Peak. Kane, Brigid, Grant and Domi volunteered to investigate, and crossed paths with Major Zuryakin and her contingent of District Twelve troopers who were engaged in the very same mission.

The man standing in the hatch began turning, but so slowly Brigid doubted he had sensed or otherwise become aware of her presence. She waited for what felt like a very long time before his face was turned to her.

He voiced a gargling cry of shock when he saw the woman lying atop the hull of the vehicle. His expression of openmouthed astonishment was so comical, Brigid nearly laughed. When she saw the man contorting himself to drop back down inside the Scorpinaut, all the amusement value vanished.

Brigid stabbed a thumb and forefinger into his larynx, driving whatever alarm he was about to raise back into his throat.

Clutching at his neck with his free hand, eyes bugging out, the man wheezed and gasped, lips writhing. Brigid pulled herself atop the turret, drawing her autopistol at the same time. Although she felt a twinge of shame, she struck him sharply on the left temple with the barrel, hoping she gauged the force of the blow correctly. She preferred him unconscious rather than dead.

The man's head fell forward and his body sagged. Brigid caught him by the thick fleece collar of his cold suit, holding him upright. Pinned to it was a small brass button. It depicted a familiar and stylized representation of a featureless man holding a cornucopia in his left hand and a sword in his right. That accessory was more than enough to identify him as an agent of the Millennial Consortium, and any regret she felt about rendering him senseless vanished.

The Scorpinaut chugged its way up the slope and paused as it gained the crest. Even over the roar of the engine, Brigid heard a thunderclap detonation from the road below. She glanced down to see the lead FCS vehicle engulfed by a roiling mushroom of flame.

The Scorpinaut beneath her lurched to a violent halt,

nearly pitching her headfirst from the turret. She was forced to release her grip on the unconscious millennialist and snatch a handhold on the upright hatch cover.

For a few seconds, the man remained caught, his shoulders jammed against the rim of the aperture. Then, by inches, he slid into the interior. Faintly, Brigid heard a medley of surprised cries and profane questions.

Hazarding a quick look down, she glimpsed a man staring upward, cradling his unconscious comrade in his arms. His face twisted first in astonishment, then anger. Dropping his comrade, he lunged upward right as Brigid slammed the hatch cover shut. She heard a gonglike impact from the underside and a new torrent of obscenities.

Resting her full weight on the cover, she jacked a round into the chamber of her TP-9, knowing that if a concerted effort was put forth from below, she could easily be dislodged from her perch. But with a sudden clenching of her stomach muscles, she realized there was no time for that to happen.

The Scorpinaut teetered on the edge of the rise, then the front end dipped sharply downward. Brigid paid little attention to the rattle of a machine gun and a second explosion from the road.

The heavy vehicle slid down the face of the slope, tires skidding, the frame yawing back and forth, all control gone. A thought flashed through her mind that the man she had struck with the hatch cover had fallen atop the machine's wheelman.

The undercarriage of the Scorpinaut clattered noisily from a barrage of loose rocks and pebbles torn up by the big tires. The vehicle was moving too fast and recklessly to be able to brake in time to avoid a rear-end collision with the other Scorpinauts. It listed up on its right side, and Brigid feared it would turn over, crushing her beneath it.

Quickly, she returned her pistol to her pocket and raised herself up to a half-standing posture, poising to leap. The Commtact hissed and Kane's voice demanded, "Baptiste, what the hell are you—?"

Brigid kicked herself off the machine's right side, flying through the air, and for a shaved sliver of a second, she felt as if she were suspended between space and the firmament. Then she landed heavily, rolling, keeping her body turning over and over to minimize injury. The snow helped to cushion the impact, but it still drove almost all the air from her lungs. She went thrashing to the bottom of the slope and lay half-buried, gasping and groaning.

Dizzily, she pushed herself up to a sitting position, brushing snow from her eyes just in time to watch the Scorpinaut swerve into a crazed fishtail at the base of the slope, its front end broadsiding an idling FCS. With a shriek of metal grinding into metal and a flurry of sparks, the two vehicles careened madly in a wild figure eight.

The out-of-control Scorpinaut flipped up on its right side, turning completely over and landing upside down atop the other machine. Both vehicles rocked to shuddering, crashing stops.

Brigid dragged in a lungful of painfully cold air and stood up, slapping her parka sleeves free of snow. She activated the Commtact frequency to Kane and inquired hoarsely, "You were saying?"

"Forget it," he said. "I guess you knew what you were doing."

"Guess again," she retorted. "But we've cut down the opposition. Maybe the others will be in a surrendering mood."

Side hatches on the upside-down Scorpinaut popped open. Amid a cloud of smoke, four millennialists clambered out. They were dazed, unsure of themselves, but apparently not seriously injured.

"Maybe," Kane said doubtfully.

The two undamaged Scorpinauts came to brake-shoe-squealing halts. The perforated snouts of the .50-caliber machine guns roared with flame and thunder. This time, the heavy weapons were not aimed at the ground but at both sides of the road.

Chapter 4

Domi, Kane and Grant crouched behind the tumble of rocks, trying to make themselves as small as possible. The process was much easier for Domi than for Kane and Grant.

A sleet storm of bullets gouged the bastion of stone, pelting them with gravel, ricochets screaming in all directions. The machine gun raked the boulders lining the road with snare-drum ferocity, explosions of snow and stone shards filling the air. After a prolonged burst, the line of fire moved on.

"Shooting blind, the stupes," Domi commented contemptuously, drawing her Detonics Combat Master .45 from the holster beneath her parka. Gloved fingers securing a tight hold on the checkered walnut grips, her thumb flicked off the safety. The stainless-steel pistol weighed only a pound and a half and was perfectly suited for a girl of her petite build.

"Shooting blind for the moment," Grant grunted, fitting the flowerpot object over the flared opening of the rocket launcher in his hands. He twisted it counter-clockwise. Lock rachets clicked loudly into place.

"Kane!" Zuryakin's angry voice blared out of the transceiver. "We're moving out...if we don't counterattack, those *styervos* will roll right over us and get away."

"Let Grant get in position first," Kane snapped.

"*Nyet.* If you want to stand around with your mouths open and *vafli lovit,* go ahead. I've given the orders to complete this mission."

The major cut the channel, and Kane gritted between clenched teeth, "Bitch."

Over the Commtact, Brigid asked, "What's happening?"

"What does *vafli lovit* mean?" Kane asked, stumbling a bit over the pronunciation.

Brigid didn't answer for a few seconds. Then she said, "Loosely translated, it means to 'catch flying dicks.' Why?"

Kane didn't answer but he spat again, "Bitch."

"Hey, you're the one who asked," Brigid shot back hotly.

"I don't mean you. Stand by. Major Zuryakin is about to make a move."

"I can see that," Brigid replied dryly.

Cautiously, Kane raised his head, looking down the road. A dozen District Twelve troopers swarmed out of the snowbank, closing in on the quintet of millennialists who had abandoned their pair of disabled vehicles. Five seemed a small number divided between two of the Scorpinauts, but Kane guessed that everyone who could climb out under their power had already gotten out.

All of the men wore dun-colored cold suits, with small black automatic rifles held across their chests. Kane recognized the subguns as Calico M-960s, the standard weapon of Millennial Consortium field operatives. Each autorifle carried full extended magazines of fifty 9 mm rounds.

The consortium operatives might have been dazed from the collision, but when they saw the approaching Russians, they darted for cover behind the Scorpinauts, firing their weapons. For a moment, the ripping snarls of the multiple Calicos firing on full-auto drowned out the drumming of the Scorpinaut's mounted machine guns.

Two of the District Twelve troopers spun in sprays of blood, scraps of white coveralls flying away from their bodies. The remaining soldiers dropped flat, opening fire with their AKSU autorifles. A hail of bullets peppered the hulls of the Scorpinauts. Sparks flared on the metal hide, leaving deep dents to commemorate the multiple impacts of armor-piercing rounds.

The rest of the troopers ran toward the pair of operable Scorpinauts, spreading out in a widening horseshoe formation to encircle them. Kane instantly grasped their strategy. The Russians' clothes were the same color as the snow and the gunners aboard the Scorpinauts were preoccupied with the skirmish by the disabled machines.

The turrets of the Scorpinauts suddenly rotated, the cannon barrels swinging around toward the D-12 troopers. The Russians fired at the vehicles, a combined full-auto fusillade. Brass arced in a glittering rain from the ejector ports of their weapons. Sparks danced on the armor of the vehicles, the clang of bullets sounding like a gang of blacksmiths hard at work.

The cannon barrels of the Scorpinauts gouted smoke, thunder and flame, more or less simultaneously. Two high-explosive rounds impacted on the roadbed, flinging up snow, stone and men in mushrooming orange-red columns.

A Scorpinaut's cannon belched flame and smoke again, but the round flew long, impacting against the right rear end of the upside-down FCS. A blossom of roiling yellow flame swallowed the bodywork of the two disabled vehicles. A series of explosions raced through the twisted frames as various volatile materials within detonated. The millennialists caught by the blasts were killed instantly by the multiple concussions. Both machines went tumbling end over end in a shower of hardware, fire and loose tires.

"Oops," Kane commented with a studied banality.

The men who survived the explosions came out shrieking, slapping at flames licking along their bodies. The District Twelve troopers shot them down ruthlessly, catching them in a triangulated cross fire. They clutched at themselves as bullets clawed open their bodies, sending fragments of bone and clots of tissue flying in all directions, propelled by crimson sprays.

The cannon of a Scorpinaut bloomed with smoke and flame. The shell exploded in the midst of the Russian soldiers. Their bodies flew up, out and apart amid a mushroom of yellow fire.

As black smoke spread a hazy umbrella over the area, Grant crawled out from behind the rocks, carrying the Dragon rocket launcher with him.

He sat on the ground, propping his elbows on his raised knees. Placing the launch tube on his left shoulder, Grant squinted through the eyepiece of the top-mounted tracker sight. He swiftly adjusted the focus, then inserted his finger into the molded bulge of the trigger on the cylinder's underside.

The Dragon was a one-man, optically tracked launcher. The projectile carrier attachment fitted over the end of the tube and ignited a Cobra 2000 one-stage rocket. The warhead contained a HEAT hollow charge. The weapon's electronic targeting system employed a command-to-line-of-sight guidance with infrared tracking.

The Dragon came from the same place as most of their other ordnance—the fantastically well-equipped armory in the Cerberus redoubt nestled deep within a Montana mountain peak.

Grant flicked a tiny switch to activate the targeting system, and the launcher emitted a faint hum. Holding his breath, he placed the nearest of the Scorpinauts in target acquisition, peering through the eyepiece, focusing the crosshairs on a small space between two of the tires. Internal engine heat emissions showed like a shimmering patch of molten lava. He took a half breath, held it, then squeezed into the trigger pull.

"Fire in the hole," he stated calmly.

Smoke and flame spewed from the hollow bore of the Dragon missile launcher. Trailing a wavering ribbon of vapor and sparks, the Cobra 2000 rocket leaped from the muzzle, accompanied by a ripping roar. Small fins popped open at the tail of the missile as it rotated, searing the air in a direct line toward its target.

The projectile lanced between two tires, and the warhead exploded in a flaring fireball. The shaped hollow charge smashed a deep cavity into the chassis on the Scorpinaut's undercarriage, and the kinetic force tipped the vehicle up and over on its left side. The echoes of the detonation rolled over the terrain, bouncing off the mountain walls.

"Standing around *vafli loviting,* my ass," Kane muttered.

"What?" Domi asked, perplexed.

The turret hatch popped open and disgorged five men, all of them cradling Calico assault rifles in their arms. As they clambered out of the vehicle, they opened fire indiscriminately, shooting in all directions.

"So much for their policy of thrift," Domi muttered.

Raising herself above the rocks, she dropped the Combat Master's sights over one of the men and squeezed the trigger. The bullet slammed through the millennialist's head, punching him off his feet and throwing him against the man beside him.

Two of the consortium men whirled toward her, their Calicos blazing. Cursing, Grant dropped the Dragon and flung himself backward, behind the shield of rocks. Rounds crashed into them, chiseling out granite splinters.

"Thanks for drawing their attention," Grant growled sourly to Domi as he crawled over to her.

The girl ignored him, squeezing off another round at one of the men. She missed him by inches as he doubled over, succumbing to a coughing fit as he inhaled smoke pouring from the underbelly of the Scorpinaut.

Kane achieved a half-standing posture, tensing his wrist tendons. The Sin Eater slapped into his waiting hand, and his index finger depressed the trigger stud.

The 248-grain bullet hit the man in the right shoulder and knocked him erect.

Aiming for his chest, Domi fired again, but the man staggered, the bullet passing through the thigh of his cold suit. It punctured the fuel tank of the Scorpinaut. A jet of gasoline squirted out and caught fire. The tank instantly exploded and enveloped the millennialists in a billowing balloon of flame.

Kane, Domi and Grant felt the blast of withering heat that melted the snow and ice for yards all around. They ducked to avoid being scorched by the rain of burning gasoline.

With a clashing of gears, the throttle open wide and the engine roaring like a terrified beast, the remaining Scorpinaut hurtled forward, fishtailing over the layer of slush on the roadbed. Kane figured the semiliquid stuff would freeze solid again within minutes. The prow hit the vehicle lying on its side and battered it out of the way. Domi stood up as the machine lumbered past and fired two ineffectual shots that spanged off the bodywork.

Hiking himself up, Grant said darkly, "Guess they don't subscribe to the old 'leave no man behind' rule."

"They're believers in loss-cutting first," Kane replied.

"Kane!" Major Zuryakin's voice shouted from behind him, not over the transceiver.

He turned to see her and a pair of D-12 troopers jogging up the road, skirting the flames dancing from the rocket-punctured Scorpinaut.

"You let them get away!" The woman's tone of voice was outraged, scandalized.

Rudely, Kane turned his back on her, watching the Scorpinaut's lumbering progress up the road.

Panting, Zuryakin came to his side. "Did you bring only the one rocket or what?"

"What about your end of it?" Kane shot back coldly. "Is there anybody who can be questioned?"

"We've taken a couple of prisoners, but when you were allowed to participate in this mission, the agreement was to let none of the consortium *zalupas* escape—"

With an earsplitting, marrow-jarring crack, the block of C-4 erupted in a nova of orange fire. A roaring wall of flame belled out from the dark throat of the overhang like a fireball flung from a catapult. The Scorpinaut rocked violently as the wall of concussive force struck it broadside like a wrecking ball.

The air continued to shiver with echoes of the explosion until the second demolition charge detonated. The entire cliff face seemed to burst outward, then topple. As the rocks fell, they sheared away the softer ledges beneath, smashing them apart. A seething cascade of stone slabs and dirt roared down the steep face of the cliff.

Flying fragments struck the Scorpinaut, making a cacophony like a work gang pounding repeatedly on the armor with sledgehammers.

Huge boulders and shattered crags poured down onto the roadway, completely engulfing the Scorpinaut. A wave of bouncing stone swept over the channel, filling it with colliding, grinding chunks of stone.

Kane, Domi and Grant shielded their faces from flying rock fragments, lowering their goggles to protect their eyes from the clouds of grit blowing over them. Zuryakin and her troopers turned away.

Slowly, the shuddering crash of tumbling, rolling stone faded as the avalanche bled itself out, although boulders continued to grate and click. No sign of the Scorpinaut could be seen in the sea of settling stone.

Fanning the dust-thick air, Kane turned toward Zuryakin. "What was that about an agreement, Major?"

Illyana Zuryakin glowered at him for a silent few seconds, her one eye glinting with angry resentment. Then the grim slash of her mouth twitched, the corners turning up in a smile. Voicing a wordless cry of triumph, she caught Kane up in a crushing embrace and kissed him on the lips.

Kane voiced a wordless cry of his own, one of horror, when he felt the major's vodka-slick tongue snake past his lips. He was struggling to fight free just as a breathless and smoke-streaked Brigid Baptiste sprinted up.

Chapter 5

Columns of gray-and-black smoke corkscrewed into the morning sky as Zuryakin led Kane, Brigid, Domi and Grant among the burst carcasses of the flaming Scorpinauts. Corpses lay everywhere, all of them maimed and riddled with bloody bullet holes.

Brigid barely managed to control the nausea roiling in her stomach. Even the smell of smoke didn't completely mask the nostril-abrading stench of burned human flesh. She managed to maintain an intellectual distance from the horror running through her mind. It was hard, even after all the pitched firefights she had been involved in over the years, to dispassionately view the aftermath of brutal combat.

Brigid tossed back the hood of her parka and freed a thick braid of red-gold hair. It fell down the center of her back almost to her waist.

"So you only have two prisoners?" she inquired.

Zuryakin shrugged. "That's enough, isn't it?"

The major stepped behind a gutted, smoke-belching Scorpinaut and gestured. Two men wearing tan coveralls lay side by side, leaning against a tumble of stone, apprehensively eyeing the gun barrels of several D-12 troopers. They were both of a type—medium-sized, brown-haired Caucasians so nondescript in appearance, they would not have been given so much as a cursory glance if they had been seen in one of the villes.

Trickles of scarlet ran down one man's face, leaking out from beneath a bandage he held pressed to his forehead. The other man didn't seem to be injured except for dark, wet stains on both of his legs.

"What are your names?" Brigid asked.

The man with the injured head shifted position slightly. "You can call me Mr. White. This is Mr. Pink."

Kane blinked in confusion. "Mr. Pink?"

"That's all you'll get out of us," White declared in a monotone. "You're only wasting your time questioning us."

A District Twelve trooper turned toward Zuryakin and spoke a few words in hard-edged Russian. The major nodded and said, "Petrovich tells me they haven't been very forthcoming."

Domi showed the edges of her teeth in a wolfish grin. "We have ways of changing that."

Reaching inside her parka, Domi withdrew a long combat knife with a nine-inch, wickedly serrated blade. It was her only memento of the six months she'd spent as Guana Teague's sex slave in the Tartarus Pits of Cobaltville. The razor-keen edge bore bloodstains from many kills, animal and human alike.

Zuryakin snorted. "We have our own ways."

Without preamble, she delivered the steel-reinforced toe of her right boot full into Mr. Pink's face. The back of his head struck the rock behind him. He fell to one side, spitting blood and splinters of teeth.

"The Russian tradition of finesse," Brigid murmured, not bothering to disguise the disgust in her tone.

Zuryakin whirled on her angrily. "What did you say?"

Brigid ignored her and stepped closer to Mr. White, gesturing to herself, Kane, Grant and Domi. "Do you know who we are?"

White swallowed hard and nodded. "The Cerberus crew."

Zuryakin's lips twisted in a sneer. "So you're famous."

Kane cast the woman a hard, challenging stare. "You have no idea."

Grant scowled down at the man, folding his arms over his massive chest. "Tell it. All of it."

The man hesitated, eyes darting back and forth between Grant and Zuryakin. He apparently was fearful of the Russian methods, even though Brigid knew that if Grant believed the millennialist was lying, he wouldn't stop short of using methods just as brutal as the major's.

Domi stood nearby, absently thumbing the blade of her knife. She could be quite creative when torture was involved, but one look into those bloodred eyes was usually sufficient to loosen even the most recalcitrant tongue.

White glanced over at the moaning Mr. Pink, who sat huddled over, hands cupping his lower face, then he sighed in resignation. "There's not that much to tell. We were sent here to check out a cave in the Gerlachov Peak and bring back what we could from it."

Kane's eyes narrowed to suspicious slits. "That's not how the consortium works."

White lifted a shoulder in a dismissive shrug. "What can I say?"

Zuryakin drew her back her left foot and the man blurted, "The intel we had was too strong to pass up. My section chief was the one who gave the orders."

"What's the name of your section chief?" Grant demanded.

A crafty gleamed flashed in White's eyes. "You know I can't just tell you. Not unless…"

He trailed off meaningfully, glancing up into the somber faces, obviously expecting one of them to ask, "Not unless what?"

Instead, Domi stepped close, her delicate, piquant features as tight and composed as a marble mask. She leaned down and casually turned the knife over in her hand, manipulating it skillfully, like a cat flicking out its claws. The milky sunlight glinted from the razor-sharp tip. The brass button bearing the symbol of the consortium flew from White's collar, attached to a tiny scrap of fabric. The man's eyes bulged out, following the play of the steel.

"Here's an 'unless' for you," the albino girl said in a soft, taunting voice. "Unless you start talking, you'll lose an ear just like you lost a button. If you still don't talk, or if we don't like what you're saying, then you'll lose another ear. Then it'll be your nose. After that, I'll move farther down."

The tip of the knife inscribed a small circle over White's crotch. "*Way* down. I'll save your eyes for last, so you can see what you're losing. Unless…"

Kane grinned appreciatively, but Brigid didn't so much as smile. She knew Domi was not bluffing or making empty threats.

"Just tell them what they want to know!" Mr. Pink bleated, his voice a liquid gurgle beneath his hands. "This op is *so* fucked! There's no profit in this. Let's cut our losses."

"*That's* the Millennial Consortium philosophy I remember," Grant rumbled.

Illyana Zuryakin stated, "You were in the vicinity of Gerlachov Peak."

White nodded. "Yes. There's a cave about three-quarters of the way to the summit. That was the objective of the mission."

Creases deepened on Zuryakin's forehead. "There are cave networks all over the Tatras…Gypsies often live in them. What was so special about that one?"

White took a deep breath, held it and released it in a sigh. "It was the base of a military operation in 1946."

"So what?" the major argued. "Even 260 years later, there are still World War II ammunition depots and listening posts found all over this part of Europe."

"Wait a second," Brigid interjected. "You said 1946."

White nodded. "Yes."

Glancing at Zuryakin, Brigid said smoothly, "The war ended in 1945, so this couldn't have been connected to any ongoing military project. Hitler was dead, the Third Reich was smashed—"

"It *was* military nevertheless," White broke in impatiently. "But it was outside of the reich's mainstream strategies, even though the plan had been formulated a couple of years before, around late 1944."

"What plan?" Kane asked.

White shook his head. "I'm not really sure. I mean, I was briefed, but it all seems like so much mystical technobabble horseshit to me."

"What did?" Kane pressed.

The man stared levelly into Kane's eyes, an expression almost of embarrassment crossing his face. "Whatever was going on up there was connected with something called the Totality Concept and Operation Chronos."

Belly turning a cold flip-flop, Kane exchanged swift looks with Brigid, who managed to keep her face composed. "Suppose," he ventured, "you tell us what you found of Operation Chronos in that cave."

"Operation what?" Zuryakin's aggressive voice punched all of their eardrums. She swept the Americans with a piercing stare. "Does that mean something to you?"

Quietly, Brigid intoned, "Yes, you might say it does."

The Totality Concept dated back to World War II, when German scientists labored to build what turned out to be purely theoretical secret weapons for the Third Reich. After the fall of Nazi Germany, the Allied powers adopted the researches, as well as many of the scientists, and constructed underground bases, primarily in the western U.S., to further the experiments.

The Totality Concept title became the umbrella designation for supersecret researches into many different yet interconnected subdivisions. The primary subdivision of the Totality Concept was Overproject Whisper, which in turn spawned Project Cerberus and Operation Chronos.

Cerberus dealt with the transfer of organic and inorganic matter from one location to another, and Chronos focused on transtemporal interphasing—time travel, or in the vernacular of the Totality Concept scientists, time "trawling."

Mr. White gestured to the burning Scorpinauts. "Everything we found that could be moved was in the wags there. To be honest, most of it seemed like antique junk to me…old machines that were beat to hell, some primitive computers, memorabilia of interest to collectors but not of any real value. A lot of it was damaged, like there'd been a big explosive energy discharge. But we found an extensive file system that was still intact and we took it, cabinets and all."

He paused, his lips twisting as if he tasted something sour. "Of course, it's probably pretty much up in smoke now."

Brigid turned to Zuryakin. "Major, please set your troops to searching the Scorpinauts and salvaging anything they find in them, particularly file cabinets."

Zuryakin frowned, not caring for the green-eyed woman's terse tone of command, but she activated her radio and snapped out orders in rapid-fire Russian.

Grant nudged White's leg with a booted foot. "Can you walk?"

The millennialist's eyes widened, startled by the query. "I think so."

Grant nodded. "Good. You can act as our guide."

"Guide to where?"

Kane saluted the Gerlachov Peak. "To the cave and the Operation Chronos facility therein. We didn't come all this way and get dressed up for nothing."

Chapter 6

"I didn't say it *was* an Operation Chronos facility," White protested, hugging himself. "I said that whatever was going on here had something to do with it. Or at least, that's what my section chief told me."

The cavern opening was a lopsided triangle, twenty or so feet tall, nearly twice that wide at the base. Boulders lay around except for an unnaturally flat expanse jutting from the yawning black cleft. The two Manta aircraft that had conveyed Grant, Kane, Brigid and Mr. White to the Gerlachov Peak sat wing-to-wing on the broad shelf of rock.

The pair of transatmospheric vehicles held the general shape and configuration of seagoing manta rays, and as such they resembled little more than flattened wedges with wings. Sheathed in bronze-hued metal, intricate geometric designs covered almost the entire exterior surface. Deeply inscribed into the hulls were interlocking swirling glyphs, cup and spiral symbols and even elaborate cuneiform markings. The composition of the hulls, although they appeared to be of a burnished bronze alloy, was a material far tougher and more resilient.

The craft had no external apparatus at all, no ailerons, no fins and no airfoils. The cockpits were almost invisible, little more than elongated symmetrical oval humps in the exact center of the sleek topside fuselages. The Manta's wingspans measured out to twenty yards from tip to tip, and the fuselage was around fifteen feet long.

Of Annunaki manufacture, the Mantas were in pristine condition, despite their great age. Powered by two different kinds of engines, a ramjet and solid fuel pulse detonation air spikes, the transatmospheric vehicles could fly in both a vacuum and in an atmosphere. The Mantas were not experimental craft, but an example of a technology that was mastered by an ancient race when humanity still cowered in trees, hiding from saber-tooth tigers. Metallurgical analysis had suggested that the ships were a minimum of ten thousand years old.

Kane squinted into the cave, noting that the sunlight slanting down from above reached only a few yards past the opening. Beyond it was darkness, and he found himself reluctant to move into it, wishing vaguely that he instead of Domi had remained behind to salvage the files from the Scorpinauts. Unfortunately the little albino couldn't pilot the two-seated craft. As it was, the unpredictable updrafts and thermals had made for tricky maneuvering as the Mantas came down for vertical landings on the ledge.

From a storage compartment in the undercarriage of the Manta he had flown, Grant removed a big box-batteried xenon flashlight. It could project a beam of three million candlepower.

Turning to Mr. White, Brigid asked, "How'd you find this place?"

The man shrugged. His superficial head wound had been treated and bandaged. "Like I told you, my section chief had the old intel that—"

"No old intel could specifically pinpoint a place as remote and hard to reach as this." A steel edge slipped into Brigid's voice. "We must've flown over and past a dozen caves just like this one on our way up here. You relied on locals to guide you here, didn't you? Gypsies."

White's eyes widened in surprise. "How did you know?"

"I saw you execute a man who looked like a Gypsy," Brigid retorted flatly.

"I didn't execute him," White protested feebly. "He wasn't even in my vehicle."

"Who was he?" Grant asked.

"His name was Janos, the *hetman* of a group of Romany we contacted."

"Why was he killed?" Brigid inquired.

"He served his purpose." White did not elaborate.

A cold, humorless smile quirked the corners of Kane's mouth. "I have the distinct feeling Janos didn't help you out of the kindness of his heart."

"Or for pay, either," Grant rumbled. "What'd you do, hold his family hostage, threaten to kill them if he didn't lead you up here?"

White cast his gaze downward, at the snow-covered ledge. "Something like that," he admitted. "We were just following orders from our section chief."

"And who was that again?" Brigid demanded.

White shook his head. "Her name wouldn't mean anything to you."

"*Her* name?" Grant echoed.

White did not respond. Instead, he took a hesitant step toward the cave entrance. "You brought me back up here so I can show you around, right?"

"That was the general idea," Kane drawled, unleathering his Sin Eater. "And I'll be right behind you so you don't get any more ideas."

The four people entered the dark throat of the cave, and within a few dozen yards they couldn't see their hands in front of their faces. The Cerberus warriors paused long enough to put on dark-lensed glasses. The electrochemical polymer of the lenses gathered all available light and made the most of it to give them a limited form of night vision.

The xenon flashlight in Grant's hand cast an almost

solid rod of yellow incandescence before them. White walked carefully on the bare, icy stone floor. Although Kane followed him closely, he instinctively slipped into the point man's persona, his eyes roaming from side to side, searching every nook and fissure.

Walking point was a habit Kane had acquired during his years as a Magistrate because of his uncanny ability to sniff out danger in the offing. He called it a sixth sense, but his point man's sense was really a combined manifestation of the five he had trained to the epitome of keenness. When he walked point, Kane felt electrically alive, sharply tuned to every nuance of his surroundings and what he was doing.

The passageway was completely featureless, but it showed signs of long-ago construction—they saw the marks of chisels and drills on the rock walls and arrangements of joists, timbers and beams shoring up the low roof. The frigid air bit at their nostrils, their lips and eyes, wherever it could find moisture.

Brigid looked around, seeing very little but rock and ice chips, mentally comparing her surroundings to the many other predark military installations she had visited over the past five years. She knew that the Totality Concept projects were usually hidden in subterranean annexes.

Almost all of the redoubts she had ever visited seemed haunted by the ghosts of a hopeless, despairing past age. The walls seemed to exude the terror, the utter despondency of souls trapped when the first mushroom cloud erupted from Washington on that chill January noon.

The cave had an oppressively empty sense about it, of having once played host to great power, but now there was only an energy vacuum, a strange sensation of absence, of sterility, of nonexistence. In some ways that emptiness felt more oppressive than a lingering atmosphere of terror, like a grave that had been exhumed.

The tunnel ended at an entranceway. A heavy metal door hung askew on warped hinges, its dull gray surface coated by a layer of ice. Playing the flashlight beam over it, Grant commented, "Looks like it was blown open from the other side."

White nodded. "Yeah, that's our guess, too."

The xenon beam lit their way down a featureless corridor. Metal frameworks and support posts were twisted and bent, as if they were composed of paraffin and exposed to extreme heat. They walked past the splintered fragments of a wooden door hanging loose in a wide frame and into a vast, bowl-shaped cavern. The air, though cold and stale, held the faint, bitter reek of superheated metal.

"Where'd the consortium find the intel that led you to this place?" Kane asked, unconsciously lowering his voice. Still, echoes of his question chased each other through the high shadows.

Mr. White sighed. "Does it make any difference?"

"I wouldn't ask otherwise." For emphasis, Kane rapped him on the back of the head with the barrel of his Sin Eater, not hard enough to cause damage, but sufficiently painful to remind the millennialist that he was in no position to withhold information.

White rubbed the rear of his skull, then his shoulders slumped in resignation. "I'm not exactly sure of the source, but I know it came back from an expeditionary op to Germany."

Brigid swung her head toward him, eyes bright with surprise. "The consortium has spread into Europe?"

"To some extent, I guess. We've established trading agreements with a couple of the provincial governments."

"Which ones?" Kane asked.

An expression of discomfort crossed the man's face. "I really don't know. I'm a field man, a pack mule, not one of the board of directors." He glanced at all of them with troubled, puzzled eyes. "Why do you care, anyway? I mean, what difference does it make to you people at Cerberus? Why do you keep coming after us?"

"Gee, I thought you knew," Grant said inanely. "We just hate you guys, that's all."

"We're trying to rebuild the world," White stated, a

defiant undercurrent in his tone. "To make it better and safer for everyone. Do you prefer anarchy?"

Brigid said calmly, "In the normal order of things, no. But for the consortium to reach its goals would mean a world of people who think alike and live alike for all time, with no deviation from a standard imposed from outside. You're trying to breed consortium thinkers, consortium conquerors, consortium dictators who will become a new aristocracy. You're seeking world peace through world domination."

"And that just doesn't seem to work for us," Kane said breezily. "Go figure. Keep moving."

Although they couldn't see very much, the crunch and grate of their boot soles sent eerie echoes darting back and forth through the darkness.

"So this was a Nazi base?" Brigid asked.

White started to nod, then shook his head. "I'm not sure…definitely it was connected to the Third Reich, but nobody knows the particulars. I would imagine the files we retrieved will give more of the story." He paused, then added bleakly, "If you and those damn Russians didn't burn them up, that is."

They walked carefully into the central chamber, the dark bulk of many machines looming out of the murk.

Brigid sniffed the air. "Old diesel-fuel electricity generators. Inefficient, but I suppose it was the best they had."

Grant glanced around, his eyes following the xenon beam. He swept it over a matte-black surface, then whipped it back. Flatly, he declared, "Not exactly."

Brigid and Kane followed the rod of light. After a few silent seconds, Kane murmured softly, wonderingly, "Huh."

A two-tiered fusion generator rose from the floor. More than twelve feet tall, it resembled two solid black cubes, a slightly smaller one balanced atop the other. Usually the top cube rotated slowly, but this particular one did not move, seemingly locked in midrevolution.

The Cerberus warriors had seen generators of the same type before in various and unlikely places around and even off the world. Lakesh had put forth the initial speculation they were fusion reactors, the energy output held in a delicately balanced magnetic matrix within the cubes.

When the matrix was breached, an explosion of apocalyptic proportions resulted, which caused the destruction of the Archuleta Mesa installation in New Mexico. The act, as inadvertent as it had been, was the first major blow struck against baronial tyranny. However, they had never seen one of the generators completely dead, drained of power before.

As it was, the presence of the generator in the cavern bespoke a definite connection to the Totality Concept projects.

After an awkward moment of silence, Brigid said, "There was a lot more to this place than just Nazis."

"You've seen something like that before?" White asked.

Brigid nodded. "We have."

"What is it?"

"Never you mind," Grant announced, passing the xenon beam over a litter of debris lying between them and the generator. It briefly cast a halo on a human face staring up from an ice-glazed scattering of half-slagged metal.

Brigid recoiled with a wordless utterance of disgust.

The face was little more than a mummified mask, the lips peeled back like old leather over discolored teeth. Although much of the scalp was completely bare, peeled down to the bone, tufts of white hair bristled upward in spots. The thick round lenses of spectacles covered the eyes, but the glass bore networks of cracks and was scorch-blackened to complete opacity.

The man's body lay crushed beneath a giant flywheel that had fallen from one of the machines.

"Something blew the big-time hell out of this place," Grant observed bleakly.

"Yeah," Kane agreed. "But it doesn't look like the damage associated with standard explosives, and the reactor didn't go critical or there wouldn't even be a mountain here, much less a cave."

With the tip of a boot, Brigid tapped a wrist-thick conduit that snaked across the floor. Visually, she traced it back to a heavy ceramic socket protruding from the base of the fusion generator. "A high-energy plasma discharge could be the culprit."

"It had to vent from somewhere, though," Grant said, shining the flashlight beam along the length of the conduit. Nearly three feet of it was melted through, adhering to the stone floor in a puddle of glistening metal that had turned molten, then hardened again. "Overloaded power lines were apparently one of their problems."

The four people strode beside the cable for a dozen yards, walking between a pair of tall Y-pronged voltage-convertor pylons. Both of them tilted to the left at twenty-degree angles, a webwork of cracks deeply inscribed into their ceramic surfaces.

The conduit terminated in a metal collar attached to the base of a free-standing console. The upper half consisted of a shapeless mass of burned plastic and melted metal. On the other side of the console, they made out a pair of chairs, both of them set in half-reclining positions.

Grant cast the xenon beam on the cadaver lying in one of the chairs, a small wizened figure with dark limbs like sticks of charred firewood. A metal framework caged a hairless skull covered by a thin, drum-tight layer of leathery flesh. The teeth gleamed in a macabre caricature of a grin.

"What the hell was this?" Kane muttered, feeling his scalp tighten with apprehension.

Brigid shook her head, confusion and frustration rising within her in equal measure. "I can't even hazard a guess. But look at the size of the body—it's a child."

Grant glared over his shoulder at White. "Where'd you find the files?"

The millennialist hooked a thumb to the right. "There's an office suite over there. It didn't suffer the same degree of damage as the rest of the place, even though there were bodies in there."

"How many?" Kane asked.

"About a dozen, all preserved better than this one. The cold contributed to that, I expect."

Brigid studied the withered body in the chair. "It almost looks like he was electrocuted."

Kane eyed a large black area beyond the chairs. "Pretty elaborate method of execution, even for Nazis."

He walked forward a few yards, then came to a halt. "Hey, take a look at this, why don't you?"

He spoke with such affected nonchalance, the nape hairs of both Grant and Brigid instantly tingled. They knew from years of experience that the stranger the circumstances, the more casual Kane pretended to be.

A huge round pit occupied most of the floor space, but it wasn't very deep—perhaps only six feet. When the outlanders saw what lay at the bottom, they experienced shuddery sensations of dread, realizing that the cavern contained far darker secrets than failed time-manipulation experiments from the twentieth century.

Deeply engraved into the rock floor was a vast geometric design, a complex series of interlocking cuneiform glyphs that formed a dizzying spiral of concentric rings a hundred yards or more in diameter.

For a second time, Kane murmured softly, blandly, "Huh."

The pattern of symmetrical hieroglyphs arched, twisted, swirled, turning, stretching out, bending in on themselves at right, then left angles, intersecting to meet in the raised center ring.

"Do you people know what that thing is?" White asked querulously. "My people couldn't figure it out, but I think it's got something to do with—"

"Shut up," Grant snapped, following the confusing pattern with the flashlight beam.

Brigid, Kane and Grant knew the design inscribed into the floor was an ancient geodetic marker, chiseled into the naked stone as a two-dimensional representation of the multidimensional geomantic vortex points that comprised the natural electromagnetic grid of Earth energies. Although they had seen similar markers in the past, in places such as Iraq, China, Brazil and even on Mars, they had never encountered one a fraction of the size of the one sunken below floor level.

Kane stared unblinkingly at the intricate labyrinth of lines. He didn't pretend to understand the scientific principles of geomantic vortex points, but he respected and feared their power, as had the ancient peoples who engraved the rock floor with the symbols. He realized that the fusion generator and the geodetic marker represented a link in a chain that stretched up from the dawn of human civilization to the very instant he came to the realization.

Brigid Baptiste cleared her throat, then stated quietly and calmly, "We *really* need to look at the files found in this place."

Chapter 7

Mohandas Lakesh Singh stepped over the threshold and onto the plateau, inhaling deeply of the fresh mountain air and then repressing a shiver. The temperature was fairly mild for so early in the spring, but Lakesh had been born in the tropical climate of Kashmir, India. Even after 250 years, his internal thermostat was still stuck there. Although he had spent well over a century in a form of cryogenic suspension, and though it made no real scientific sense, he had been very susceptible to cold ever since.

The sprawling plateau surrounding the Cerberus redoubt was broad enough for the entire population of the redoubt to assemble without getting near the rusted remains of the surrounding chain-link fence. The flat expanse of tarmac was bordered on one side by a grassy slope rising to granite outcroppings and on the other by an abyss that plummeted vertically for nearly a thousand feet to the rushing waters of the Clark Fork River.

The tarmac still glistened with the residue of that morning's dew, making the uneven areas slippery underfoot as Lakesh crossed it, skirting the members of Cerberus Away Team Alpha. Led by a former Magistrate named Carr, three men and three women were engaged in their daily program of calisthenics. Carr exhorted them to suck it up and learn to love the burn. Lakesh wasn't sure what the tall man meant, but he was sure it wasn't anything he would find pleasant.

Lakesh had initially opposed the formation of the three Cerberus away teams, made uncomfortable by the concept of the redoubt's own version of the Magistrate Divisions. Indeed they were composed of former Magistrates. However, as the canvas of the redoubt's operations broadened, the personnel situation at the installation also changed.

No longer could Kane, Grant, Brigid Baptiste and Domi undertake the majority of the ops and therefore shoulder the lion's share of the risks. Over the past year, Kane and Grant had set up Cerberus Away Team Alpha, Beta and Delta. CAT Delta was semipermanently stationed at Redoubt Yankee at Thunder Isle, rotating duty shifts with the Tigers of Heaven, and CAT Beta had been assigned an extensive security patrol in the foothills.

The road leading down from the plateau to the foothills of the Bitterroot Range was little more than a cracked and twisted asphalt ribbon, skirting yawning chasms and cliffs. Acres of the mountainside had collapsed during the nuke-triggered earthquakes of two centuries ago.

A network of motion and thermal sensors surrounded the Cerberus installation, expanding in a six-mile radius from the plateau, following an attack on the redoubt staged by Overlord Enlil.

Although a truce had been struck, a pact of noninterference agreed upon by Cerberus and the nine overlords, no one trusted Enlil's word, and so the security network was constantly monitored and periodically upgraded.

Noticing Mariah Falk standing off to one side at the base of the slope, Lakesh approached her. She dabbed at a film of perspiration on her forehead with the corner of a towel. Like the other people out on the plateau, she wore a sweat suit, but she was not exercising.

"Malingering, Dr. Falk?" Lakesh inquired, his cultured voice underscored by a lilting East Indian accent.

The woman cast him a quick but slightly annoyed glance with her brown eyes, but when she realized he was teasing, a smile touched her lips. A former geologist from the Manitius Moon base, Mariah wasn't particularly young or particularly pretty, but she had an infectious smile and a relaxed, easy manner. Her short chestnut-brown hair was threaded with gray at the temples.

"Strained a hamstring," she replied. "When I stopped

enjoying the burn, I decided not to suck it up. What's your excuse, Dr. Singh?"

Lakesh shrugged. "Malingering is a subject upon which I have sometimes thought of writing a monograph. So I'm always researching it."

Mariah laughed in appreciation. "Since both of us spent over a century malingering in stasis, it's a subject we should collaborate on."

Lakesh nodded. "Us and about seventy percent of the personnel here."

Mariah Falk did not respond to the oblique reference. Like the other lunar colonists, Mariah had been born in the twentieth century but spent nearly all of the twenty-first and twenty-second centuries in a form of cryogenic stasis.

"It's still not easy turning academics into Magistrates, even fake ones," Mariah said, pointing to the members of CAT Alpha.

Lakesh frowned at her. A well-built man of medium height, with thick, glossy black hair, a dark olive complexion and a long, aquiline nose, he looked no older than fifty, despite strands of gray threading his temples. In reality, he had celebrated his 250th birthday a few months before. He wore a one-piece white zippered bodysuit, the unisex duty uniform of the Cerberus personnel.

"That's not what we're doing," Lakesh said a bit more harshly than he intended.

Mariah glanced over at the men and women jogging in place and raised an ironic eyebrow. "No? After the jumping jacks is a weapons drill, you know."

"Things are very different now," Lakesh shot back defensively.

For three-plus years, the Cerberus resistance movement had struggled to dismantle the machine of baronial tyranny in America. They had devoted themselves to their work, and victory over the barons, if not precisely within their grasp, did not seem a completely unreachable goal. Unexpectedly, nearly two years before, the entire dynamic of the struggle against the nine barons changed.

The Cerberus warriors learned that the fragile hybrid barons, despite being close to a century old, were only in an early stage of their development. Overnight, the barons changed. When that happened, the war against the baronies themselves ended, but a new one, far greater in scope, began. As the barons evolved into their true forms, incarnations of the ancient Annunaki overlords, their avaricious scope expanded to encompass the entire world and every thinking creature on it.

"Speaking of things being different, is there any word from our people in Slovakia?" Mariah said.

Peeling back the cuff of his sleeve, Lakesh consulted his wrist chron. "Not yet, but they're not scheduled for a report for an hour yet."

Mariah eyed him closely. "You seem nervous anyway."

Lakesh opened his mouth to voice a denial, then forced a smile to his face. "Am I that obvious?"

"You usually don't take outdoor constitutionals so early in the day," she replied. "You're normally in the op center, reviewing reports that came in during the night. Domi is the most competent young woman I've ever met. I don't think you have to worry about her so much."

Lakesh sighed. "Perhaps not—or not since I promised to stop expressing my worry to her whenever she went out into the field. It became a serious point of contention between us."

Mariah nodded. "I know."

Lakesh narrowed his eyes suspiciously. "You do? May I ask how?"

The trans-comm in Lakesh's pocket shrilled for his attention. Pretending to ignore Mariah's expression of relief, he withdrew the little radiophone and flipped open the plastic cover. "Lakesh here."

"We've received a message from Brigid," Donald Bry's crisp voice responded. "She needs to talk to you. It's urgent."

Lakesh felt chill fingers of dread stroke the buttons of his spine. "She's ahead of schedule."

"Apparently the team is already on its way back."

The man's voice acquired a note of impatience and amusement. "Oh, and she told me to inform you that Domi is just fine."

"That was the furthermost thing from my mind," Lakesh retorted gruffly, folding the cover over, but not quite quickly enough to cut off Bry's snorting laugh of derision.

He nodded curtly to Mariah and turned away. "Carry on malingering, Dr. Falk."

She returned the nod. "You too, Dr. Lakesh. Learn to love the burn."

Chapter 8

Knowing Mariah watched him, Lakesh deliberately adopted a gait so casual it was almost leisurely. In truth, whenever Domi was away from the installation for an extended period of time, he did not sleep well and he found relaxing an almost impossible task. He felt somewhat embarrassed by his mother-hen tendency, so he did his best to disguise it.

As he walked across the plateau, he pretended to study the great gray peak looming overhead, the base of which held the entrance to the redoubt.

Constructed at the end of the twentieth century, no expense had been spared to make the installation, the seat of Project Cerberus, a masterpiece of concealment and impenetrability. Although official designations of all Totality Concept-related redoubts were based on the phonetic alphabet, almost no one stationed in the facility had ever referred to it as Bravo. The mixture of civilian scientists and military personnel simply called it Cerberus.

The thirty-acre, three-level installation had survived

the nukecaust with its operating systems, radiation shielding and fission reactors in good condition. The redoubt contained two dozen self-contained apartments, a cafeteria, a well-equipped armory, a medical infirmary, a gymnasium complete with a swimming pool and even holding cells on the bottom level.

When Lakesh had secretly reactivated the installation more than thirty-five years before, the repairs he made had been minor, primarily cosmetic in nature. Gradually he had added an elaborate security system. He had been forced to work completely alone, so the upgrades had taken several years to complete. However, the location of the redoubt in Montana's Bitterroot Range had kept his work from being discovered by the baronial authorities.

In the generations since the nukecaust, a sinister mythology had been ascribed to the mountains, with their mysteriously shadowed forests and deep, dangerous ravines. The wilderness area was virtually unpopulated. The nearest settlement was located in the flatlands, and it consisted of a small band of Indians, Sioux and Cheyenne, led by a shaman named Sky Dog.

Planted within rocky clefts of the mountain peak beneath camouflage netting, were concealed the uplinks from the orbiting Vela-class reconnaissance satellite and the Keyhole Comsat.

Lakesh walked down the main corridor, a twenty-foot-wide passageway made of softly gleaming vanadium alloy and shaped like a square with an arch on top. Great curving ribs of metal and massive girders supported the high rock roof. He passed a number of people who greeted him either with a deferential nod or with a polite "Good morning, Dr. Singh."

He appreciated the respect. For many years he received very little of it, nor had he felt he deserved it. As a youthful genius, Lakesh had been drafted into the web of conspiracy spun by the overseers of the Totality Concept during the last two decades of the twentieth century. A physicist and cyberneticist with multiple degrees, he served as the administrator for Project Cerberus, a position that meant he survived the global megacull.

Lakesh entered the op center, the largest room in the redoubt. Two aisles of computer stations divided the long, high-ceilinged room. A dozen people sat before the terminals. Monitor screens flashed images and streams of code.

The operations center had five dedicated and eight shared subprocessors, all linked to the mainframe computer concealed behind a shielded far wall. Two centuries before, the machine had been one of the most advanced models ever built, carrying experimental, error-correcting microchips of such a tiny size that they even reacted to quantum fluctuations. Biochip technology had been employed when it was built, protein molecules sandwiched between microscopic glass-and-metal circuits.

The information contained in the main database may not have been the sum total of all humankind's knowledge, but not for lack of trying. Any bit, byte or shred of intelligence that had ever been digitized was only a few keystrokes and mouse clicks away.

A huge Mercator relief map of the world spanned the entire wall above the door. Pinpoints of light shone steadily in almost every country, connected by a thin glowing pattern of lines. They represented the Cerberus network, the locations of all functioning gateway units across the planet. As he walked in, Lakesh gave an over-the-shoulder glance at the map. No lights blinked, so none of the indexed mat-trans chambers were in use.

On the opposite side of the operations center, an anteroom held the eight-foot-tall gateway unit, rising from an elevated platform. Six upright slabs of brown-hued armaglass formed a translucent wall around it. Manufactured in the last decade of the twentieth century, armaglass was formed of a special compound that plasticized and combined the properties of steel and glass.

It was used as walls in the jump chambers to confine quantum energy overspills. The redoubt's particular unit was the first fully debugged matter-transfer inducer built after the prototypes. It served as the basic template for all the others that followed, and Lakesh still felt a strong degree of fondness for it.

In 1989, Lakesh himself had been the first successful long-distance matter transfer of a human subject, traveling a hundred yards from a prototype gateway chamber to a receiving booth. That initial success was replicated many times, and with the replication came the modifications and improvements of the quantum interphase mat-trans inducers, reaching the point where they were manufactured in modular form.

In the dim light the huge room hummed with the quietly efficient chatter of the system operators. The control center was almost always well-manned, but inasmuch as the complex was the brain of the redoubt, it naturally drew personnel from all quarters. Most of the people sitting at the various stations were émigrés from the Manitius Moon base. The only long-term Cerberus staff members Lakesh saw were Donald Bry and Farrell.

Sitting before the communications station, Bry glanced toward him and said sourly, "Took you long enough."

Donald Bry, a round-shouldered man of small stature who acted as Lakesh's lieutenant and apprentice in matters technological, had curly copper-colored hair and a perpetual expression of consternation, no matter his true mood.

Lakesh paid no attention to the man. His eyes went immediately to the medical monitor, where the telemetry transmitted from Kane's, Brigid's, Grant's and Domi's biolink transponders scrolled upward. The Comsat kept track of Cerberus personnel by their subcutaneous transponders when they were out in the field.

The icons that represented the vital signs of the four people displayed no signs of stress; their blood-pressure and heart-rate readings were well within the normal range. The four symbols were superimposed over a map, inching across a computer-generated Pacific Ocean. The Mantas were whisking the team back at the maximum cruising speed of Mach 20.

Feeling that he had successfully masked his surge of relief when he saw Domi's strong vitals, Lakesh turned his attention to the comm station.

Bry said into the microphone of his headset, "It's himself, at long last."

Lakesh was accustomed to Donald Bry's acerbic manner, so he didn't respond to his sarcasm. Slipping on another headset, he said, "I'm here, Brigid. Where are you?"

"Somewhere over the Baltic Sea," Brigid Baptiste replied curtly. "And before you ask, everybody is fine."

"Then why are you—?"

"I have a preliminary report to make."

A little taken aback by Brigid's brusque attitude, Lakesh simply said, "Proceed."

In her characteristic clear, concise way, Brigid outlined all the events since the last check-in, beginning with their arrival in Slovakia and ending with the exploration of the cave within Gerlachov Peak.

"Frankly, I'm stumped," Brigid concluded. "The geodetic marker is certainly the largest we've ever seen, so you'd think a vortex node of corresponding size would have been in the Parallax Points index—which it isn't. Couple that with White's contention that the facility itself was constructed by the Germans and was connected with time-dilation experiments, we're dealing with something that has the potential to be pretty horrifying."

Despite the queasy sensation Brigid's report had invoked in his belly, Lakesh managed to keep his voice calm and steady. "Were you able to salvage any of the files?"

Brigid's sigh of frustration was conveyed over the channel. "Not many. They were very old, so they went up like flash paper. About ninety percent were pretty thoroughly burned. The other ten percent we had to share with District Twelve."

"That's rather generous of them, all things considered."

"Not really. We also had to let them keep the two millennialists. Major Zuryakin is very keen to learn more about the consortium. Anyway, I've been skimming over a couple of the files and—"

Brigid's voice trailed off. Lakesh cast Bry a sharp, questioning glance. "What's happening?"

"Nothing." The small man pointed to a glowing indicator light. "The channel and frequency are still open. She just stopped talking for some reason."

"Dearest Brigid," Lakesh said loudly. "Are you there? Are you all right?"

"I am…I'm just trying to collect my thoughts." Brigid's uncertain tone suddenly acquired its usual crisp, matter-of-fact edge. "Apparently the Slovakian operation wasn't strictly a Third Reich undertaking, since it was implemented a year after the war ended. The group involved was some sort of offshoot of the SS who called themselves the Brotherhood of the Black Sun, and an occult group known as the Ordo Templi Orientis."

Lakesh felt his eyebrows knit together at the bridge of his nose. "The OTO I remember was some sort of pseudo-occult group, a not-so-secret society that was popular among black-magic-minded morons with too much time and money to spend. But I don't believe I ever heard of the Brotherhood of the Black Sun."

"It rings a distant bell with me," Brigid replied. "An obscure reference I came across several years ago during my research into the occult roots of Nazism, but it was out of context. Judging by what I've read so far, the OTO and the brotherhood were working on something called a trans-temporal inversion chronoscope. I think that may have a familiar ring."

Lakesh felt his stomach muscles clench. "As I recall, it was the designation for the prototype temporal dilator that Operation Chronos developed for the Totality Concept decades later."

"Exactly. And we also know that the Totality Concept had its hooks into a number of secret societies."

"Or vice versa." Lakesh knew that in the rarefied atmosphere of high security surrounding the Totality Concept, many secret societies networked with government intelligence agencies. He remembered meeting representatives of the Knights of Malta, the Order of Thule, the Priory of Awen and even envoys from the Vatican.

"I can consult the database," Lakesh told her, "and see if anything is there regarding such a bizarre alliance and hopefully have something for you by the time you arrive."

"Good." Brigid hesitated, then said, "There's something else."

"That always seems to be the way," Lakesh commented, striving for a lighter note. "What is it this time?"

"Remember you telling me that a few of the overprojects reached out to some pretty strange people as consultants?"

Lakesh snorted. "Yes, a lot of mentally damaged adherents to crackpot scientific theories came and went over the years."

"I haven't gone through all the files, but one name keeps showing up, figuring very prominently on just about every page."

"Who?"

Brigid took so long to answer that Lakesh was on the verge of repeating the question. Then she said flatly, unemotionally, "Crowley. Aleister Crowley."

Chapter 9

Lakesh's shoulders jerked in reaction to the pronounce-
ment. "Crowley?" he echoed hoarsely.

"You know that name?" Brigid asked.

Lakesh did not respond for a long moment. He knew
the name very well. Of all the madmen involved with
the initial underpinnings of the Totality Concept bureau-
cracy, none had been more loathed by the scientific personnel than the depraved Englishman.

Crowley had died several years before Lakesh was
born, but he knew it was nearly a cause for official cele-
bration among the scientific staff of the various Totality
Concept divisions when the man expired in 1947. They
had despised him.

"Lakesh?" Brigid sounded more impatient than
concerned.

"Yes, I've heard of him...the so-called world's wickedest man." Lakesh forced a scornful chuckle. "Of
course, that was an appellation foisted upon him by
English newspapers, and he exploited it to the fullest.

He gloried in boasting about his sexual conquests, his devil worship, his—"

"I'm not interested in his reputation," Brigid broke in. "It's his connection to Operation Chronos and maybe even the Archons that has me bothered."

"Technically," Lakesh pointed out, "there wasn't an Operation Chronos in 1946."

"Regardless," said Brigid dismissively, "we found an Archon generator in the cave, even though it was dead. And I remember reading that Crowley claimed to be in contact with an otherworldly entity he called Lam, whom, as you might recall, had a very strong familial relationship with the Archons."

"I'm aware of Crowley's claims," Lakesh countered stiffly, not caring for Brigid's patronizing tone. "He made countless assertions about himself, most of which were unverified boasts made for the benefit of the news media. He was extremely conscious of his public image. And if he indeed had contact with Lam, how is that important now? Crowley died in 1947."

"Reportedly died," Brigid said impatiently. "Lakesh, at the moment I'm not too interested about Crowley's reputation in the twentieth century. We've got a giant geodetic marker, but no indexed vortex point, a powerless Archon fusion generator, a dead little boy and evidence that places an offshoot of the SS, an alleged Satanist and time-travel experiments all in one place.

You may not see that any of it is worth much at this late date, but I and the Millennial Consortium beg to differ."

Tamping down his rising anger due to Brigid's manner, Lakesh said, "I'll have some of our people put together a briefing jacket. What's your ETA?"

A faint murmur filtered over the transceiver as Brigid consulted with someone, then announced, "About another hour, give or take. I'm flying in with Grant. He'll drop me off at Redoubt Yankee and then scoot over to New Edo for some downtime."

"Drop you off at Redoubt Yankee? Why?"

"Can you think of a more appropriate place to investigate early time-travel experiments than the seat of Operation Chronos?"

Lakesh assumed the query was rhetorical, so he didn't address it. "Hopefully I'll have solid information for you to work with by then."

"Hopefully. When you do, have Brewster gate over to Thunder Isle with it. I can use his help on this."

"Dr. Philboyd is already at Redoubt Yankee."

"He is?" Brigid sounded slightly surprised. "Why?"

"The staff there noticed an energy fluctuation on a couple of the instruments. He was asked to offer an opinion. You know how we scientists are."

Twenty of the former Moon base scientists were stationed on Thunder Isle in the Cific, working to refurbish the sprawling complex that had housed Operation

Chronos two centuries before, although the place technically fell under the jurisdiction of the government of New Edo.

"As a point of fact," Brigid replied dryly, "I do know how you are. I'll contact you again when I arrive at the installation."

Lakesh cut the connection and Bry remarked, "Seemed a little stressed-out, didn't she?"

"With her day's activities, I don't blame her too much," Lakesh said distractedly as he stepped toward a computer station networked to the main database.

"She sure wasn't letting you off the hook," Bry stated, a slightly mocking edge in his voice. "Why do you figure that is?"

Lakesh refused to be baited. He sat down before the keyboard and stared fixedly at the monitor, as if he found the screen-saver image of a chimpanzee using a cell phone utterly fascinating.

When Brigid Baptiste, Grant, Kane and Domi first arrived at Cerberus as fugitives fleeing baronial justice, Lakesh had been the final authority in the redoubt, planning the missions and all of the operating protocols.

Several years after that, Kane, Brigid and Grant staged a mini-coup d'état. Lakesh hadn't been completely unseated from his position of authority, but he became answerable to a more democratic process. At first he bitterly resented what he construed as the usurping of his power by ingrates, but over a period of time, he accepted sharing his command with the other Cerberus exiles. It was the only fair position to take, since the majority of them were exiles due to his covert actions.

Except for the former Moon colonists, almost every person in the redoubt had arrived as a convicted criminal—after Lakesh had set them up, framing them for crimes against their respective villes. He admitted it was a cruel, heartless plan, with a barely acceptable risk factor, but it was the only way to spirit them out of their villes, turn them against the barons and make them feel indebted to him.

This bit of explosive and potentially deadly knowledge had not been shared with the other exiles. Only Kane, Grant and Brigid were aware of it and they kept the information to themselves, not so much as a tool for blackmail, but because they genuinely feared Lakesh might be lynched, out on the very plateau upon which the personnel exercised.

Fingers clattering over the keys, Lakesh accessed the historical files and input the words "Crowley, Aleister, Ordo Templi Orientis."

"Who was this Crowley slagger supposed to be?" Bry asked.

Lakesh started to answer, then shook his head. "To

be frank, I'm not sure. I don't know if anyone does. He was a true enigma, the classic walking contradiction."

Bry arched a skeptical eyebrow. "The wickedest man in the world?"

Lakesh's lips quirked in a humorless smile. "That label was applied to him when the standards for wickedness were a little less broad than they became a few years later."

"Could he really have had contact with the Archons?" Bry pressed. "Lam in particular?"

Lakesh began a denial, then thought better of it. "It's possible. We know that Lam walked in very odd circles during his long life."

Strictly speaking, Lam was not an Archon, but rather one of their forebears, a custodial race known as the First Folk, created many millennia before as part of a pact between the Annunaki and the Tuatha de Danaan.

The First Folk were determined to guide humankind. If nothing else, they still possessed the monumental pride of their race and devotion to the continuity of their people. To accomplish their goals, they retreated into the subterranean kingdom exalted in Tibetan legend as Agartha.

Lam was the last of the pure-blooded First Folk. He rallied his people, becoming a spiritual leader, a general and a mentor. He knew his folk could not stay hidden forever, nor did they care to do so. The human race could not be influenced without interaction.

Under Lam's guidance, he and some of his people ascended again into the world of men. Lam was known throughout human historical epochs, but by names such as Osiris, Quetzacoatal, Zarathustra, Tsong Kaba and many others.

Although Lakesh was aware of Aleister Crowley's writings in regard to Lam, he had never taken them seriously, simply because he viewed the British occultist as more of a headline-grabbing showman than a genuine Satanist. Lakesh assumed Crowley's black magic was of the dime-store variety.

However, Lakesh did recall being struck by an account of how Crowley conducted a series of experiments in what would many decades later be termed as channeling. Although he couldn't remember the details, it seemed that at some stage during the proceedings Crowley underwent a form of contactee experience involving an entity he called Lam. He often cited Lam's guidance and counsel.

The notion wasn't quite as mad as it seemed on the surface. During his years spent investigating the hidden history of humanity, Lakesh reached the conclusion that several of the First Folk, or the Archons, maintained a telepathic communication with various visionaries, most of whom were believed by their contemporaries to be mad.

The computer beeped, signaling it had completed the

search through the files in the database. On the screen flashed a dense block of copy and a black-and-white portrait of a bald-headed man dressed in a flowing, elaborately decorated robe. His long fingers were crooked and held in contorted, double-jointed positions that Lakesh assumed were some sort of eldritch signs.

The face looked pale, even in the monochromatic photo. The square-jawed head was completely hairless. The eyes were round like a doll's. The whites showed all around the irises and gave a mesmeric quality to the hard, challenging stare. The mouth, although full-lipped, was compressed, like the edges of a wound.

Meeting Aleister Crowley's unblinking stare, Lakesh felt a tension building between his shoulder blades. Almost reluctantly, he scrolled down to a smaller picture below the one of Crowley. The tension became almost painful.

The black-and-white watercolor image depicted a close-up view of a large head, the cranium smooth and hairless, tapering to a pointed chin. The slit of the mouth was pursed and the big eyes extended partway around the sides of the face. There was no suggestion of clothing beyond what appeared to be a cloak buttoned at the neck.

Done by Crowley's hand, the rendering was crude, almost childish, but the portrait still exuded a power that set Lakesh's nape hairs to tingling. In a voice barely above a whisper, he said, "Lam…for the love of God, what kind of guidance and counsel could you have possibly given that man?"

Chapter 10

The early-morning sun felt good on Brewster Philboyd's shoulders, even though he knew that within an hour he would be cursing it. As it was, the humidity that perpetually seemed to surround Thunder Isle had already drawn sweat out of him.

As Philboyd paused to sip from his water bottle, Edwards growled, "Can't you drink and walk at the same time, techie?"

Philboyd cast the big shaved-headed ex-Mag a coldly appraising stare. "I could, but I didn't want to make you feel inferior since I know you have trouble walking and farting at the same time. And that's Dr. Techie to you."

In his mid-forties, Brewster Philboyd was a little over six feet tall, long limbed and lanky of build. Blond-white hair was swept back from a receding hairline. He wore black-rimmed eyeglasses and his cheeks appeared to be pitted with the sort of scars associated with chronic teenage acne.

Edwards was only a couple of inches taller but considerably broader of build with overdeveloped triceps, biceps and deltoids. He and Philboyd were dressed similarly in drab-olive T-shirts, green-striped camou pants and high-laced jump boots.

Edwards cradled an M-14 rifle in his arms, and a Colt Government Model .45 rode at his right hip in a paddle holster. A small backpack held spare ammunition, as well as food and water.

Philboyd was armed with a Copperhead, but the stunted subgun dangled from a clip on his web belt. In his right hand he held a rectangular power analyzer, a device designed to measure, record and analyze energy emissions, quality and harmonics. He swept the extended sensor stem back and forth in short arcs.

Edwards eyed it distrustfully. "You Moonies sure are dependent on your little toys."

Philboyd didn't outwardly react to the derogatory term for the Manitius émigrés. "And you Mags sure are dependent are your little popguns. You ought to be more like Nakai…he depends only on his steel."

Nakai listened to the exchange between the two men with no particular expression on his swart face. Neither Philboyd nor Edwards was sure if the samurai understood English, or if he preferred to conceal the fact that he did. He hadn't spoken a word since embarking from Redoubt Yankee forty minutes before.

Edwards hadn't concealed his annoyance when Sela

Sinclair, the shift officer at Redoubt Yankee, ordered him to accompany a scientist and a Tiger of Heaven out into the tangled green hell of Thunder Isle.

A short, stocky man, Nakai wore only a partial suit of his samurai armor, not the full battle dress of the Tigers of Heaven. A lightweight *hara-ate,* consisting of lacquered metal wafers linked together by tiny chains, covered his torso. Coarse-clothed shorts fell to mid-thigh and a pair of *sune-ate,* shin protectors made of tough leather, extended down from his knees to his ankles.

Two scabbarded swords, a long-bladed *katana* and a shorter *tanto,* were strapped crosswise across his back. A strip of white cloth bearing the red ideograph of New Edo bound his forehead.

The LCD window display on the face analyzer flashed with numbers, scrolling up and down as Philboyd passed the sensor stem back and forth. The digits suddenly held steady and he announced, "That way."

Edwards looked at the distant tree line and shifted from one foot to the other. "Isn't that in the direction of the swamp?"

A supercilious smile creased Philboyd's lips. "A big badass Mag like you isn't afraid of a few leeches, are you? Takes one to know one, I guess."

Edwards scowled down at him. "Watch your mouth, techie."

"No, I'd say it's you who should watch yours," Philboyd countered waspishly. "You're here as a bodyguard, nothing more."

Edward indicated Nakai with a backward jerk of his head. "And him?"

"I'm here to escort you both," Nakai said in a surprisingly mild, unaccented voice. "This is New Edoan territory and you are our guests. Please conduct yourselves accordingly."

Both Philboyd and Edwards stared at him in silent surprise. The former Magistrate's lips worked as if he struggled to bottle up a stream of profanity. He jerked his head in the direction the sensor stem pointed. "Let's get on with this."

Philboyd performed a parody of a gracious bow and began walking, repressing the urge to laugh. Despite his dislike of Edwards, he couldn't deny the man's presence was a comfort. As an astrophysicist by training and trade, Brewster Philboyd knew from painful prior experience that physical action was not his forte. The few times he had traipsed out into the field had resulted in injury, captivity or both.

However, when an anomalous energy signature appeared on a hitherto-dead sensor array in the Operation Chronos control cortex, he was invited to look into the matter. The source of the power emission, although faint and sporadic, was triangulated to emanate from a central area of Thunder Isle, one that hadn't been visited either by the New Edoans or the Cerberus personnel.

Although the last stroll Philboyd had taken away from the relative safety of Redoubt Yankee ended with him being pursued by a ravenous Daspletosaurus christened Monstrodamus, he wasn't about to back down in front of CAT Beta or the Tigers of Heaven.

For one thing, Monstrodamus was dead, although two of the creature's offspring had been sighted a few times, and for another he was weary of being dismissed as a chair-bound academic who couldn't go anywhere without clutching the hand of Brigid Baptiste. The population of the Western Isles region wasn't large, but as more contact was made with the inhabitants, he didn't relish the notion of earning a reputation as a coward.

The term "Western Isles" was something of a misnomer—it was more of a catch-all to describe a region in the Pacific of old and new landmasses. During the nuclear holocaust, seismic bombs known as earthshakers fractured the fault lines of the Pacific coastal regions. When the most intense tectonic shifts abated, the Pacific coast was barely twenty miles from the foothills of the Sierra Nevada.

During the intervening two centuries, the sea receded somewhat, leaving islands where high points of the landmass had once been. Undersea quakes raised new volcanic islands. Because the soil was scraped up from the seabed, most of the islands became fertile very quickly, except for the Blight Belt—islands that were originally part of California but were still irradiated.

New Edo and its companion islet, Thunder Isle, were part of the Santa Barbara or Channel Island chain. Many of the other Western Isles were overrun by pirates and Asian criminal organizations known as tongs and triads.

Thunder Isle wasn't irradiated, but in the short time New Edo had been settled, a body of legends had sprung up about the island. A cyclical phenomenon was said to occur on the island. Lightning seemed to strike up, accompanied by sounds like thunderclaps, even if the weather was clear.

On the heels of the phenomenon often came incursions of what the more impressionable New Edoans claimed were demons. Brigid was shown the corpse of one such demon, and she tentatively identified it as a Dryosaurus, a man-sized dinosaur.

She was able to identify other artifacts found on the shores of Thunder Isle—a helmet from the era of the conquistadors, and a stone spearhead that resembled a Folsom point, so named for Folsom, New Mexico, the archaeological site where the first spearhead was found. It was evidence of a prehistoric culture, many thousands of years old.

After walking less than half a mile, Philboyd, Edwards and Nakai reached the edge of the swamp. To their collective relief, they did not have to slog through it. Instead, they skirted its outer edges, traveling through desolate stretches inhabited by ground lizards, snakes and swarms of insects.

Beyond the swamp lay a dense tangled jungle that climbed the sides of small hills. All around were growing plants, most of them ferns. The size ranged from tiny seedlings to monstrous growths the size of oak trees. Tangles of creeper vines carpeted the jungle floor.

Philboyd stopped and consulted the power scanner again. "We're still on the right track."

He made a move to step forward, but Edwards restrained him with a heavy hand clapped on his shoulder. "Hold on that."

Philboyd cast him an annoyed glance, on the verge of ordering the man to keep his hands to himself. Then he noticed the intense glint in his eyes, a gleam mirrored in the gaze of Nakai.

"What?" Philboyd asked, unconsciously lowering his voice.

"Get down, techie," Edwards said quietly, exerting pressure on his shoulder.

Philboyd knelt behind a copse of undergrowth. Edwards and Nakai crouched on either side of him, studying the tree line. Within a few seconds, Philboyd glimpsed a shifting of shadows. Heavy-set figures pushed through the foliage.

Four people emerged from the jungle, although if they actually qualified as human was open for debate. The males were about five feet five with very rounded shoulders, and foreheads that bulged out like the edges of cliffs. Their eyes were set deeply under thick supraorbital ridges. They wore loincloths made of a tough fabric and at a distance, they looked almost like kilts. They carried wooden-hafted spears angled over their shoulders.

Philboyd knew he should not have been surprised to see the primitive humans on the island, since Kane reported an encounter with them several years before and he himself had seen a couple of pelt-wearing brutes in the redoubt's temporal-stasis chamber.

He studied their harsh, simian features. Their hair ranged in color from dark to fair and a few of the men wore grizzled beards. The one woman wore her unruly mop of hair bound up with rawhide thongs. A necklace of painted bone and animal teeth banded her throat. All of them, men and the woman alike, had the bearing and feral expressions of animals.

"Hunting party, must be," Philboyd whispered. "The others must be somewhere else."

"Maybe," Edwards replied. "Or these are the last survivors of the group. The others might have been eaten by now."

With a twinge of sadness, Philboyd realized Edwards could be speaking the truth. Since Kane's discovery of the primitives, attempts had been made to communicate with them, but to no avail, since they spoke no language but a grunting dialect of their own. Foodstuffs and even the clothing the subhumans wore had been left for them to find. Like almost every other bit of flora and fauna on the island, the subhumans were abductees.

When the Cerberus warriors first explored the Operation Chronos installation, they discovered that the temporal dilator's chronon wave guide conformals ran wild on random cycles. They either reconstituted trawled subjects from the holding matrix or snatched new ones from all epochs in history. Thus everything from people, to animals and plants were randomly trawled from past epochs.

The three men remained hunkered down behind the scrub until the primitives had trudged out of sight into the swamp.

Standing up, Philboyd commented, "You surprise me, Edwards."

"Why's that, Dr. Techie?"

"I figured you'd shoot those poor bastards down just on the off chance one of 'em might slobber at you one day."

Edwards lifted the broad beam of his shoulders in a shrug. "Maybe I would have if they'd been closer. Or given you to them as lunch."

Philboyd looked up from realigning the power analyzer, his eyes slitted suspiciously. Then he caught the faint smile ghosting over Nakai's lips and he muttered, "Very whimsical, Edwards."

The path the three men followed broadened into a narrow trail enclosed between walls of deep green. The tree ferns grew to great heights, and their glossy trunks stood close together. The bushy crowns of the trees were so heavy, so dense, that by looking up from the ground Philboyd could not see them individually. Through occasional brief openings in the canopy he saw shafts of green-hued sunlight.

Thick, flowering vines hung in loops from the trees, some of them festooned with fragrant, multicolored garlands. Broken tree trunks lay on the ground entangled with one another by the vines or leaned against other trees, covered by luxuriant moss from which sprang beautifully tinted orchids. Cup-shaped palms sprang from the soil, competing for growing room with the gigantic tree ferns. All the plants reached toward the light, struggling upward to be touched by the sun.

The cornucopia of plant life produced a musky perfume and the oppressively humid air enclosed the three men in a hothouse atmosphere, making their breathing labored. Perspiration formed dark crescent moons at their armpits and necklines. Palming a film of sweat away from his forehead, Philboyd wryly recalled his

reasons for turning down Brigid's invitation to join the
Slovakian mission: "Way too cold."

The three men continued along the narrow, twisting
trail, sometimes taking short detours around tangled
thorns and clumps of shrubbery. Frequently they heard
rustles in the underbrush and once a deep-throated
grunt, but they saw nothing.

The heat of the day turned stifling even in the shade
of the forest. The strident chirps of the birds suddenly
stopped and nothing seemed to stir in the jungle. Eyes
on the LCD readout, Philboyd stumbled slightly in a de-
pression underfoot and nearly fell. Biting back a curse,
he looked down and his breath caught in his throat.

He saw a set of deep parallel tracks that had crushed
and flattened the vegetation on the jungle floor. The outside edges of the prints showed a pattern resembling
splayed, three-toed feet. They were twice the length
and breadth of Edwards's size-thirteen feet.

The instant Philboyd saw the tracks, he felt a cold
wash of fear and an awareness that death could be breathing down all of their necks. He husked out, "Monstrodamii."

Chapter 11

Nakai dropped to a knee beside one of the footprints and probed the edges with careful fingers. "These tracks were made at least a day ago, possibly longer."

Edwards favored Philboyd with a smirk. "Now you don't have to piss in your pants, Dr. Techie."

Philboyd swallowed a shudder. "You wouldn't take that attitude if you'd ever been chased by one of those devil lizards. They're the ancestors of the *T. rex* and as far as we know, we're right in the middle of their nesting territory."

Nakai stood up, brushing the dirt from his fingers. "I agree…we must be extremely cautious from now on."

Edwards looked to be on the verge of responding to Nakai's warning with a contemptuous remark, but instead he hefted his rifle and nodded. "Good idea."

The three men moved on down the trail, alert for any unusual sound or even a fleeting glimpse of stealthy movement in the jungle. A second's carelessness could result in blindness from the lash of poison-tipped thorns across the eyes, or a bloody death from a crouching predator.

The path they followed was like a tunnel cutting through the tall ferns overhanging either side of it. The world was a primeval, menacing green with blooming epiphytes and flowering creepers stretching down from overhead to snag them if they weren't watchful.

After another half hour of travel, the jungle gradually thinned and they emerged from the tree line. They stood on the edge of a savanna of dried grass and reddish, dusty soil. The terrain sloped gently downward. To the west, Philboyd saw the glimmer of the Pacific, and he calculated they had reached the center of the island.

The power analyzer in his hand suddenly emitted a steady electronic buzz. The LCD window glowed with three digits: 000. Edwards frowned, first at the device then at the barren terrain stretching before them. "This must be the place—wherever it is."

Philboyd's eyes scanned the area, noting but not caring for its resemblance to the dead zone surrounding the Redoubt Yankee complex. A flat, sandy plain at least a half mile in diameter enclosed the Operation Chronos facility. At its leading edge, the vegetation and shrubbery dropped away as if the foliage dared not cross an invisible boundary. The open place marked a zone of demarcation across the ground. The dead zone was the result of radiation poisoning.

Philboyd passed the sensor wand back and forth in wide sweeps, but the analyzer's energy reading did not change. Taking a deep breath, he stepped forward. "Let's see what we can find."

Edwards restrained him with one arm, holding him back. "My job, Doc."

Philboyd did not bother disguising his surge of relief. "You're absolutely right. I stand corrected."

Edwards moved carefully into the clearing, walking heel-to-toe, rifle held crossways across his broad chest. Philboyd and Nakai silently watched the big man's methodical progress, not speaking or even daring to breathe deeply.

When Edwards reached a point nearly thirty yards away from them, he paused, staring at the ground. He gazed downward for what seemed like a long time, then tentatively raised his right boot and stamped down hard.

"What's he doing?" Philboyd whispered, mystified.

Just as tentatively, Edwards reversed his grip on the M-14, using the butt to tap the ground several times. Nakai and Philboyd heard a faint chime of metal against metal.

Not able to contain his burgeoning curiosity, Philboyd called, "What is it?"

Edwards hesitated, then answered, "I don't know. Maybe you can tell me. Come on over…it seems safe enough."

The scientist and the samurai exchanged brief, wry smiles.

"Sounds like the winning entry in a famous-last-words contest," Philboyd said.

Nakai nodded dolefully, reaching up behind him and drawing his *tanto* with a rasp of steel on wood. "I agree."

Without the shade provided by the trees, the heat felt like a physical assault. Globes of sweat sprang out on Philboyd's forehead, and he blinked constantly to keep it from flowing into his eyes. He was blinking when he stumbled over an irregularity in the ground and would have fallen if not for a steadying hand extended by Nakai.

Looking downward, his first impression was that he stood in the bull's-eye of an immense, horizontal target. He heard himself mutter, "What the hell—?"

He, Edwards and Nakai gazed down at a series of giant, concentric rings, two wheels within a larger outer band, the circular center raised in a half dome like a hub. Composed of a gray alloy, perfectly round and more than a hundred yard's in diameter, each of the wheels was etched with numerical strings.

Philboyd had no doubt that the colossal series of rings was man-made, since its surface gleamed with countless tiny crystal facets all of the same size and hexagonal shape. The pattern laid out was as pristine and meticulously complex as a fractal Mandelbrot set. The facets glowed with a cold blue light, not at all intense but exuding a shimmering quality like heat waves rising from a desert blacktop road at high noon.

"What is this thing?" Edwards demanded.

Philboyd shook his head in frustration. "I wish I could tell you."

"I thought you were a scientist."

"And I thought I was a techie."

With the tip of his sword, Nakai traced several of the numbers engraved into the metal. "The numbers are English...perhaps this is connected with Operation Chronos."

Philboyd refrained from sneering. Instead he said dryly, "Obviously. But I never—" He broke off and cocked his head. "Listen."

"To what?" Edwards asked.

"Hush," Nakai ordered.

The men fell silent. A faint electronic hum reached their ears. Brewster Philboyd dropped to his hands and knees, lowering his head and pressing an ear against the metal surface of the hub. With a tone of self-satisfaction he announced, "Yep, *definitely* some kind of activity going on inside this thing. Or beneath it."

Edwards took an involuntary step back. "Activity? What do you mean?"

Philboyd rapped on the ring with his knuckles. "Solid."

"I asked you a question," Edwards snapped peevishly.

Philboyd glanced up at him. "I don't know if I can answer it. All I can tell you is that it's generating enough power to be picked up on a hand scanner from three miles or so away. Why, I have no idea, but I'll try to find out."

Edwards's face locked in a scowl. "My assignment was to accompany you out here to pinpoint the source of the energy signature. We've done that. Hanging around while you do your techie thing wasn't part of the mission profile. Let's head on back and report."

"You can make a comm-call and report."

Edwards nodded, reaching into his pocket. "I'll do that very thing."

Pulling out the small radiophone, he thumbed up the cover and pressed the transmit key. "Edwards to Cube. Do you copy?"

Only squawks, pops and the hashy crackle of static filtered over the comm. Edwards repeated the hail several times before he closed the cover. "Interference. My guess is the thing we're standing on is jamming the frequencies. All the more reason to get out of here."

Philboyd shook his head in mock incredulity. "Don't be a bigger idiot than you've shown yourself to be already."

Edwards's scowl deepened. "You heard me. We're going."

Before Philboyd could formulate an appropriately insulting response, a low bass hum floated from the metal beneath him. At the same time, the blue glow within the crystalline hexagons increased in intensity. A vibration passed through the ring upon which the three men stood. Philboyd scrambled to his feet, uttering a wordless cry of alarm.

The outer wheel suddenly began rotating clockwise. An instant later, the second ring spun in a counterclockwise motion. The hum rose in pitch and the light exuded from the crystals brightened even more.

Edwards, Philboyd and Nakai looked around frantically for a means of getting off the surface of the spinning wheels without losing their footing. Only the center hub remained motionless, so they climbed atop it. Tension felt like a length of heavy wet rope coiling in Philboyd's bowels. A static electricity discharge prickled his flesh like the legs of a thousand climbing ants.

"What the fuck is going on?" Edwards snarled, hands tightening around his M-14.

The wheels continued rotating in opposite directions for nearly a minute, like a gigantic combination lock. Then, with two loud clanks, like tumblers catching, the rings suddenly halted. The dome upon which the three men stood began to split open in precise V-shaped sections, and they hesitated no longer. With Edwards in the lead, the men ran across the metal rings and onto solid ground.

Breathing hard, faces sheened with perspiration, they watched as the hub opened like the iris of an impossibly huge camera lens, spilling out a column of blue light. It stretched upward fifty feet or more, a pillar of spinning energy that reminded Philboyd of a maelstrom or a whirlpool confined by an invisible container. It created the illusion of a tunnel of corsucating light.

Thousands of threads of energy crackled up and down its length, forming a luminous aura around the center ring. The halo dancing around the shaft of energy exuded curling, flaring strings. The tendrils spit outward in all directions, one of them passing by Philboyd's cheek, fanning it with a hot, tingling shock. He clapped his hand to his face, crying out.

Edwards grabbed Philboyd by the upper arm, hauling him backward. "*Move,* you dumb ass!"

At that instant, the column of light burst with eye-searing brilliance. A brutal shock wave crashed into Nakai, Philboyd and Edwards, picking them up and rolling them headlong over the arid ground in backward somersaults. The concussive report was so loud the men only heard the first fraction of a second of it.

The silence that followed was filled with a profanity-seasoned tirade from Edwards.

Philboyd could see nothing but a painfully bright radiance. Even with his eyelids screwed up tight, his optic nerves had been overwhelmed by the incandescent blaze.

"I can't see a fuckin' thing!" Edwards snarled.

"Nor can I," Nakai said with an eerie calm.

Philboyd, striving to sound confident, said, "Relax, guys. I'm sure it's only a temporary effect."

Even as he spoke, Philboyd's vision returned by degrees. His surge of relief was replaced by disbelief. His blurred eyes fixed upon a tall blond woman wearing a scarlet tunic that clung to her statuesque torso in enticing curves.

Beneath the visor of a black, peaked cap, her dark blue eyes glinted with amusement. A cold smile etched her classically beautiful features into a mold of iciness. Although a pistol was snugged into a holster at her hip, she held a black rawhide riding crop between the slim, tapering fingers of her right hand.

As Philboyd stared in openmouthed astonishment, the smiling woman stepped close and lashed him across the face with the hard, knotted length of the whip.

Chapter 12

Brigid Baptiste backed away and shielded her eyes as, with a droning whine, the Manta slowly lifted from the ground. A small, brief blizzard of dust swirled beneath it. The tripodal landing gear retracted automatically into the TAV's underbelly.

The ship's ascent halted at one hundred feet, and Grant waggled its wings in a farewell. Then the ramjet engines engaged and the Manta hurtled across the sky like an arrow flying from a bow, lancing in the direction of New Edo. The full-throated roar of the afterburners sounded like a protracted thunderclap over the Redoubt Yankee compound.

Parka folded over one arm and a metal-walled box tucked under the other, Brigid turned to face a gargantuan, almost featureless monolith rising from the ground an eighth of a mile away. The Cube resembled a black fortress looming above a collection of smaller structures like a squared-off mountain peak towering over foothills. Made of a very dark stone, it bulked upward in a series of arches and overhanging buttresses.

As Brigid walked toward the huge building, she eyed the position of the sun in the bright blue bowl of the sky, noting it was just beginning its descent to afternoon. Although her shadow suit kept her comfortable, she still felt the heat and humidity that were hallmarks of Thunder Isle. She reflected wryly on her fear a few hours before that she would never feel warm again, figuring the current temperature was a minimum of ninety degrees warmer than that of Slovakia.

A broad blacktop avenue ran inward toward the Cube. The asphalt had a peculiar ripple pattern to it and weeds sprouted from splits in the surface. She had seen the rippling effect many times before, out in the hellzones. It was a characteristic result of earthquakes triggered by nuclear bomb shock waves.

The long-ago ground tremors damaged a number of the smaller outbuildings around the Cube and some had fallen completely into ruin. A few storage buildings scattered around the outer perimeter of the walls remained intact.

The avenue widened inside the walls, opening into a broad courtyard filled with great blocks of basalt and concrete that had fallen from the buildings. Secondary lanes stretched out in all directions, a spokelike pattern of streets, bike paths and pedestrian walkways.

All along the streets stood the empty husks of former classrooms, laboratories, testing facilities and liv-

ing quarters. One of the largest of the structures had collapsed entirely, folded in on itself like a house of domi-
nos, with the fallen rear wall knocking down all the
interior sections one by one. Even the dark exterior of
the Cube showed damage, but very little of it was
caused by the nukecaust.

Within the imposing mass of dark stone lay the seat
of Operation Chronos and the temporal dilator itself. A
few years before, when the dilator had reached critical
mass, the resulting explosion had blown out chunks of
the facade.

In the intervening years, the wall surrounding the
main complex had been repaired, and a network of intruder deterrents and a video monitor system had been
installed. Armed guards stood upon elevated watch
posts at equidistant points surrounding the Cube, hands
resting on the triggers of swivel-mounted U.S. MG-73
heavy machine guns.

The guards were drawn from both Cerberus and New
Edo personnel, since the security and maintenance of
Redoubt Yankee was a cooperative effort. However, all
of the ordnance was supplied by the Cerberus armory,
quite likely the most fully stocked and outfitted arsenal
in postnuke America.

Lakesh himself had assembled the arsenal over several decades, envisioning it as the major supply depot
for a rebel army. The army never materialized—at least

not in the fashion Lakesh hoped it would. Therefore, Cerberus was blessed with a surplus of death-dealing equipment that would have turned the most militaristic overlord green with envy, or given the most pacifistic of them heart failure—if they indeed possessed hearts.

Brigid reached the set of wide steps leading up to the entrance of the Cube. There was only a single doorway in the featureless face of the monolithic building. When she first saw the place years before, there hadn't been a door, only a twisted, blackened metal frame hanging askew on sprung hinges, but Wegmann, the Cerberus engineer, had fabricated one out of sheet metal. It opened easily.

A big plastic sign from predark days was still bolted to the wall on the right of the doorway. Despite two centuries' worth of chem storms, fallout and weathering, the words imprinted on it were still legible. It bore a familiar warning: Entry To This Facility Strictly Forbidden To All Personnel Below B12 Clearance. Below the legend was the symbol of a stylized hourglass, the top half of it colored red, the bottom black.

She entered a large lobby, with walls of black-speckled marble that showed deep crisscrossings of cracks. The Tiger of Heaven who occupied a guard station bowed formally when Brigid approached.

The medium-sized Japanese man wore a full suit of battle armor, his torso enclosed by a segmented *yoroi* made of flattened wafers of metal, the interlocked and overlapping plates trimmed in scarlet and gold. Between flaring shoulder epaulets, a war helmet fanned out with sweeping curves of metal resembling wings. The full-face visor presented the inhuman visage of a snarling tiger.

A quiver of three-foot-long arrows dangled from one of his shoulders, and a bow made of red-lacquered wood was strapped to his back. The samurai carried two swords in black scabbards swinging back from each hip.

The Tigers of Heaven declined to use firearms, but their skill with swords and bows was such they didn't really need them. Ammunition was hard to come by, and New Edo didn't have the natural resources to manufacture it themselves.

Cerberus had offered to supply the Tigers with guns and ammunition from the armory, but had been politely refused. The samurai code practiced by the Tigers considered firearms unmanly weapons, despite the fact they did have a few old World War II-vintage carbines in storage.

The Tiger said softly, respectfully, *"Domo arigato, Brigid-chan."*

She returned the bow, murmuring, *"Konnichiha, ekiyuu."*

Due in part to her eidetic memory, Brigid Baptiste

spoke a dozen languages and could get along in a score of dialects, but knowing the native tongues of many different cultures and lands was only a small part of her work. Aside from her command of languages, Brigid had made history and geopolitics abiding interests in a world that was changing rapidly.

She entered a long hallway lined on both sides with wooden, card-keyed office doors. All of the doors had been forced open in the years since Cerberus and New Edo had established a permanent presence on the island. The glow of the fluorescent lights inset into the ceiling provided illumination.

After a number of turns, the corridor began to slant downward. It dead-ended at a heavy metal door without a knob or a latch. Brigid waved to the lens of the vid spy-eye bracketed to the wall just above the frame. Machinery clanked, and with a prolonged hiss of pneumatics, the door slid to the right. She walked into a room dominated by a huge flat-screen vid monitor. The screen was divided into twelve square sections, displaying various views of the Operation Chronos facility and its exterior perimeter.

A pair of Moon base émigrés, Fisher and O'Keefe, sat before it, and they greeted her with friendly questions.

"Did everybody make it back from Slovakia?" Fisher asked.

Brigid nodded. "As far as I know."

"What was it like working with Russians?" O'Keefe wanted to know. Despite his Irish surname, the man had strong Latino features and coloring. "Are they easier to get along with than the twentieth-century models?"

"I couldn't say," Brigid answered, striding past them toward a door on the opposite end of the monitor room. "But it was a test of diplomatic endurance—that much is for certain."

As she stepped into a narrow accessway beyond, sensors in the walls reacted to her motion signature and the door opened automatically. She walked down a passageway toward a bright light glimmering just beyond a tall arch. As the corridor stretched through the archway, it became a catwalk overlooking a vast chamber shaped like a hollow hexagon. A dim glow shone down from the high, flat ceiling, two faint columns of light beaming from twin round fixtures, both the size of tires. Massive wedge-shaped ribs of metal supported the roof.

The shafts of luminescence fell upon a huge forked pylon made of burnished metal alloy that projected up from a sunken concave area in the center of the chamber. The two horns of the pylon curved up and around, facing each other. Mounted on the tips of each prong were jagged shards of what appeared to be blackened quartz crystal.

The pylon was at least twenty feet tall, with ten feet

separating the forked branches. Extending outward from the base of the pylon at ever decreasing angles into the low shadows stretched a taut network of fiber-optic filaments. They disappeared into sleeve sockets that perforated the plates of dully gleaming alloy sheathing the floor.

Many of them were buckled here and there, bulging and split. The faint odor of superheated and slagged metal still hung heavy in the air, even after two and a half years. The pylon itself was canted forward, about ten degrees out of true.

As Brigid Baptiste strode along the elevated platform, she couldn't help but recall the last time they had seen the temporal dilator functioning. It had been encapsulated, cosmic chaos with sparks sizzling through the facets of the prisms, crackling fingers of plasma energy darting from one sphere to the other and back again like snakes made of electrical current.

The pent-up energies built to critical mass and when they were vented, the floor supporting the pylon ruptured, rivets popping loose and the crystal spheres exploding. It could have been far worse—the Archon fusion reactor that powered the complex could have hit critical mass itself.

But fortunately, only the temporal dilator's individual power source melted down and left the machine itself somewhat intact. It was composed of a blend of conductive alloys and ceramics that made it virtually indestructible. The dilator itself operated as essentially a giant electromagnet, creating two magnetic fields, one at right angles to the other. Both of the fields represented two planes of space and a third field was reproduced through the principle of sound manipulation.

The catwalk led directly into the round, bileveled Chronos control center. Banks of glass-covered consoles formed the perimeter of both levels. Overhead lights gleamed on alloys, the glass, the numerous CPUs.

Inset computer terminals followed the curve of the walls. Almost all of the instrument boards were manned, the drive units of the machines humming with a steady drone. On the far side of the room stood the familiar arrangement of armaglass slabs enclosing a mat-trans jump chamber. The translucent armaglass was tinted a smoky gray, the hue of old lead.

Inside the horseshoe curve of the central control module sat Sela Sinclair, speaking briskly into the microphone of her headset. At first, Brigid caught only her terse tone, an impression of agitation, then as she walked closer she heard her demand, "How can that be? An explosion but with no sound?"

A wiry, lean-muscled black woman in her midthirties, Sela Sinclair wore a sleeveless gray T-shirt, camou pants and high-topped jump boots. The image of a stylized eagle, wings outspread beneath the letters USAF, was tattooed on her rope-muscled right bicep. Her long black hair, plaited and beaded, was bound up at the back of her head.

Unlike most of her fellow Manitius scientists, Sinclair had served in the United States Air Force and had earned the rank of lieutenant colonel shortly before being assigned to the Moon base. Her military bearing was more akin to the demeanors of the former Magistrates than the lunar colony personnel.

When Sinclair saw Brigid, she held up one finger, indicating she wanted her to wait while she concentrated on the voice filtering in through the earpiece. She said sternly, "Under no circumstances are you to check it out, Orcutt. Stand by until you hear from me."

The woman punched a button on the arm of her chair. "Cube to Edwards, come in."

Her dark, full-lipped face remained as impassive as a teak mask for a long tick of time, then she repeated the call. "Edwards, this is Sinclair. Please respond."

"What's going on?" Brigid asked Nguyen, one of the techs.

The pudgy Asian woman shrugged. "All I know is that Dr. Philboyd, Edwards and Nakai went out into the bush a couple of hours ago to trace the source of an anomalous energy signature. About five minutes ago, one of the observation posts reported seeing and hearing something."

"Something?" Brigid echoed impatiently. "Like what?"

Sinclair swiveled her chair to face her. "Like an explosion, but one with no sound or smoke. I've tried raising Edwards and all I get is static."

"Are you the one who ordered Brewster into the field?" Brigid demanded.

"He was the most qualified," Sinclair answered smoothly. "And you know I could only make a request. I don't have the authority to order him to do anything. But Dr. Philboyd knows how important it is to maintain the security of this installation."

Brigid wanted to argue with the woman but realized she spoke the truth. The seat of Operation Chronos, even if the temporal dilator no longer functioned, was potentially the most dangerous place on Earth, prowling Monstrodamii notwithstanding. Pirates from the other Western Isles had made a couple of previous incursions.

"What instruments registered the anomalous signature?" she inquired.

Nguyen gestured to a small freestanding console. "That one. None of us are quite sure what it's supposed to do. We thought it was burned out."

Tossing her parka over the back of a chair, Brigid stepped over to it. She noted that all the indicator lights on the surface were dark, but beneath a transparent glass cover, a needle gauge swept madly back and forth, then subsided into a series of short oscillations. A few seconds later, it began ticking wildly to and fro again.

"The spikes have become a lot more active in the past few minutes," Nguyen continued.

"About the time Orcutt reported seeing an explosion," Sinclair interposed. She cocked her head quizzically at Brigid. "Any ideas you care to share, Baptiste?"

Brigid nodded. "A couple. This is an automatic sensor board, designed to react to and register fluctuations in the electromagnetic field of the island."

Nguyen slitted her eyes skeptically. "How do you know that?"

"I studied all the specs on this place once we got the computer systems back up and running. I remembered what everything was supposed to do."

As a former archivist in the Cobaltville Historical Division, Brigid's knowledge on a wide variety of subjects was profound, due in the main to her greatest asset—an eidetic memory. She could instantly and totally recall in detail everything she had read, seen or experienced, which was both a blessing and a curse.

"The fact that this board is registering anything after all this time," she went on, "tells me the wavelength is exceptionally strong."

Brigid turned toward Sinclair, striving to maintain her calm expression and tone. "Furthermore, it tells me the spikes are being artificially generated."

She paused, took a breath and added, "That's *not* a good thing, in case you were wondering."

Chapter 13

The navigational computers of the Manta brought the ship on a direct trajectory across the Pacific, then over the forbidding peaks of the Cascades and within half an hour, the small craft crossed winged over Montana.

Holding the handgrip control, Kane kept to the wilderness areas, skirting mesas and mountains, forests and waterfalls, basins and plateaus. Although settlements were few and far between in the territory, maintaining a low profile was part and parcel of Cerberus policy.

The low altitude ride control—LARC—subsystem fed him turbulence data. The controls automatically damped the effects of unstable air pockets by the deflection of two small fins extending down from beneath the cockpit area.

Once the Bitterroots came into view, Kane dropped the Manta's altitude to ten thousand feet and cruised above a panorama of open grassland and the silvery windings of the Elk River. Gilded by the noonday sun, the rolling terrain looked peaceful, almost bucolic, much as it had over three centuries earlier.

Lifting his gaze, Kane looked out over the blunt prow of the Manta at the rugged foothills spreading out beyond the tableland. The coordinates scrolled across the inner curve of his helmet's visor, and he reduced the TAV's airspeed to under one thousand knots.

Kane wore a bronze-colored helmet with a full-face visor. The helmet itself was attached to the headrest of the pilot's chair. A pair of tubes stretched from the rear to an oxygen tank at the back of the seat. The helmet and chair were a self-contained unit. A dozing Domi sat strapped into a small jump seat in the rear of the cockpit.

The instrument panel of the Manta was almost comical in its simplicity. The controls consisted primarily of a handgrip, altimeter and fuel gauges. All the labeling was in English, squares of paper taped to the appropriate controls. But the interior curve of the helmet's visor swarmed with CGI icons of sensor scopes, range finders and various indicators.

Both Kane and Grant had easily learned to pilot the Mantas in the atmosphere, since they resembled the Deathbird gunships the two men had flown when they were Cobaltville Magistrates. But when they flew the first of the four TAVs down from the Manitius Moon colony they came to the unsettling realization that the Mantas could not be piloted like winged aircraft while in space.

A pilot could select velocity, angle, attitude and other complex factors dictated by standard avionics, but space flight was a completely different set of principles. It called for the maximum manipulation of gravity, trajectory, relative velocities and plain old luck. Despite all of the computer-calculated course programming, both men learned quickly that successfully piloting the TAV through space was more by God than by grace. But so far, the Mantas had proved to be trustworthy in all maneuvers and atmospheres.

Static hissed over his Commtact, and Farrell's laconic voice said, "Manta One, this is Cerberus flight control. We have you on our scopes. What is your projected ETA? Over."

"Flight, this Manta One. I estimate five minutes. Over."

"Copy that, Manta One. Will apprise the ground crew. Out."

The channel to Cerberus closed and Kane announced, "Almost home." His voice echoed hollowly within the confines of his helmet.

He sensed rather than heard Domi stirring in the jump seat, rousing from sleep. Her headset comm conveyed a sighing yawn. "'Bout damn time."

"What do you mean?" Kane asked irritably. "We flew almost a quarter of the way around the world in less than three hours. And you slept almost the entire way."

"Then it's about damn time I woke up," Domi retorted, sounding just as irritable. "And I've got to pee big-time."

"Didn't I tell you to go before we left Slovakia?"

"I tried, but I couldn't make water...could only make ice."

Kane couldn't completely suppress a chuckle. "Well, you don't have to hold it much longer."

"Good thing," she replied. "For everybody concerned."

The mountain peaks seemed to rush toward the Manta. The aircraft flew well above the summits but just below the cloud cover. Kane saw no vegetation to speak of on the lower slopes, just a vast litter of stone. Even under the bright sunlight, the Bitterroot range looked menacing, and the deep, dark gorges between the peaks filled with forest were not much more inviting. He attributed the sense of foreboding to a lingering residue of skydark, the generation-long nuclear winter.

Repressing a shudder, Kane swung the Manta toward a gray peak and within seconds, the flat black expanse of the redoubt's plateau appeared directly below.

At the point where plateau debouched into the higher slopes, the bright sun gleamed off the white headstones marking more than a dozen grave sites. The fabricated markers bore only last names: Cotta, Dylan, Adrian and many more. Ten of them were inscribed with the names of the Moon base émigrés who had died defending Cerberus from the assault staged by Overlord Enlil.

Kane engaged the vectored-thrust ramjets, hovered for a moment, then dropped the TAV straight down on the far side of the grassy slope, bringing it gracefully to rest between another pair of the ships covered by camouflage netting. Fine clouds of dust puffed up all around.

He switched off the engines and they cycled down from high- to low-pitched whines. Opening the seals of his helmet, Kane unlatched the opaque cockpit canopy and slid it back. Domi climbed out first, snatching off her headset and clambering over him, then sliding down the starboard wing to the ground. She shed her parka as she did so.

"Later!" she said.

Kane sighed and lifted off his helmet, figuring that by the time Domi reached the sec door she would be stark naked—a condition that would not be all that unusual where the albino girl was concerned.

During her first few weeks at Cerberus, Domi often strolled through the redoubt wearing only a pair of red stand-ups and a smile. At that point in time, the girl wasn't accustomed to wearing clothes unless circumstances demanded them, and then only the skimpiest concessions to weather, not modesty.

Born a feral child of the Outlands, Domi was always

at ease being nude in the company of others, and if those others didn't share that comfort zone, she couldn't care less. However, she had not taken any naked strolls through the redoubt in quite some time. Kane wasn't quite sure how he felt about that.

As Kane heaved himself out of the cockpit, he saw Banks struggling up the face of the slope, carrying Domi's parka under one arm. The slender black man with the neatly trimmed beard had been assigned TAV ground crew duty for the week.

Most of the people who lived in the Cerberus redoubt, regardless of their skills, acted in the capacity of support personnel. They worked rotating shifts, eight hours a day, seven days a week. Often their work consisted of the routine maintenance and monitoring of the installation's environmental systems, the satellite data feed, the security network.

However, everyone was given at least a superficial understanding of all the redoubt's systems, so they could pinch-hit in times of emergency. At one time, the small number of residents had been a source of constant worry to Lakesh, but the arrival of the Moon base personnel presented a larger pool of talent from which to draw.

Grant and Kane were exempt from cross-training, inasmuch as they served as the enforcement arm of Cerberus and undertook far and away the lion's share of the risks. On their downtime between missions, they made sure all the ordnance in the armory was in good condition and occasionally tuned up the vehicles in the depot.

Brigid Baptiste, due to her eidetic memory, was the most exemplary member of the redoubt's permanent staff, since she could step into any vacancy. However, her gifts were a two-edged sword, inasmuch as those selfsame polymathic skills made her an indispensable addition to away missions.

Banks handed the hooded garment to Kane. "Domi must not have noticed she dropped this, I'm assuming."

"You are?" Kane replied. "I wouldn't."

Banks flashed him an appreciative grin, hooking a thumb over his shoulder. "As soon as the flight control picked you up, Lakesh asked me to have you meet him in his office before you do anything else."

"Why his office?"

"A private confab—that's all I know."

Kane quashed a surge of annoyance, attributing his reaction to the feud that had begun the day he and Lakesh had first exchanged words, some five years ago. Displacing the man from his position of total authority hadn't improved their relationship much.

"All right," he said, moving toward the crest of the slope. "Anything else I should know about?"

Banks shrugged, eyeing the contours of the Manta

for damage. "Dr. Philboyd gated over to Redoubt Yankee a couple of hours ago. I don't know why exactly, but I didn't get the impression it was anything urgent."

"Wouldn't that be a welcome change," Kane commented wistfully.

Chapter 14

Before entering the redoubt, Kane stripped off his own parka and gusted out a sigh of relief at the freedom of movement and lack of weight. As he strode down the main corridor, he noticed heads of men and women turning toward him, the glances deferential and even embarrassingly admiring. Kane, Brigid, Grant and Domi were considered something special among the personnel. The actions performed by the four of them had quite literally saved the world, more than once.

Kane turned down a side passageway and walked toward Lakesh's office. The man's request to meet with him in his private office didn't arouse his suspicions, but it was definitely a change in routine. Normally, when Domi returned from a field op, Lakesh was on hand to meet her, whether she had traveled by gateway, interphaser or Manta.

Kane felt tempted to stop by his quarters change out of the shadow suit, but decided to indulge Lakesh's whim for the time being. He opened the door without knocking.

The office was small, not much larger than an alcove containing a desk, two chairs and a computer terminal. The overhead lights were not on and a peculiar tension was palpable in the room. Lakesh, seated at his desk and staring fixedly at the monitor screen, swung a startled gaze in his direction. For an instant, his face did not register recognition.

"Yes?" The strained, reedy quality of his voice sent prickles of apprehension up and down Kane's spine.

"You wanted to see me, right?"

"Yes, come in. Close and lock the door." He added "Please" as a quick afterthought.

Kane did as he said, dropping his and Domi's cold-weather gear into a corner. He came around the desk, staring over Lakesh's shoulder at the black-and-white images flickering over the monitor screen. They flashed by with such rapidity Kane could make little sense of them, although he glimpsed men in dark uniforms and symbols he recognized as swastikas.

"What are you looking at here?" he asked. "A collection of Nazi memorabilia?"

"I wish it were only that simple, friend Kane." The older man's voice was soft, haunted. "I started out doing a bit of research for dearest Brigid, and it took me to areas I did not expect or wish to go."

"Explain."

"I don't know if I can." Lakesh pressed a key and a

harsh monochromatic photograph appeared on the screen. The image showed two views of a beautiful woman with heavy blond hair done up in sophisticated braids on both sides of her head, one a full-length shot and the other a full frontal view.

The woman was obviously tall and splendidly built, wearing an extremely tight-fitting silver-lamé evening gown and spike-heeled black pumps A pendant of stones fell from her slim throat, falling across the wide shelf of her breasts. Kane would have guessed her to be a twentieth-century model or actress attending a glamour-drenched function, if not for the riding crop she held in her long-nailed right hand.

A small brooch could be discerned on the left breast of the gown's revealing bodice, showing a simple black disk against a gray background with a number of straight lines radiating from it.

Kane would have allowed himself to be impressed by the woman's truly statuesque beauty had her eyes not seemed to blaze with a fanatical luminance. Noncommittally, he said, "Quite the babe, if you like big blondes with scary eyes who carry whips."

"I don't," Lakesh said. "Nor should you. Not this particular babe, at any rate."

"Who is she?"

"Her name is Countess Paula von Schiksel. I found this picture in our historical database...it's one of several dozen taken of various Nazi personnel associated with Germany's Totalitat Konzept."

"Totalitat Konzept?" Kane echoed, stumbling over the pronunciation. "You mean the Totality Concept?"

Lakesh nodded. "The personnel files were confiscated from the Third Reich High Command at the end of World War II."

"That still doesn't tell me who she is," Kane pointed out impatiently.

Lakesh hesitated, then whispered, "The Scarlet Queen."

Kane's eyebrows rose toward his hairline. "The who?"

Under his breath, Lakesh murmured two strained syllables of anguish. "Kali."

KANE WAS BY NOW accustomed to Lakesh's tendency to indulge in melodramatics, but familiarity didn't make it any easier to tolerate—nor the man's fondness for filtering every experience through a mythological frame of reference.

"Kali?" Kane repeated. "What the hell has a Hindu goddess got to do with anything? What's got you so wound up now?"

Lakesh regarded him reprovingly. "Nazis, which should be apparent. I'm sure you remember them."

"Not personally."

Lakesh angled challenging eyebrows. "Oh, really?"

In fact, Kane, Brigid and Grant had come across the residue of Nazi Germany on more than one occasion. A few years before, they had found a subterranean installation beneath the Antarctic ice. Kane knew Lakesh was making an oblique reference to Otto Skorzeny, the crazed German officer they had found in the base.

Also in the Antarctic they explored the hidden realm of Ultima Thule, the Teutonic version of Atlantis, and learned the Nazis had unsuccessfully tried to conquer its people. Kane also knew that the Totality Concept researches were deeply rooted in the Third Reich.

"Brigid told me a bit about what you found in Slovakia," Lakesh stated. "You don't seem too concerned about it."

Kane shrugged. "That's because it dates back to World War II. You might want to finally get around to accepting the fact that it happened a very long time ago."

"To paraphrase the Bard of Avon, the evil that men do lives on after their bones are interred."

Kane rolled his eyes ceilingward. "Do you have a specific idea you're trying to get across? If you do, I wish you'd just spit it out."

Lakesh scowled up at him, then manipulated the mouse attached to the computer's keyboard. The image of the woman's cleavage swelled on the screen. Kane watched him do it in mystified silence. Under Lakesh's careful touch, the view zoomed in on the brooch.

"Do you know what that is?" he inquired.

Kane squinted, then said, "No."

"What does it look like?"

"A squashed spider."

In a tone of aggrieved patience, Lakesh said, "Look harder."

Kane did so, and though he was slightly distracted by the curve of the woman's left breast, he ventured, "A sun symbol, maybe."

Lakesh nodded in satisfaction. "Exactly, friend Kane. A *black* sun, to be precise."

"And that's important?"

"I fear so. The Brotherhood of the Black Sun was an elite Nazi secret society of which the countess was a high-ranking member."

"So what?" Kane challenged. "Like I said, that all happened a very long time ago."

Lakesh shook his head in frustration. "I assumed you knew by now that the Nazi party was not just a military machine. The Nazis brought a completely new culture into prominence almost overnight and with the passive acceptance of most of the general populace of Germany. It was a capital mistake of people in my own time who believed that the military defeat of the Nazis was the same as the cultural defeat of their ideas."

"What's this got to do with the Brotherhood of the Black Sun and the bimbo with the whip?"

"Historians claim that the abbreviation 'SS' stood for *Schutzstaffel,* but to Third Reich insiders, the abbreviation represented the words *Schwarze Sonne.*"

Kane stared at him expectantly, refusing to play straight man to Lakesh's academic performance.

After a few seconds, Lakesh intoned, "*Schwarze Sonne* means Black Sun in English."

"Tell me again why I should give a shit what it means in English or Urdu?"

"To the members of the society, the Black Sun represented a kind of energy source that radiated light that was invisible to the human eye. The very concept of it seems to have bordered upon the religious. The Brotherhood of the Black Sun was usually represented symbolically as a black sphere out of which eight arms extended."

Lakesh tapped the image of the brooch that filled the screen. "Something like that, I imagine."

Folding his arms over his chest, Kane said, "I already know that the Nazis believed in a lot of hocus-pocus and superstitious horseshit. This doesn't seem much different from the rest of their master-race garbage."

Lakesh tugged at his long nose, a habitual gesture that meant he felt a great deal of inner agitation. "Hear me out."

"Go ahead, but I'm pretty sure I won't be hearing anything too surprising. Just make your point so I can go take a shower."

"The point is that the concept of the Black Sun is not just the standard Nazi mumbo-jumbo. Their thesis was that it existed somewhere on Earth as a cold, collapsing implosive vortex. It generated unseen radiation in the form of cosmic, gamma and x-ray radiation. In spite of the stereotypical view of mad Nazi scientists, the Black Sun was indeed a very real phenomenon. In fact, I believe you found it in that cave in Slovakia. Furthermore, the phenomenon in the cave was associated with a German scientific undertaking called Projekt Kronoscope. I'm assuming you don't need a translation."

Kane stared at Lakesh, at a loss for words.

Lakesh forced a smile, but it did not reach his eyes. His face was lined with apprehension. "Did you hear anything *too* surprising, friend Kane?"

Chapter 15

The bathhouse was surrounded by artfully trimmed thickets and tidy little rock gardens. The exterior looked like a storage building made of stone and wood. The Spartanly furnished interior contained only a few benches and a large aboveground tub. The far wall was made of the oiled paper and lathwork, common in New Edo construction.

The circular tub was about ten feet in diameter, with a bench running around the inside, all of it made of planks of seasoned hardwood and sealed with pitch. It rose three feet above the floor, and although normally filled with steaming water, a considerable amount had sloshed over the edge onto the floor, due to the vigorous activities of Grant and Shizuka.

Grant sat on the bench and Shizuka sat upon him, straddling his thighs. A little over five feet tall, her luxuriant blue-black hair framed a smoothly sculpted face of extraordinary Oriental beauty. Her complexion was a very pale gold with peach and milk for an accent. Beneath a snub nose, her petaled lips were full. The dark, almond-shaped eyes that usually held the fierce, proud

gleam of a young eagle were liquid pools of pleasure
and lust. Grant cupped the firm swell of her small but
perfectly shaped breasts, feeling the gem-hard nipples
pressing against his callused palm. He showered her
face and the slender column of her throat with kisses.

Panting, Shizuka clasped her hands at the back of his
neck, her forearms resting on the broad yoke of his
shoulders, her hips moved back and forth. Grant's hands
slid from her breasts and cradled her buttocks as she set
a steady rhythm, thrusting up and down gasping, whimpering and moaning. She clutched at his biceps, her
fingernails digging into the flesh.

Steam and lust and sweat blinded them both, the
scented water roiling around their bodies. He tongued
the desire-hard nipples of her breasts, and Shizuka cried
out uncontrollably with each of his long, deep lunges.
The sound of her passion, her pleasure in heat, nearly
drove Grant out of his mind, the need for his own release swelling with every passing second.

Back arching, Shizuka suddenly convulsed and
shuddered in a spasming orgasm. Grant allowed his
own climax to begin and he burst deep inside her, an
eruption of liquid fire that seemed to last forever. Shizuka sucked in her breath noisily as she ground out her
final throes of orgasm against him. Grant embraced her
tightly, while both of them trembled through the aftermath of their mutual release.

His senses slowly returned to him, and Shizuka breathed a long, final sigh of satisfaction. Her brown eyes gazed steadily into his and she whispered, "Grant-san, it has been far too long a time since we did this."

Grant was too out of breath to respond, enjoying her petite body pressed against him like a comfortable blanket. He wrapped his arms around her, luxuriating in the feeling of repletion that trickled through him.

At length he husked out, "We've been busy...both of us."

With a sigh, Shizuka lifted herself off his softening shaft. "Duty has no sweethearts."

Grant heard the bitterness edging her tone, but he could think of nothing to say. He watched her move to the small table bolted to the rim of the tub, admiring her grace and the play of taut muscles beneath satin-smooth skin. Her glossy black hair fell halfway to the firm rondure of her buttocks.

Shizuka poured hot tea from a small, fragile pot into a pair of eggshell-white, eggshell-thin cups. As she turned to hand Grant one of the cups, he reflected again how such a delicate, refined-looking woman bore no resemblance to the fearsome armored samurai he had first met on a dark night in the California badlands.

Shizuka waited for Grant to take the first sip before bringing her own cup to her lips. She said with a touch of pride, "It is a new blend, grown right here in New Edo."

For better or for worse—and New Edo was certainly far better than most of the Western Isles—the island was Shizuka's home. Dangerous, but still hers. Moreover, she considered the well-being of its citizens her responsibility. And after she had saved the island both from internal rebellion and outside invaders, the citizens of New Edo obeyed her every command, appeased her every whim with a kind of devotion different, yet more powerful, than that which they would have given a man. Shizuka was not viewed as a woman, or even a Tiger of Heaven—she was revered almost as a goddess.

Grant well understood that devotion to Shizuka, since he felt it himself. A couple of years before, it had been his intent to leave Cerberus and live in the little island monarchy with her. He felt—or hoped—the new recruits from the Manitius lunar colony would alter the dynamics of the struggle against the barons.

But after being captured and tortured by the sadistic Baroness Beausoleil, Grant realized the struggle remained essentially the same, there were just new players on the field. The war itself would go on and would never end, unless he took an active hand in it, regardless of his love for Shizuka.

But Grant's heart was still pledged to her, and they were determined to spend a couple of days together a month, despite their respective duties that kept them apart most of the time.

"It's not too late," he said suddenly.

Shizuka eyed him with a mixture of surprise and wariness. "For what?"

Grant found it difficult to formulate an answer. His tongue felt clumsy and thick as he said, "Not too late for us...to be together permanently."

Shizuka's face did not change expression. "We have discussed that many times."

Grant frowned at her frostily formal tone. "But we never reached a conclusion, only a compromise."

Sighing, Shizuka replaced the cup on the tray and reached for a blue silk kimino from a hook on the wall. As she thrust her arms into the belled sleeves, she said in a soft, sad whisper, "I fear a compromise is the best we can hope for. If duty does not allow sweethearts, nor does it permit children."

Grant declined to respond directly. He knew she referred in an oblique way to their hope to one day start a family. In the baronies, children were a necessity for the continuation of ville society, but only those passing stringent tests were allowed to bear them. Genetics, moral values and social standing were the most important criteria. Generally, a man and a woman were bound together for a term of time stipulated in a contract. Once a child was produced, the contract was voided.

A number of years before, Grant and a woman named Olivia had submitted a formal mating application. Both of them had entertained high hopes of the application being approved and they managed to convince themselves that it would be. After all, babies still needed to be born, but only the right kind of babies. A faceless council determined that he and Olivia could not produce the type of offspring that made desirable ville citizens.

Once their application was rejected, he and Olivia had drawn attention to themselves. Their relationship became officially unsanctioned and could not continue lawfully. In the years since Olivia, Grant had never given much thought to fathering children. But since pledging himself to Shizuka, he'd started thinking about it more seriously. He wondered if creating a new life might not be a way to balance out the ones he had taken over the years.

Certainly Lakesh had tried his hand at bringing new lives into the world as a way to cleanse his soul of guilt over his involvement in the Totality Concept conspiracies. Kane and Brigid might not have even existed if not for his efforts to clean his conscience by manipulating the in vitro human genetic samples in storage.

"I'm tired of sharing you," Grant declared, heaving himself out of the tub.

Shizuka made a short, sharp gesture of impatience. "Share *me?* Do I not share you with Cerberus? Even if we wed, even if we had children, would I still not have to share you with Kane every day of my life?"

Grant shrugged into a quilted, pearl-gray robe. He regarded the woman stonily from beneath knitted brows. "No."

Shizuka uttered a short, weary laugh of exasperation. "One of the reasons I love you so much is that you are such an awful liar."

"I'd have new responsibilities," he retorted. "I'd be a father, not an explorer or a warrior."

Shizuka's dark eyes glinted with the sparks of a warrior's inner fire. "And as a mother, would you demand I lay down my sword, surrender my obligations to my people?"

Grant opened his mouth to reply, then realized he could think of nothing to say. He and Shizuka stared at each other steadily for a long moment, then a faint, sad smile ghosted over her lips. She extended her right hand and he took it.

"Let us go back to the palace," she said quietly. "We'll have some dinner and perhaps discuss this matter further."

"Perhaps," Grant muttered bleakly, and allowed himself to be led out of the bathhouse.

The two people slipped on sandals and walked hand-in-hand across the palace grounds. The noonday sun shone brightly, but the sea breezes wafting in from the Pacific kept the temperature comfortable The gravel path wound up and around a series of gently rolling hills, all green with rich grass. Cattle grazed inside split-rail fences. Cultivated fields made a patchwork pattern over the terrain.

Some of the hedgerows had been trimmed into interesting shapes resembling cranes and snakes. Gardeners and groundskeepers they encountered bowed deeply whenever eye contact was made. A contingent of Tigers of Heaven guarded his Manta ship, to keep it safe from the curious.

The palace was not particularly tall, but it sprawled out with many windows, balconies and carved frames. The columns supporting the many porches and loggias were made of lengths of thick bamboo, bent into unusual shapes. The upcurving roof arches and interlocking shingles all seemed to be made of lacquered wood.

To Grant's eye, the palace was well laid out, strategically designed with deep moats on three sides and cliffs on the other. At the top of the walls were parapets and protected positions for archers and spearmen.

Grant was deeply impressed, not just with the size of the fortress and its architecture, but with the knowledge the citizens of New Edo had accomplished so much in only ten years. Most of the Outland settlements he had seen, even those that had existed for decades, always resembled the temporary camps of nomads. A memory of Domi's squalid settlement on the

Snake River drifted through his mind, and he repressed a shudder at the thought.

Michi, one of the Tigers of Heaven, greeted Shizuka at the portal leading to the inner gate. Instead of the elaborate armor, he wore a billowy green *kamishimo*, the formal attire of the daimyo's personal guard. His hair was clubbed back, tied at his nape. He looked with a certain distaste at Grant, but bowed to him anyway.

He spoke to Shizuka in a hurried, agitated whisper, gesturing toward the interior of the fortress. Shizuka stiffened, inhaling sharply in surprise. Grant sensed her sudden tension and asked, "What is it?"

"Come with me." Shizuka strode swiftly through the door and down a passageway made of highly polished panels of wood.

With Grant on her heels, she scaled a flight of stairs and entered a room with a balcony overlooking craggy rocks and a small bay. The rocks thrust up out of the foaming surf like blunt fangs. At the balcony's railing stood a tripod-mounted telescope. On the shelves of a bookcase built into one wall rested a curious collection of artifacts, all of which had been found on Thunder Isle.

On one shelf was a dented and dull metal casque from the days of the conquistadors, and on another were crude knives made from flakes of flint, the handles wrapped with leather thongs. The blades were shaped somewhat like laurel leaves, with deep grooves along either side. A brace of rusty flintlock pistols lay beside them. There were other items less recognizable.

Stepping to the telescope, Shizuka leaned down and squinted through the eyepiece. After a moment, she sank her teeth into her full lower lip and exclaimed, "No way!"

"What's going on?" Grant demanded.

Stepping aside, Shizuka waved him toward the telescope. "See for yourself."

Grant bent and peered through the eyepiece. At first all he saw was Thunder Isle, which resembled a saucer crafted from volcanic rock but with thick vegetation sprouting all over the top of it.

"What am I looking for?" he asked.

Before Shizuka could answer, light flickered and flashed in the center of the green-and-black saucer. It wasn't an optical illusion. Squinting through the eyepiece, he tightened the focus. Light flickered again, white and bright, far too bright to be a reflection. A dazzling white column burst upward. In the distance he heard a rumble.

At first he thought the sound was thunder, but then the realization sank in. He cast a questioning glance at Shizuka. The expression on her face was strained.

Grimly, she intoned, "It is happening again."

Chapter 16

A black-gloved fist caught Philboyd on the right side of his face. His teeth cut into his lower lip, filling his mouth with salt and blood. Another closed hand smashed into his face and his glasses went flying. Then the fists moved down to his stomach. The sun overhead was unrelenting, and his own sweat blinded his blurred vision.

Philboyd fell heavily to the ground and felt a boot pound viciously into his midriff, rolling him over on the brown scrubby grass. He thought he heard Edwards cry out in either anger or pain.

"Enough," snapped a male voice touched with a British accent. "I want a live source of information, not a corpse."

Philboyd felt hands close around his upper arms and jerk him upright, and for a painful moment he hung limply before he set his feet and straightened. He tried to keep his head from wobbling on his neck, but it wasn't easy. Every bone in his body ached.

After the blond Amazon had struck him with the rid-

ing crop, she shouted orders in a language that was unmistakably German. He, Edwards and Nakai were
swarmed over by a bizarre collection of helmeted,
black-masked men, their goggled eyes lending them
the frightening resemblance to a hive of outraged hor-
nets. Philboyd assumed his companions had been disarmed swiftly, if not completely incapacitated.

A multitude of black shapes stood everywhere he
looked, like shadows somehow given life and dimension. Sunlight glinted from the goggles covering their
eyes. A broad figure moved into Philboyd's field of vision and he squinted in order to bring the details into
focus.

A pair of unblinking eyes buried deeply within
pouches of fat bored into his own. The heavyset man
wearing a voluminous robe made of black, gold and red
silk moved toward him in a slow, shuffling gait, rolls of
fat jiggling beneath the layers of fabric.

His round head looked to be completely hairless,
with even his eyebrows missing. He intertwined his
thick, beringed fingers at his belly, sunlight winking
from silver skulls, onyx spiders and gold five-pointed
stars. Philboyd gazed at him, his mind trying to process
the information his eyes fed to his brain. The fat man
was a caricature, something dug out of a theater trunk.

"What is your name, dear fellow?" he asked, his lips
creasing in a Buddha smile. The man spoke with an

NO POSTAGE
NECESSARY
IF MAILED
IN THE
UNITED STATES

BUSINESS REPLY MAIL
FIRST-CLASS MAIL   PERMIT NO. 717-003   BUFFALO, NY

POSTAGE WILL BE PAID BY ADDRESSEE

GOLD EAGLE READER SERVICE
3010 WALDEN AVE
PO BOX 1867
BUFFALO NY 14240-9952

Get FREE BOOKS and a FREE GIFT when you play the...

LAS VEGAS GAME

Just scratch off the gold box with a coin. Then check below to see the gifts you get!

YES! I have scratched off the gold box. Please send me my **2 FREE BOOKS** and **gift for which I qualify**. I understand that I am under no obligation to purchase any books as explained on the back of this card.

▼ DETACH AND MAIL CARD TODAY! ▼

366 ADL EF6L

166 ADL EF5A
(GE-LV-07)

FIRST NAME	LAST NAME

ADDRESS

APT.#	CITY

STATE/PROV.   ZIP/POSTAL CODE

7	7	7	Worth TWO FREE BOOKS plus a BONUS Mystery Gift!
🍒	🍒	🍒	Worth TWO FREE BOOKS!
🔔	🔔	♣	TRY AGAIN!

Offer limited to one per household and not valid to current Gold Eagle® subscribers. All orders subject to approval. Please allow 4 to 6 weeks for delivery.

upper-class British accent that sounded comically incongruous.

The Englishman invoked a distinct but uneasy sensation of familiarity within Philboyd. He turned his head and spit a little jet of blood on the ground, then glanced to the left and right, looking for Nakai and Edwards. He saw only the black-garbed men, and the spindly barrels of submachine guns he recognized as Schmeissers.

"I asked you a question," the bald man said, his voice silky soft.

"Where are my friends?" Philboyd demanded.

The tall blond woman stepped forward to stand beside the robed man. Her left hand flourished a six-inch-long ivory cigarette holder with a filterless cigarette jammed in the end of it.

Philboyd couldn't help but stare. He hadn't seen a woman smoke since the late 1990s. The tendril of tobacco smoke curling from the glowing tip of the cigarette smelled exceptionally strong and pungent.

"Answer Herr Crowley's question," the woman said in a voice that held all the warmth of a hollow echo within a glacier.

"My name is—" Philboyd broke off, a surge of recognition constricting his throat. He thrust his head forward and whispered hoarsely, "Crowley?"

The fat man beamed at him, not speaking.

"Aleister Crowley?"

Surprise flickered in the man's eyes as they widened. "You know me?"

Philboyd cleared his throat. "I know *of* you."

"How can that be, dear boy?"

"Mainly from old photographs."

Aleister Crowley drew himself up in parody of prideful preening. He cast a superior smirk at the woman and said, "Old photographs, you say. How old?"

"I don't understand," Philboyd said haltingly.

"Perhaps you will be good enough to tell me the year as well your name?"

Philboyd started to answer, then shook his head. "Where are my friends?"

"The Nipponese and the colonial thug?" Crowley's lips pursed in distaste. "They are right behind you."

Philboyd started to turn, but the black-garbed troopers tightened their grips on his arms. He strained against them until Crowley said, *"Los lassen."*

The men released him and Philboyd turned. Even without his glasses, he had no problem seeing Edwards and Nakai kneeling a few yards away, their hands clasped at the backs of their necks. The faces of both men bore abrasions and a dark bruise purpled Edwards's right cheek. They had been disarmed, their weapons tossed to one side. A pair of uniformed men stood on either side of them, subgun barrels aligned with their heads.

"Are you guys all right?" Philboyd asked, hoping the relief he felt wasn't too evident in his tone.

"Hell no, we're not all right!" Edwards snapped. "We've had the crap kicked out of us and been taken prisoner!"

The blond woman removed the cigarette holder from her mouth and demanded, "Why is a Nipponese in the company of two Amerikanners?"

It took a couple of seconds for the oddity of the question to penetrate Philboyd's haze of confusion. He glanced toward the woman. "Why shouldn't he be?"

She regarded him scornfully. "The Japanese are renowned for their long memories and nurturing grudges. I would not have thought they would ever forget about August 6, 1945."

Edwards's brow furrowed. "Why? What happened then?"

The woman speared him with an icy blue stare of contempt. "You mean you do not know?"

Before Philboyd could shush him, Edward retorted angrily, "Why should I? That was over 260 years ago."

"*Two* hundred—!"

At the note of panic in Crowley's voice, Philboyd turned to face him. The Englishman's complexion paled, his lips turning the color of lead. Clapping a hand to his chest, he began breathing laboriously through an open mouth. He stared wildly around, looking first at Philboyd, then up at the sky. He suddenly appeared to be a very old man.

The blond woman wheeled on him, a torrent of outraged German bursting from her mouth. She spoke too quickly for Philboyd to pick out more than a few words until she uttered two words that sent needles of terror stabbing into the base of his spine. "Projekt Kronoscope," she said.

She swung on Philboyd, pointing the riding crop like an accusatory finger. "The year! What year is this?"

Philboyd hesitated and watched as the woman's beautiful face changed from an icy mask to a grimace of bare-toothed rage. She stalked over to Nakai, secured a tight grip on his hair and yanked his head back.

As she glared challengingly at Philboyd, she poised the glowing tip of her cigarette less than an inch from Nakai's eye. "Year!" she shouted. *"Location!"*

"The year is 2203," Philboyd blurted. "You're on an island off the California coast."

The woman stared at him, eyes seething with cobalt fury. "Names. Give me your names."

"I'm Brewster Philboyd. That's Nakai. The other man is Edwards."

Crowley croaked, "It's 2203? How can that be? Lam said we would jump only a century ahead when the Archons would be in control. That was the plan."

Skin prickling with a chill, Philboyd managed to

prevent the shock he felt from registering on his face at the utterance of the words "Lam" and "Archons."

"What government do you represent?" the woman asked. "The United States?"

"You're from the past," Philboyd stated, sidestepping her question. "From World War II or thereabouts, aren't you? Who the hell are you? How did you get here?"

Releasing Nakai's hair, the woman said, "I am Countess Paula von Schiksel." She paused as if waiting for an astonished reaction. When it did not come, she added, "I take it that name is not familiar to you."

Philboyd shook his head. "Afraid not."

Her lips worked as if she were going to spit. "But you recognize the name of a fat homosexual drug addict?"

Before Philboyd could respond, the countess called, *"Anbringen Tshaya! Mach schnell!"*

A masked trooper marched forward, dragging a small pale figure with him.

Philboyd's belly lurched sideways at the sight of the little girl. She wore a shapeless white cotton shift that was actually more suited to the climate than the clothing worn by the soldiers, Crowley and the countess.

The girl's face was a marble oval between two straight falls of black hair. Philboyd guessed her to be no more than ten years of age. At first he thought her eyes were closed, then realized the irises of her eyes were the color of opals or moonstone with little to distinguish them from the whites. Her blind stare suddenly fixed on his face, and he sensed an electric thread stretching taut between them.

"This is Tshaya," Crowley said, patting the child's head. "In many ways, *she* brought us here."

Philboyd did not reply, continuing to stare at the child. His head hummed with a faint and distant voice, a feathery whisper that slid along the edges of his mind. He stiffened, shaken by an eerie foreboding. The tiny voice grew louder, a call from a million miles away where no ear could possibly hear it, yet he did.

Then a terrified wail bounced from the inner walls of Philboyd's skull and he winced, checking the reflex to lift a hand to his head.

Where is Heranda? the voice cried. *Where is my brother? Why is it so hot? Why does it smell so funny? Where is Heranda?*

Philboyd glanced from the faces of Crowley and the countess. Their expressions had not altered, and he understood only he had heard the plaintive voice.

I'm lost, I can't find my brother!

Philboyd stared at the little girl, filled with disbelief and a mounting horror.

Can't someone help me?

With effort, Philboyd mentally formed words and

sent them skittering across the thread he sensed stretching between himself and Tshaya. *Help you do what?*

Take me back to my brother, my people, the desperate voice wailed. *Take me back before more bad things come through the hole!*

He received an impression, a fragmented flash of a pulsating black aperture. *What hole?*

The hole in the cave, the black sun! Will you help me?

A stinging blow twisted Philboyd's head around on his neck. Tendons twinging, he focused his vision on the angry face of Countess Paula von Schiksel.

"How dare you ignore me when I address you!" she shrilled.

Probing the laceration on the tender lining of his cheek with his tongue, he muttered, "Sorry, my mind was elsewhere."

The countess nodded with savage satisfaction. "*Ja,* and soon your body will be, too. Six feet under the ground. I asked you what you and your friends are doing here."

Philboyd deliberately averted his gaze from Tshaya. "I asked you first. How did you get here?"

The countess uttered a scoffing laugh. "You would not understand."

"Does it have something to do with the black sun?"

The woman's eyebrows curved down to the bridge of her nose and her lips peeled away from her teeth. She struck Philboyd at the angle of neck and shoulder with the riding crop, hitting a clump of nerve ganglia.

Clutching at his throat, Philboyd collapsed and for a long moment writhed on the ground at her feet. Trying to breathe felt like inhaling the flame of a blowtorch. Over his labored gasps he heard Crowley bleat, "Something is happening!"

Philboyd managed to open his eyes and see a blue bolt of energy blazing up into the sky, spreading out into a funnel. Ripples of light shimmered around it, the cascade of incandescence whirling and spinning like a cyclone.

Everyone stared up at it, except for Tshaya, whose sightless eyes were still fixed upon him. Brewster Philboyd came to a swift decision. He hurled his body into a roll, snatching up the little girl in his arms and springing to his feet, shoulder-slamming one of the black-clad troopers aside. He glimpsed Nakai and Edwards staring at him in openmouthed shock.

Drawing in a deep lungful of air and staring directly at Edwards, he shouted, "*Move,* you dumb ass!"

Then he heard the staccato burst of gunfire.

Chapter 17

"Kronoscope?" Kane growled, resenting the fact he had given Lakesh the satisfaction of seeing him startled into silence, even for a few seconds. "A Nazi version of Operation Chronos?"

Lakesh nodded. "In essence, yes, apparently using the so-called Black Sun as the propagation medium. I postulate it is a singularity. Or was."

Kane felt his lungs seize for a painful instant. "I know what that is, at least."

Lakesh eyed him critically. "Do you, indeed? Can you explain it to me?"

Trying to tamp down his rising temper, Kane said, "You know damn good and well I'm talking about that thing Lord Strongbow put together. I saw it in operation, even traveled through it. You didn't."

Lakesh lifted one shoulder in a shrug. "I concede your point. However, Strongbow created an artificial black hole by combining the working principles of the quantum interphase inducers I developed for Project Cerberus with the temporal dilator capacitors of Operation Chronos."

Kane didn't need to be reminded. Despite the passage of nearly five years, he could easily recall the huge orb of absolute, impenetrable blackness floating in the center of a complexity of electronic consoles, relays and snaking power cables. It was like a bubble of burnished obsidian, but its surface reflected no light whatsoever.

Although he was loath to admit it, he also remembered Brigid Baptiste's explanation of its existence, later expanded upon by Lakesh. Hyperdimensional physics depended on the directed acceleration and deceleration of subatomic particles. Powered by a small thermonuclear generator, the singularity was the black maw of eternity, potentially the hub of a wheel to every time, place and person.

Kane knew the madman who called himself Strongbow envisioned the singularity as a method to wring order from chaos by channeling the energies of the quantum stream into the artificial black hole. Once that was accomplished, Strongbow believed he could impose true order on all humanity simply by willing it, as a stone thrown into a pond sends ripples to the farthest shores.

"So you think the Nazis managed to build a singularity long before Strongbow did?" he asked.

"Not exactly," Lakesh answered. "It appears that what lay within the cavern you visited was a naturally occurring vortex point, perhaps the most powerful one on this or any other planet."

Kane crooked an eyebrow. "I'll go along with the fact it *was* a vortex point, but as far as we could see it was just a hole in the ground."

"Yes, now. But I've reached the provisional hypothesis that its energies were completely drained over two hundred years ago."

Kane frowned. "Is that even possible?"

"Who knows? After all, working out the relationship between our interphaser and the parallax points is an ongoing process."

Several years before, Lakesh had constructed a small device designed to interact with naturally occurring hyperdimensional vortices, which were indexed by the Parallax Points Program. The program actually a map, a geodetic index, of all the vortex points on the planet.

The interphaser Lakesh designed interacted with the energy within a naturally occurring vortex and caused a temporary overlapping of two dimensions. The vortex then became an intersection point, a discontinuous quantum jump, beyond relativistic space-time.

Evidence indicated there were many vortex nodes, centers of intense energy, located in the same proximity on each of the planets of the solar system, and those points correlated to vortex centers on Earth.

Lakesh knew some ancient civilizations were aware of these symmetrical geo-energies and constructed monuments over the vortex points in order to manipulate them. Once the interphaser was put into use, the Cerberus redoubt reverted to its original purpose—not simply a sanctuary for exiles or the headquarters of a resistance against the tyranny of the barons, but a facility dedicated to fathoming the eternal mysteries of space and time.

When making phase transits from the redoubt, they always used the mat-trans chamber because it could be hermetically sealed. The interphaser's targeting computer had been programmed with the precise coordinates of the mat-trans unit as destination zero. A touch of a single key on the control board would automatically return the device to the jump chamber.

Kane exhaled a weary breath. "You're playing connect-the-dots again."

Lakesh did not seem to be offended. "The few notes that remained about the Black Sun society indicate they believed the physical manifestation of the *Schwartz Sonne* could be activated by the use of machines and psionics. Our galaxy acts as a centrifugal vortex, does it not? It is the same kind of implosive vortex from which the Nazis dreamed of building a new science based upon living energy."

"Yeah, but—"

The door to the office suddenly opened and Domi stepped in. "What's going on? You up to something secret? Good."

Closing the door behind her, Domi sauntered over to Lakesh, leaned down and planted a smacking kiss on his lips. "Miss me?"

Lakesh took her by the hands. "You have no idea. But friend Kane and I are discussing a matter of greatest gravity."

Domi gazed down at him with eyes wide in mock fear. "More doom around the corner. This makes the third time this year, right?"

Kane held up four fingers. "Fourth, actually."

Domi laughed and ran a playful hand over Lakesh's hair. The dim lighting rested on her white skin like frosting on a cake. Her face held an open, childlike frankness beneath its unruly mop of bone-colored hair. She wore high-cut khaki shorts, and a clinging yellow tank top showed the nipples of her pert breasts as little buttons under the thin cloth. She wore no shoes.

"Darlingest one," Lakesh said, forcing a patient smile to his face, "friend Kane and I are involved in a briefing about what you found in the cave in Slovakia."

"Good!" Domi rested a hip on the corner of desk. She smiled mischievously. "Been wondering what that was all about."

"It's rather technical," Lakesh said.

"He thinks the hole in the ground we found in the cave is another Singularity, like the one Strongbow had," Kane declared.

Domi gave Lakesh a dubious look. "You do?"

Lakesh shook his head in frustration. "Not exactly. Kane, you claimed that the Nazis believed in all sorts of mumbo-jumbo, but their concept of the Black Sun is the most esoteric theory they ever came up with. To the brotherhood that bore the name, it represented the void of creation itself, and therefore was the most ancient archetype imaginable. They believed the force of life itself was derived from the Black Sun, a big ball of Prima Materia that supposedly existed just out of phase with our dimension.

"After World War II and the subsequent occupation of Germany, Allied military commanders were stunned to discover the penetrating depth of the Nazi regime's state secrets. They discovered massive and meticulous files on secret societies, eugenics and other scientific pursuits that boggled the imagination of the Allied forces."

"I'm aware of all that," Kane said stiffly.

"You're aware of some of it," Lakesh corrected. "Behind all of these mysteries was an even deeper element—a secret order known to initiates as the Brotherhood of the Black Sun, an organization so feared that it became illegal to even print their symbols and insignia in postwar Germany."

"Why was that?" Domi inquired, idly scratching a bare thigh. "Who came up with this thing?"

"In 1917 four people met in a café in Vienna. There was a very young woman and three men. They met under a veil of mystery and secrecy and discussed secret revelations about a new source of power—the Black Sun, a secret philosophy thousands of years old that provided the foundation on which the occult practitioners of the Third Reich would later build."

"Who were the people?" Kane asked, trying not to sound too interested.

Lakesh touched the keyboard and the image of the blond woman in the evening gown flashed there. "Countess Paula von Schiksel was the woman obviously, but not a countess then—only a very ambitious but telepathically gifted teenager."

"Just a Scarlet Princess," Kane remarked dryly. "She hadn't been crowned queen?"

Lakesh ignored the query. At a touch of another key, a frowning middle-aged man's face appeared, crew cut, square jawed, and with a monocle jammed into his left eye socket. "She was the mistress and later the wife— and shortly thereafter, the widow—of Count Eckhart von Schiksel, an enormously wealthy industrialist."

A second man's face appeared on the screen, thin, sallow but with a lock of black hair falling over his high forehead. A narrow smudge of a mustache occupied the space between his upper lip and nose. Domi shifted on the desk, murmuring wordlessly. Kane recognized him, too.

"Adolf Hitler," Lakesh continued, "a man who needs no introduction. And finally, *this* personage—"

On the screen appeared a head-and-shoulders shot of a bald, heavyset man with wide staring eyes and thick lips curved in a supercilious smile. "Aleister Crowley, who apparently effected a trade between the Brotherhood of the Black Sun and his own Ordo Templi Orientis. The two groups swapped rituals and shared the same goals."

"Goals of what?" Kane asked.

Lakesh cast him a patronizing glance. "What do you think?"

Kane blew out a disgusted sigh. "Oh, yeah. All that master-race and tomorrow-the-world shit. So, you're trying to tell me that this cast of wackos got together over 250 years ago and cobbled together a time machine?"

Lakesh nodded, relieved that Kane finally seemed to grasp the concept. "Exactly. They used an Archon generator to activate all the quantum energies pent up in the vortex point and open a temporal conduit."

"It apparently didn't lead anywhere," Kane commented dryly. "The last time I looked, no storm troopers or blond bimbos with whips have fallen out of the sky."

"True," Lakesh admitted. "But that doesn't mean—"

The trans comm on the wall suddenly uttered a discordant beep and Bry's voice blared, "Lakesh, are you in there?"

Swiveling his chair around toward the unit, Lakesh called, "I'm here, Mr. Bry, with Kane and Domi."

"Good. I've just received two emergency hails, one from Brigid in Redoubt Yankee and the other from Grant on New Edo." Bry paused, then said in a rush, "Something's happening on Thunder Isle…wild energy signatures, electronic interference and even gunfire. All hell is breaking loose."

Lakesh jerked his head toward Kane, eyes alight with sudden fear, but satisfaction glinted there, too. "Would you care to ask him about blond bimbos falling out of the sky?"

Chapter 18

Grant dropped the Manta's altitude to three hundred feet and cruised above a panorama of grassland and jungled valleys. The interior of Thunder Isle looked peaceful, almost bucolic. But he knew from painful experience that the jungle held exceptionally nasty surprises.

"Anything?" Brigid asked, her voice echoing hollowly within the confines of Grant's helmet. "You should be in visual range of the electromagnetic disturbance by now."

"Nothing yet," Grant replied. "I'll keep you apprised. Stand by."

A little less than an hour earlier, he and Shizuka had taken off from New Edo and set down on the grounds of Redoubt Yankee. Inside the Cube they conferred with Brigid and Sela Sinclair regarding the disturbances. Although Sela didn't care for having her authority summarily usurped upon the arrival of Shizuka, she handed over command of the facility without complaint, as per the terms of the agreement between Cerberus and New Edo.

After a brief discussion and another attempt to raise either Philboyd or Edwards on their trans-comms, Shizuka dispatched Grant on an aerial sur-veillance mission, following the coordinates supplied by Brigid.

So far, Grant had seen no sign of life on the forested isle except for a few birds. He scanned the overgrown vastness below and maintained a slow, steady respira-tion rate to dispel the anxiety building within him.

His apprehension mirrored that of Shizuka's, who feared a return of the phenomena that had given Thun-der Isle its name. Although she knew that the original cause of the events had been the temporal dilator of Op-eration Chronos activating at random intervals, either reconstituting subjects from the holding matrix, or snatching new ones from all epochs in history, the de-vice hadn't functioned in years.

Grant looked out beyond the bow of the Manta, past the tangled tops of the tree ferns to the deep blue of the Pacific. Thunder Isle was about five miles long by three miles wide. It rose to a jagged series of hills and vine-covered cliffs that overlooked the sea, the highest of which was barely a hundred feet.

The shoreline alternated between marshland and jut-tings of black, volcanic stone. Here and there, white sand beaches swept up to the edge of the jungle. At low tide, there was very little surf, just a low curl of foaming combers that hissed over the sand and flowed around the boulders.

Grant's pulse suddenly quickened when the bright sun gleamed on a reflective substance below. He cut back the Manta's speed and tipped the craft up slightly on the port wing, directing it in a wide spiral, soundless but for the hum of the low-power gravity modifier field. He stared down, at first confused by what he saw. Seeming to float in the air between his eyes and the visor, a column of numbers appeared, glowing red against the pale bronze. When he focused on distant objects, the visor magnified them and provided CGI readouts as to distance and dimension.

He looked down into a clearing, surprisingly barren in the middle of the lush green foliage. The ground was littered with bodies. Most of the corpses wore dark khaki uniforms, many of them blotched with dark, damp stains. Ribbons of blood seeped from beneath the bodies. They were scattered everywhere, primarily on the surface of what appeared to be a round metal ring that resembled an impossibly huge shield. Grant picked out a few black uniforms mixed in with the khaki. Among the two score bodies he counted, not a single one stirred.

Slowly he circled the clearing, getting a closer look at the corpses and the definitely outdated weapons he saw scattered among them. Most of the khaki-clad men wore ridiculous-looking helmets that reminded him of mushroom caps. He did, however, recognize the style.

"This is Grant," he said into the helmet's transceiver. "I have something to report."

"Go ahead," Brigid's crisp voice responded.

"Dead bodies," he stated flatly. "Lots of them."

There was a long silence, then Shizuka demanded, "How can that be?"

"It be," he answered. "They look like soldiers...but their helmets are of the Doughboy style and the rifles are British Enfield repeaters."

"How is that significant?" Shizuka asked impatiently.

"Those rifles were first manufactured in 1902 and saw the most action in World War I." Grant paused and added darkly, "I don't know about you, but that fits my definition of significant."

Neither Shizuka nor Brigid questioned him on his knowledge of firearms. Both women knew he was a scholar of predark weaponry.

"It fits mine, too," Brigid interjected, her voice tight. "Is there anything else unusual around there?"

"As a matter of fact, there's a big-ass metal ring on the ground. Actually, a ring within a ring."

"Can you land and take a closer look?" Brigid asked.

"I could," he replied slowly. "Depending on what the New Edoan commander thinks is best."

For a long moment, Grant heard only his own respiration within the helmet and he smiled. He easily pictured the curt conversation going on between Brigid and Shizuka. Then Shizuka said, "I think it is best, but do not take any unnecessary risks."

"Do I ever?"

"Hai," she retorted grimly. "You do, otherwise I would not caution you against it."

"Kenka uten noka," he muttered sourly.

Engaging the ramjets, Grant dropped the Manta straight down and rested it on the extended landing gear. Unsealing his helmet, he unlatched the cockpit canopy, pushed it back and made a wordless utterance of dismay at the stifling heat and cloying humidity. He climbed out of the TAV, sliding down the starboard wing.

Before leaving New Edo, Grant had decided against putting the shadow suit back on, since extended wear often resulted in a skin rash. Instead, he selected clothing from the limited wardrobe he kept in the palace. He wore a sleeveless black T-shirt, with camou pants tucked into the tops of high-laced jump boots. Grant's Sin Eater was holstered to his right forearm, and a Copperhead subgun hung from a strap around his left shoulder.

The sun was high and dazzling, its heat pressing into the back of his neck like a hot poker. Putting on a pair of sunglasses, he carefully walked over to the nearest group of bodies, alert for any movement or sound from the wall of greenery enclosing the clearing. The humid air was redolent with the coppery tang of blood. Scarlet runnels cut crusted channels through the ground. Already flies buzzed over them.

Grant toed the wooden stock of a rifle, noting that his first assessment as to its make and model was correct: a British-made Lee-Enfield .303 with a 10-round magazine.

Spent cartridge cases glinted underfoot and he saw two different types, one much smaller than the other. Leaning down, he picked up one of small cylinders, revolving it between thumb and forefinger, identifying it as a 9 mm.

Static hissed and Brigid's voice came through the Commtact. "Grant, do you read me?"

"Reading you," he responded. "I'm down on the ground, but I don't have any better idea of what went on than when I was airborne. All I can say is that it looks like a squad of World War I soldiers was slaughtered here."

"That's impossible," came Shizuka's sharp objection.

"I'm only telling you what I see, sweetheart," Grant replied mildly. "So it's not impossible."

Brigid declared, "For it to be possible would mean that the temporal dilator is—"

She broke off, then a few seconds later said brusquely, "I'm going to check something. Stand by, please."

"I'm not going anywhere—yet."

As he spoke, Grant gave one of the black-clad corpses a visual inspection, seeing no weapon nearby. Beneath a coal-scuttle helmet, a black knit balaclava completely concealed his features. Tinted goggles covered the eye holes.

He glanced around alertly, then he squatted, working the helmet free and stripping off the mask. He winced at the sight, almost closing his eyes against the sudden surge of nausea in his belly.

The man's face was a grotesquerie of fire-scarred, hairless flesh. The bright sunlight made black hollows in which his glazed eyes glittered. His face was a skull-like travesty of tight, red-hued tissue, his mouth a lipless gash. It gaped open and behind the square, dull yellow teeth, Grant saw only a cauterized stub of flesh.

With the short barrel of the Copperhead, he nudged the man's head to one side, realizing he had no eyelids. They, like his tongue, had been surgically removed. He had no idea if the facial scars were due to a deliberate act of mutilation, but obviously someone had been pretty deft with a scalpel.

Straightening, Grant took a step and heard something crunch beneath his boot. Lifting his foot, he saw a pair of black-rimmed eyeglasses, half crushed into the ground. He picked them up and a cold fist of dread knotted in his chest. He recognized them as Brewster Philboyd's.

Brigid's voice returned, "Grant, do you see any insignia or rank on the bodies?"

Slipping the glasses into a pocket, Grant moved to a nearby khaki-uniformed corpse and eyed a triangular patch worked in red thread on a yellow background, sporting a stylized image of two crossed rifles. "Yeah," he said, squinting to read the words. "The First-Fourth Norfolk, B."

Brigid didn't gasp, but her quietly intoned "Oh my God" was more meaningful than if she had.

"What is it?" he demanded.

"The metal rings," Brigid said. "Can you check those out?"

"Sure," he said uncertainly, walking among the corpses, placing his feet carefully between them. Fresh, uncoagulated blood squashed beneath his boot soles. Although he knew Thunder Isle's high humidity would prevent blood from drying some hours, he was sure the massacre had occurred less than half an hour before.

Just as Grant reached the rim of the outer ring, he felt a hand clasp his ankle. He didn't jump or kick free, but he instinctively tensed his wrist tendons and the Sin Eater popped into his hand. He pointed it downward. A face stared up at him sightlessly from beneath the overhang of his helmet. The domed crown of it bore a bullet perforation, and a layer of wet scarlet glistened on the upper half of the man's face, blinding him.

"'Ullo there, guv," he said in a husky whisper. "Even if yer one of the *boche,* d'ya think ya can spare an ol' soljer a drink o' somethin' wet?"

The man was middle-aged, and despite the head wound he managed to grin, exposing red-filmed teeth. "Anything ya can spare, guv. I'm as dry as General Hamilton's conscience."

Grant didn't know to whom the man referred, and he wasn't inclined to ask for clarification. Kneeling, he glanced at the dark stains spreading around the grouping of bullet holes on the man's chest and said, "Wouldn't help."

"Aye," the soldier wheezed in resignation. "So yer a Yank…didn't know there was any American divisions out here."

"Out where?"

"Gallipoli, where the hell else?" The man's voice acquired a note of suspicion. "What division are y'with?"

Due to his visits to the British Isles, Grant easily identified the soldier's accent as English, but a thick brogue he hadn't heard before blurred his pronunciation of some words.

"What division are you with?" Grant asked, sidestepping the man's question.

"The First Battalion of the Fifth Norfolk infantry," he half gasped, a note of pride in his strained voice. "Staff Sergeant Olney at yer service, sar."

"What happened here, Sergeant?" Grant asked.

With effort, Olney managed to half lift his head. "Fightin' out of m'class, looks like. Y'seen m'mate, Dickie?"

"Dickie?"

"Dickie Bates…" Olney's voice trailed off, and he laid his head down. Abruptly he stopped breathing and was still.

Rising, Grant tried to tamp down the pity he felt for the hapless Sergeant Olney, who died desperate to find his friend.

Although Grant's upbringing as a Magistrate had taught him that any personal bonds he made with his comrades chipped away at his worth and loyalty to the baron, he understood Olney's anguish. It was one thing to go into battle prepared to die, but watching friends die was another thing entirely.

The Mag command had seen the bonds growing between Kane and Grant back in Cobaltville, which was why the decision had been made to break them up. But that bond had kept Grant alive as much as it had Kane.

Silently, Grant studied the gray alloy of the giant

wheel within a wheel, trying to make sense of the numerical strings etched into the surface. Inset into the metal were hundreds, if not thousands of tiny crystal hexagons, none of them any larger than his thumbnail.

He activated the Commtact. "I'm at the ring thing."

"What's it look like?" Brigid responded promptly.

Grant described it in detail. "Beats the hell out of me what it is," he concluded, "but it's pretty damn obvious it has something to do with bringing the soldiers here." He hesitated and added, "I spoke to one of them, right before he died."

"What did he say?"

"He claimed he was with the First Battalion of the Fifth Norfolk infantry…in a place called Gallipoli. That's in Turkey, right?"

"Right." Brigid's voice held an unsteady note. Someone who didn't know her would not have detected it at all. "So, there's no sign of Brewster?"

Grant considered not telling her about finding the man's eyeglasses, but before he could make up his mind, the tiny crystal facets suddenly exuded a cold blue glow. At the same time, his head filled with a crash of static.

"Brigid, do you read me?" he asked.

When no response was forthcoming, he stepped away from the giant disk, assuming the crystals radiated the interference. Then, his scalp tightened and his neck flushed cold. Swiftly, he pivoted on one foot, leading with his Sin Eater, eyes darting back and forth.

Grant saw nothing but the scattered bodies, the Manta and the wall of foliage enclosing the clearing, but he didn't relax. Forcing himself to walk, he strode toward his ship, trying not to step in blood.

He had crossed only half of the distance before he heard the ululating, croaking bellow from behind him.

Chapter 19

Grant came to an immediate halt, exhaling a slow, disgusted breath followed by a faint, but very heartfelt *"Shit."*

The dull reverberations of a heavy weight slamming repeatedly against the ground sent shivers up his spine, despite the heat and humidity. He knew the Monstrodamii was attracted to the heavy scent of so much fresh blood, like an ant drawn to spilled honey. He also knew the creature's vision was keyed to movement, so he stood completely immobile, like a statue carved from teak.

He took a small comfort in the fact that the carnosaur's thudding footfalls were fairly slow and methodical—he hoped it meant the creature checked out the killzone for threats instead of charging in after moving prey.

Grant heard it panting like a laboring steam engine as it advanced cautiously into the clearing. The three-toed, talon-tipped feet squealed like fingernails dragged over a blackboard as they sought purchase on the slick metal of the double disks.

A looming shadow fell across him, and he felt a gust of scalding breath on his back. Although his perspiration-filmed flesh crawled, Grant maintained his motionless posture. The revolting odor of rotten meat and the sour stench of the reptile clogged his nostrils. Absently, he realized the creature's effluvium was extraordinarily virulent; otherwise he wouldn't have been able to detect a whiff of it.

Grant's nose had been broken three times in the past, and always poorly reset. Unless an odor was remarkably pleasant or violently repulsive, he was incapable of catching subtle smells, unless they were right under his nostrils.

The carnosaur stepped into view on his right side, passing so close to him its scale-pebbled hide rasped painfully against his bare arm. Grant followed its movements with only his eyes. The Daspletosaurus stood upright on a pair of enormously overdeveloped legs. A long, muscular tail trailed out from behind it. The creature's body was completely armored by dark brown scales.

The Monstrodamii stood fifteen feet tall, the clawed forelegs small in proportion to the rest of its barrel-shaped body, but the curving, steel-hard talons tipping each of the three fingers were at least six inches long. They jerked spasmodically. Grant figured nervous gnawings of hunger caused it, but to him it looked as if the carnosaur were clapping its hands delightedly over the feast spread out before it.

Grinning jaws bared rows of glistening fangs and from between them darted a black, slimy tongue, tasting the air. The saurian snout bore a pair of flared nostrils that dilated and twitched. The head, twice the size of a bull's, turned back and forth upon an extended scaled neck. Huge, cold eyes like those of a serpent's a hundred times magnified, stared unwinkingly from beneath a pair of scaled, knobby protuberances.

The Monstrodamii lumbered past him, lowering its head to sniff at the ground, dust and mistings of blood puffing up around its nostrils. It stood spraddle-legged over a dead English soldier, its tongue continuing to flick in and out of its mouth, head tilting from side to side, taut with quivering muscles. Grant figured so many corpses were the equivalent of a smorgsabord, and the carnosaur didn't know which dish to sample first.

As bile rose up his throat, he watched as the creature's huge jaws opened and closed, crunching noisily on the hip and pelvic bones of the dead man. The giant saurian ripped out a chunk of cloth, flesh and viscera from the corpse's midsection and tugged at the intestines as if they were strands of pasta.

Grant watched impassively as the Monstrodamii fed and when it shifted position so its back was to him, he carefully began crab-walking toward the Manta. He did not move fast and stopped every couple of yards to get his bearings, to make sure there was no obstruction that would trip him up.

His head pounded, sweat stung his eyes beneath the lenses of his sunglasses and twice he stopped to wipe them clean. The crunching of fangs into bone and the moist sound of flesh being chewed seemed unnaturally loud to him, but he hoped the noise would cover the scuff of his feet on the ground.

When he was within six feet of the Manta's port-side wing, the painful constriction in his temples began to ease. Even if the Daspletosaurus became aware of him as he climbed into the cockpit, he felt fairly certain it couldn't force its way through the canopy before he was able to launch.

Suddenly, the Monstrodamii jerked erect with a startled snort. It scuttled around, facing Grant, and he came to a complete halt, freezing in midstep. The loose flesh at its throat pulsed, and from it issued a hissing, rumbling snarl. Then the carnosaur thrust its head forward, opened its jaws wide and voiced a roar that combined the worst aspects of a trumpet, steam valve and the howl of a dying dog. Its tail lashed back and forth.

To Grant's shock and horror, the roar was answered from the far side of the clearing. Vegetation swished and crashed, saplings snapped and then a twin of the Daspletosaurus bounded out of the undergrowth, hopping kangaroolike. The creature lowered its head and bellowed at the Monstrodamii that had reached the feast first.

The two Daspletosaurs trumpeted challenges at each other. Grant noted that the newcomer was smaller, leaner with numerous scars crisscrossing its body, yet it projected an air of cockiness, like an overconfident back-alley brawler. The creature began advancing across the clearing, its high-stepping gait reminding Grant of a rooster's strut, sickle-like talons digging deep gouges in the ground.

The larger Monstrodamii suddenly bounded forward, moving far more swiftly than Grant would have dreamed, due to its bulk. The carnosaur's smaller rival lunged to meet it, uttering a liquid, hissing snarl. The two beasts collided breast to breast.

Grant didn't wait to see which Monstrodamii delivered the first bite or disemboweling kick. He sprinted to the edge of the Manta's wing and vaulted atop it. As he clambered frantically toward the open cockpit, he glimpsed the pair of Daspletosaurs snapping and tearing at each other, screaming in red rage.

The smaller of the pair suddenly lowered its head and slammed the top of its skull into its opponent's chest, piledriving the creature backward. The larger Monstrodamii staggered and crashed into the rear engine assembly of the Manta, its tremendous weight jarring it, tipping it upward.

Unable to keep from shouting a curse, Grant toppled from the wing, striking the ground heavily and raising a cloud of dust around his body. He rolled desperately to one side, fearing that the battling carnosaurs could manage to turn the TAV completely over.

As he began to climb to his feet, he became aware of a sudden cessation of sound. The snarls and growls of the enraged saurians had stopped, replaced by panting, labored respiration. By degrees, Grant hitched around and froze in a crouch. His gaze slid to the two sets of eyes that regarded him coldly. The deep breathing of the Monstrodamii slowly became a steady, menacing growl.

Grant didn't so much as blink. He was prepared to remain locked in a crouching posture for as long as possible, as long as necessary. Then the smaller of the pair of dinosaurs opened its jaws and let loose a thundering bellow of anger.

The big Monstrodamii pounced, its talon-tipped toes tearing out great clots of dry earth. Grant flung himself in a headlong somersault beneath the TAV. The Monstrodamii whirled and stooped, trying to jam its huge head under the Manta.

Raising his Sin Eater, Grant squeezed off a triburst, the reports barely audible over the beast's snarls. The snarls were replaced by a howl and it scuttled backward, blood spurting from the wounds on its snout.

Grant crawled toward the rear of the ship and the smaller carnosaur raced around to cut him off. As he lifted his pistol, the Monstrodamii leaped straight up, as if shot from a cannon, and landed atop the Manta. The landing gear creaked alarmingly and the undercarriage sagged beneath the Daspletosaur's weight.

Grant did not hesitate. Adrenaline ignited a fuse in his heart, firing a fear that bordered on wild terror, an emotion he had experienced only a couple of times in his life. He shoulder rolled out from under the Manta's starboard wing, came to his feet and pounded across the clearing.

He heard the bawling of the two creatures behind him, but he kept running, his gaze fixed on the wall of undergrowth. Lungs straining with the effort of breathing in the thick, humid air, Grant warred with the fear that ate away at his nerves like acid. He forced himself to remember that Kane had survived two close encounters with the parent of the monsters, so he knew he had to evade the pair of them. If he failed and was eaten, Kane would never let him hear the end of it.

The ground trembled underfoot as the carnosaurs pounded after him in roaring pursuit. He burst through a barrier of foliage, ignoring the sting of thorns on his bare arms and hands. The Monstrodamii came crashing after him like out-of-control locomotives.

Gliding under a canopy of overlapping ferns, Grant dived to the right, then dodged between the legs of the large Monstrodamii, evading by a handbreadth a snap of the giant jaws. He spun and ran in the opposite direction and heard the smaller of the two beasts wallowing through a tangle of creepers and densely packed shrubbery.

Grant put all of his energy and concentration into running, changing direction several times and tearing his way through webworks of vegetation. The needled tips of the coniferous shrubs stabbed at him, and only his sunglasses saved his eyes. Lianas snagged him but he ripped at the growth with his powerful hands. Penetrating the jungle became like burrowing his way through to the bottom of a wet, green haystack.

Grant lost his footing and tripped, falling heavily on his right side. Panting, he pushed himself to his feet and went on. At his back he heard the crash of undergrowth and deep-throated grunts.

Grinding his teeth against the rib ache, he raced through a copse of ferns, slapping the fronds aside. He nearly pitched into empty space, digging in his heels and rocking to an unsteady stop. Directly in front of him the lip of a gully sloped downward for ten feet. At the bottom of it spread a very smooth and invitingly open space of dark green. Hearing a frustrated, angry bellow from behind him, he leaped down. The instant he did, he realized there was something ominous about the flat expanse of green below.

With a painful contortion of his body, he overcame the natural instinct to drop feetfirst. Instead he twisted and turned in midair, spread-eagling himself. He fell on his back with a moist slap and a splash of dark green ooze.

Grant realized that if his snap judgment had been wrong, the shock of impact would have knocked all the air out of him or even seriously injured his back. Instead, he was wet and covered in slime, but unhurt. He lay perfectly still, hearing the tramp of heavy feet and the snuffling grunts of the hunting Monstrodamii. He hoped if he remained motionless, the odor of the muck would overwhelm his own scent and the giant saurians would pass him by. The reptiles stomped in the vicinity, sniffing for their quarry.

After five minutes of more grunts and a diminishing rustle of undergrowth, Grant heard only silence. By then, the foul mixture of soil, water and slime was up to his ears and although it felt cold and wet, it was not a relief from the heat. He moved toward the opposite side of the gully, then realized he could move only in one direction—down.

The word "quicksand" flared in his mind like a fireball of panic, but he smothered it with cold determination and a swift, mental inventory of the well-spring of information he had gathered in the course of his life. He knew quicksand did not actually suck anything down.

Victims of quagmires died by drowning, by thrashing around in mindless terror until they sank beneath the fluidized surface.

Carefully, he extended both of his arms, dispersing his weight over the largest possible area. He would still sink, but not quite as quickly. He glanced around at his surroundings, cursing the fact that his leap had dropped him virtually into the center of the morass. The fingertips of both hands were at least six feet from anything that fit even the loosest definition of solid footing.

Although he knew it was possible to swim in mud, he also knew the progress was excruciatingly slow and swiftly burned up an enormous amount of energy. The odds of becoming too exhausted to do anything but flounder around and drown were very high.

Slowly, carefully he squirmed about, threshing, clawing aside the semiliquid sludge lying atop the surface. The opposite side of the gully was closer, by perhaps a foot. It rose from the mire as a sheer wall of rock, seven feet high. The slime crept up to the corners of his mouth as he studied the rock face. He calculated that he could not possibly struggle across the quagmire and reach it before he sank.

After a long moment of silent examination, he intoned with a flat resignation, "Well…here I am."

"Yeah, me too," a man's voice drawled from above him. "And a damn good thing, too."

Chapter 20

Kane opened his eyes, struggling against a spasm of nausea, striving and straining for inner balance as always after a mat-trans jump. He blinked against vision-clouding vertigo, glimpsed the silvery shimmer fading from the hexagonal disks on the ceiling and felt the pins-and-needles static discharge from the metal floor plates. Beneath them he heard the emitter array's characteristic hurricane howl fading away to a high-pitched whine.

His head swam. The vertigo was routine by now, a customary side effect of rematerialization. He knew better than to sit up until the light-headedness went away completely. All things considered, temporary queasiness and dizziness were small prices to pay in exchange for traveling hundreds, sometimes thousands of miles, in a handful of minutes.

Occasionally, the toll exacted was terrible, as when he, Brigid and Grant jumped to a malfunctioning unit in Russia. The matter-stream modulations couldn't be synchronized with the destination lock, and all of them suffered a severe case of debilitating jump sickness, which included hallucinations, weakness and vomiting.

Kane gingerly eased himself up on one elbow, looking around slowly, making sure the transparent plastic CD case had made the transition with him. One of the many baffling features of mat-trans jumps was how travelers could start it standing up and end it by lying flat on their back.

The floor plates lost their silvery shimmer and the last wisps of spark-shot mist disappeared even as he looked at it. Kane sat up, making sure the armaglass walls enclosing the jump chamber were tinted gray, which meant he had reached his preset destination. The six-sided chambers in the Cerberus gateway network were color-coded so authorized jumpers could tell at a glance into which redoubt they had materialized.

It seemed an inefficient method of differentiating one installation from another, but Lakesh had once explained that before the nukecaust, only personnel holding color-coded security clearances were allowed to make use of the system. Inasmuch as their use was restricted to a select few units, it was fairly easy for them to memorize which color designated what redoubt.

Kane had learned that the use to which the Cerberus process had been put was at variance with the original mission statement. Under the aegis of the Totality Concept, utilizing bits of preexisting technology, the aim of Project Cerberus was essentially matter-to-energy conversion and back again to matter. The entire principle behind matter transmission was that everything organic and inorganic could be reduced to encoded information.

The primary stumbling block to actually moving from the theoretical to the practical was the sheer quantity of information that had to be transmitted, received and reconstituted without making any errors in the decoding.

The string of information required to program a computer with every bit and byte of data pertaining to the transmitted subject, particularly the reconstruction of a complex biochemical organism out of a digitized carrier wave, ran to the trillions of binary digits. Scientists labored over a way to make this possible for nearly fifty years, financed by "black funds" funneled away from other government projects.

Project Cerberus, like all the other Totality Concept researches, was classified above top secret. A few high government officials knew it existed, as did members of the Joint Chiefs of Staff of the military. The secrecy was believed to be more than important; it was considered to be almost a religion.

A device that could transmit matter—particularly soldiers and weapons—was a more important offensive weapon than America's entire nuclear stockpile.

The matter transmitter had other, less destructive applications, as well. Given wide use, it could eliminate inefficient transportation systems and be used for space exploration and colonizing planets in the solar system, without the time and money involved in building spaceships.

However, matter transmission had been found to be absolutely impossible to achieve by the employment of Einsteinian physics. Only quantum physics, coupled with quantum mechanics, had made it work beyond a couple of prototypes that transported steel balls only a few feet across a room. But even those crude early models could not have functioned at all without the basic components that preexisted the Totality Concept.

Mohandas Lakesh Singh, the project's overseer, experienced the epiphany and made that breakthrough. The mystery of the origin of the technology, which made the entire system viable, haunted Lakesh. It would be many years before he came across the shocking fact that although the integral components were of terrestrial origin, they were constructed under the auspices of a nonhuman intelligence—or at least, nonhuman as defined by late-twentieth-century standards. Nearly two centuries would pass before Lakesh learned the entire story, or a version of it.

Kane slowly climbed to his feet, flexing his fingers, not able to repress a sign of relief at finding himself whole and in one piece. No human being, no matter how thoroughly briefed in advance, could be expected to remain unflappable on a hyperdimensional jump. No matter how many times it was performed, a trip through the gateway was unsettling to the mind, to the nerves and, Kane often suspected, to the soul itself.

An odd, muffled warbling on the fringes of audibility puzzled him, but he attributed it to a hitherto unexperienced symptom of jump sickness. Then, with a start, he realized he was hearing Redoubt Yankee's intruder alert signal.

Chapter 21

Carefully, Grant tried to wipe the muck-occluded lenses of his sunglasses clean. When that failed, he inquired gruffly, "Brewster?"

Philboyd's forced chuckle wafted from a point somewhere above him, but in the direction he was facing. "I didn't expect to find you here, but then I didn't expect any of what happened today."

Twisting his head up and around, Grant raised his sunglasses and saw Philboyd kneeling on top of the rock wall. He winced at the sight of the man's bruised face and swollen, split lip.

"What the hell happened to you?" he demanded.

Philboyd grinned feebly, then grimaced and dabbed at the blood trickling from the laceration at the corner of his mouth. "That probably should be my line. I thought you were in Transylvania or someplace. What are you doing here?"

"Looking for you."

"You found me, sort of…but it looks like you're

sinking in a bog, or am I mistaken about that?" Philboyd squinted. "Hard to tell without my glasses."

"I've got your glasses in my pocket."

"Then I guess I'd better find a way to get you out of there."

"Fair to say," Grant retorted dourly. "I don't suppose you have a rope handy?"

Philboyd shook his head. "Sorry, no…and the vines around here aren't very sturdy." He paused, then snapped in a voice quivering with almost accusatory frustration, "Goddammit, Grant, you're supposed to be superfucking resourceful! That's how you've repped out since the day we met!"

Realizing how profoundly frightened the man really was, Grant told him calmly, "Ease up on it…you won't have to stand there and watch me be sucked to my death, if that's what you're worried about. I may not be superfucking resourceful, but I always have an idea."

The tension tightening Philboyd's face relaxed a trifle. "Yeah?"

"Yeah. I'm packing a Copperhead. If I can unhook one end of the strap, I'll throw it up to you."

"Then what?"

Grant scowled. "What do you think? Anchor it to something and I'll climb out."

Philboyd matched his scowl. "You make it sound so simple."

"I didn't mean to, because it sure as hell won't be."

Taking and holding a deep breath, Grant nerved himself, rolled over to his left and plunged his hands beneath the semifluid surface of the quagmire. He fumbled to unhook the canvas strap of the subgun. Because of his mud-coated fingers, it took him a couple of attempts and by then he had sacrificed his reserve of buoyancy. He felt himself sinking fast.

With the stinking slime clinging to the ends of his mustache, he freed his right arm with a wet pop. "You ready, Brewster?" he called.

"Yeah," the man answered uncertainly. "Guess so."

Holding one end of the strap, Grant hurled the Copperhead toward the gully lip. It clattered loudly against stone and small rocks rained down all around him. He glimpsed Philboyd lunging forward, flailing with his arms. For a heart-stopping instant, he feared the skinny scientist would topple from the ledge and splat down headfirst in the bog.

Then Philboyd announced triumphantly, "Got it!"

Holding both ends of the small subgun, Philboyd jammed it into a deep horizontal fissure, then stood up and stamped on the frame, securing the weapon inside the crack. "Try it now."

Grant dragged on the strap steadily with his right hand, transferring all of his weight by cautious degrees. Then he gripped it with his other hand and heaved upward. The bog clung to his body, but he pulled himself along the strap, hand over hand, shoulder muscles protesting under the strain. Philboyd kept one foot on the subgun, pressing it in place with all of his weight.

Biceps bulging, Grant pulled his upper body free of the sludge. With trembling limbs he laboriously climbed up the strap, placing one hand over the other until his waist and then his hips came loose from the mire with a protracted sucking sound.

His wrists, forearms and shoulders burned as if they were filled with molten lava. He missed a hold and hung for an agonized few seconds by one slipping hand until he could secure another grip. Gritting his teeth, he fought his way upward until he felt Philboyd's fingers closing over his right wrist, then his left.

Grunting with exertion, the scientist hauled Grant the last few inches up to the ledge, then fell backward and the big man came with him, dropping flat atop him. A wheezing curse burst from Philboyd's lips. For a moment, the two men lay there, gasping and panting, Grant's limbs too numb to move.

"Get off me," Philboyd grunted, squirming beneath him. "I don't want Edwards to come along and find us like this."

The possibility didn't appeal to Grant, either, so he elbowed himself onto the bare stone and lay there, trying to moderate his breathing and massage feeling back into his fingers and arms.

After a moment, he sat up, scraping at the mud caking his arms, neck and face. "So Edwards is still alive. What about Nakai?"

Philboyd's brow creased. "He's alive, too, but he's wounded. Took a slug in the hip. Edwards is tending him."

"Where are they?"

The man rose and waved toward their right. "Off that way, with Tshaya."

Grant swung a suspicious stare toward him. "Tshaya? Who the hell is that? Or is it a what?"

Philboyd chuckled, but it sounded strained. "A who—a little girl."

Setting his teeth on a groan, Grant stood up. "What's a little girl doing on Thunder Isle?"

Philboyd shrugged and held out a hand. "I'm still trying to figure that out. Can I have my glasses?"

Grant fished them out of his pants pocket and placed them in the man's palm. They weren't completely coated by muck, but when Philboyd seated them on the bridge of his nose the right earpiece fell off.

"I forgot to tell you," Grant said. "I found them when I stepped on them."

Philboyd glared at him, but said nothing. He used the hem of his T-shirt to clean the lenses of mud. "You saw those metal rings?"

Grant nodded. "And about two dozen bodies…the smell of the blood drew the Monstrodamii twins."

Slipping his glasses back on, Philboyd replied, "I halfway figured those bastards would show up. I saw you make the flyover, so I was coming back to the site when I heard you talking to yourself."

"A bad habit."

"A good one this time," Philboyd retorted, turning and pushing his way through the undergrowth. "Let's get back to the others."

Bending, Grant wrenched at the Copperhead jammed into the crack and with a screech of metal scraping against rock, managed to work it free. He checked the action of his Sin Eater, relieved to find out that the ooze hadn't interfered with the spring mechanism.

As he fell into step beside Philboyd, he asked, "What was with those deformed bastards in black?"

Philboyd's eyebrows rose. "Deformed?"

"Yeah…they'd been mutilated…faces burned, eyelids and tongues removed."

Philboyd's mouth pursed in distaste. "I don't know about that, but they're Germans."

"Germans?" Grant echoed incredulously. "From Germany?"

"Where they're from isn't as important as when."

Grant nodded tersely. "Tell me everything that happened, but table the speculation until the end."

Philboyd spoke quickly and quietly. Grant listened without interjecting comments or questions, not even when he mentioned Aleister Crowley, Countess Paula von Schiksel and the little blind girl who communicated with Philboyd telepathically.

After he was done, Grant considered Philboyd's words for a thoughtful moment, then said, "Now you can speculate your ass off."

In a rush, Philboyd declared, "It's obvious this bunch of Germans and Crowley are from 260 years in the past. Somehow they established a link, a conduit between the Operation Chronos tech of the twentieth century and the temporal dilator system here. I'm not sure how, but I'll bet the girl, Tshaya, figures into it."

Grant nodded in reluctant agreement. "Even so, why would they do it?"

Philboyd shook his head. "I don't know, but I got the distinct impression they expected to show up some-where and somewhen else."

He took a breath and declared, "Apparently, Lam gave them the impression they'd be welcomed by the Archons."

Grant's stomach muscles tightened. "Lam, Balam's father?"

"I think so. Needless to say, they weren't happy when all they found was me, Nakai and Edwards…and then when those other soldiers came through the ring or the gate, we were able to get away into the jungle. Sounded like a hell of a firefight. We've been hiding ever since."

Philboyd's words trailed off and he ran a hand over his perspiration-filmed brow. "I don't know what the hell is going on, I truly don't."

Grant's mind raced with conjecture and wonder. Over the past few years all of the Cerberus warriors had learned "Archon" was a Gnostic term that described both guardians of spiritual planes and jailers of the divine spark within humanity. Ultra-top-secret groups within the U.S. military and intelligence agencies applied the word to Balam, the last of the so-called Archons.

The two men headed out to join Edwards and Nakai.

The close-growing tree ferns draped and looped with braids of flowering liana vines seemed to contain the heat. The humidity kept the mud on Grant's body from drying completely, making him feel as if he were still trapped in the bog.

Insects buzzed above their heads in the muggy air. Bright-plumaged birds cheeped at them from the branches of the trees. Once Grant sighted a creature that looked like a snake with stumpy legs, but it scuttled and slithered into the brush before he got a good look at it.

Philboyd came to a halt, looked to the left and right, then he pursed his lips and whistled softly. After a moment, the whistle was repeated, but from a thicket a dozen yards to their left.

Philboyd let out his breath in a sigh of relief, then cast Grant an abashed smile. "I thought I was lost. I'm not much of a woodsman, I'm afraid."

"You're doing fine," Grant replied.

Parting a clump of foliage, Philboyd stepped into a small glade surrounded by saplings and intertwined vines. Nakai and Edwards started up, eyes glinting with apprehension, then their faces registered relief when they recognized Grant under the coating of mud.

Edwards, finger on the trigger of an M-14 rifle, said earnestly, "I'm damn glad to see you, sir."

"Don't be and don't call me sir," Grant growled. "I'm in the same situation as you three."

"Four," Nakai corrected, reaching around behind him and gently pulling a little girl into view. "Brewster calls her Tshaya."

"I call her Tshaya because that's her name," Philboyd said in an aggrieved tone. "She told me so."

Edwards snorted. "She's blind, deaf and mute. How can she tell you anything?"

Grant gazed at the black-haired child. Despite her sightless eyes, she looked up at him gravely. Then she took a half step toward him, reaching out, groping with both hands. Kneeling, Grant allowed the girl to lightly caress his face with her fingers. His mind suddenly felt a whispering touch, like an invisible, wispy cobweb brushing him with ectoplasmic tentacles.

Grant drew in a sharp breath, resisting the urge to slap the girl's hands away. Like everyone else raised in and around the villes, he was familiar with the tales of doomies, or doomseers. Human mutants possessed of a telepathic second sight, they were exceedingly rare. Most of them had been exterminated during the Program of Unification, although the rumor mills had placed a few of them working secretly for the barons.

The vague mind-touch disappeared and the blank mask of Tshaya's face twitched. The lips of her small mouth curved up in a smile. She glanced toward Philboyd and out of the corner of his eye, Grant saw him stiffen in surprise. Then the girl leaned her head against Grant's shoulder.

After a few seconds, Grant asked gruffly, "What's going on?"

"She just spoke to me," Philboyd said unsteadily. "Telepathically."

"What did she say?"

Philboyd hesitated, coughed, cleared his throat and intoned, "'Daddy's here.'"

Chapter 22

Alarm Klaxons blared discordantly, echoing all over the Cube. Standing at the master monitor screen in the control center, Brigid Baptiste divided her attention between the exterior and interior views. The screen was divided into a dozen square sections, each one showing a different black-and-white view. People ran through the Cube's corridors in apparent panic, but in actuality they were racing to appointed emergency stations as per the red-alert drills.

Two squares showed views transmitted from the outer perimeter wall. Black-clad, featureless figures flitted back and forth, taking advantage of the sparse cover available in the dead zone.

Almond eyes narrowed to slits, Shizuka declared, "They appear to be armed."

"And wearing helmets and masks," Brigid replied, touching the screen's control keyboard. "Let me see if I can bring up the magnification without losing resolution."

Shizuka cast a backward glance at Sela Sinclair,

seated at the control console. "Colonel, I think we've had enough of the alarm now."

As the woman turned off the Klaxon, Shizuka saw a shadow-suited Kane step out of the jump chamber, pushing open the heavy door on its counterbalanced hinges. He made his way swiftly across the room to join Brigid and Shizuka at the monitor screen, exchanging terse nods with Sinclair.

"What's going on, Baptiste?" he asked.

"Intruders," Brigid replied, still manipulating the images. "Did you bring what I asked for?"

Kane tapped the plastic CD case against his palm. "One digital briefing jacket, as ordered. Lakesh seemed fairly shook up by what's going on, which might disturb me if I actually had any idea in hell of what *is* going on."

"If it's half of what I suspect is happening," Brigid retorted curtly, "then Lakesh has every right to be shook up."

"Maybe you can let me in on it when you have a free moment." Kane didn't even try to soften the peevish, sarcastic edge in his voice. "For starters, who are the intruders? And where's Grant?"

Shizuka sighed and Kane turned toward her. The Japanese woman wore a partial suit of samurai armor, her *katana* and *tanto* blades sheathed crosswise at her back. Inclining her head toward a view of the jungle, she said grimly, "Out there. He took the Manta to locate Dr. Philboyd, Edwards and my man Nakai. We lost contact with him about fifteen minutes ago."

"But not before he reported coming across a few items of interest," Brigid interposed.

"Like what?" Kane inquired, feeling tension knot at the base of his neck.

"Apparently a brigade of time-trawled soldiers."

Kane stared at her, too surprised to speak for a moment. At length he demanded, "How is that possible? You caused the dilator to go critical a couple of years ago."

Brigid nodded. "The dilator, yes, but not the main matrix conduit. It was apparently still functioning…it just needed another propagation medium."

"What?" Kane snapped peevishly.

"The intruders are moving again. All of the sentries have been alerted," Shizuka said.

They returned their attention to the figures darting across the screen. They approached the north wall of the complex in a Delta-V formation, moving very swiftly and professionally across the open ground.

Kane studied the images with narrowed eyes. "Those are the soldiers?"

"The ones Grant reported were apparently from the World War I era," Brigid answered matter-of-factly.

"They don't look like World War I soldiers to me," Kane replied.

"That's because they're not," Sela Sinclair announced from behind them. "The submachine guns they're carrying are Schmeissers...World War II vintage."

Kane turned to face her. He didn't know the tall woman very well, but since she reminded him of his Mag small-arms instructor, he tended to trust her, despite the fact there had been no female Magistrates in any division.

"You're sure?" he asked, hoping he didn't sound as if he were challenging her assertion.

She nodded. "Yes, sir. I've seen Schmeissers. They definitely weren't in use before the late 1930s."

Kane scowled, starting to reprimand her for addressing him as "sir" but instead turned to Brigid. "World War I or World War II—which is it, Baptiste?"

Crisply, Brigid said, "Grant found World War I soldiers...a British unit, the so-called Lost Battalion."

Kane dry-scrubbed his hair in frustration. "What are you talking about?"

"It's a mystery dating back to the end of World War I," Brigid stated, eyes still on the monitor screen images. "According to eyewitnesses serving with the New Zealand army, during a battle with Turkish forces on August 28, 1915, a strangely dense cloud seemed to form on the ground across a creek on the Suvla Plain."

"Where is that supposed to be again?" Kane asked.

"The Gallipoli peninsula, Turkey. The New Zealand regiment observed a British battalion, the First-Fourth Norfolk, marching up a dry creek bed and into the cloud. They marched straight into it, with no hesitation." She paused, then added, "None of the soldiers ever came out."

Kane frowned. "Where'd they go?"

Brigid lifted a shoulder in a half shrug. "Nobody ever knew. After the last of the soldiers disappeared into it, the cloud lifted off the ground and, like any cloud or fog would, slowly dispersed. Officially, the First Norfolk was listed as being wiped out, the soldiers killed or captured. But after the war, Turkey denied they had any of the bodies or prisoners. Turkish officials claimed that they didn't even know the battalion existed. The disappearance of a Norfolk infantry unit's officers and men has been a mystery for nearly three hundred years and it became part of twentieth-century UFO lore, as if they'd been victims of a mass abduction. Now I think we have the solution."

Kane's throat constricted. "They were time trawled."

"Accidentally, I'm sure, and they ended up here— today—on Thunder Isle." Brigid swiveled her head toward him, face pale, her eyes haunted emerald pools. Despite her terse, scholarly tone, Kane knew she struggled to stay on top of a mounting fear.

"Are you sure they weren't released from the zero-time buffer? It wouldn't be the first time."

Brigid acknowledged his oblique reference to what had happened to Domi with a head shake. Several years before, it appeared as if Domi had been vaporized by an implode gren. A short time later, during their first visit to the Operation Chronos installation, the Cerberus warriors found video evidence that Domi hadn't been killed—she had been time trawled.

They learned that at the precise micro instant before Domi was swallowed by the full lethal fury of the grenade, she was trawled and then suspended in a noncorporeal matrix. Brigid had activated the instruments of the temporal dilator that retrieved the girl from the holding buffer, but Domi had no recollection whatsoever of what had occurred.

"Who are those guys, then?" Kane asked, nodding toward the dark figures on the monitor screen. "Time trawled, too?"

She shook her head again. "Time *traveled*. They didn't come here accidentally but deliberately."

"How can you be sure of that?" Shizuka asked skeptically.

Brigid didn't answer the woman's question for a long moment, then she stated, "I'm not, but I will be."

Her long fingers stroked a sequence of keys, and the frozen image of a black-clad figure swelled on the screen. Kane examined it, feeling apprehension grow within him at the sight of the coal-scuttle helmet, featureless masked face and goggle-covered eyes. He counted ten oddly shaped cylinders hanging from a leather bandolier about the man's torso.

Sinclair said, "*Stellhandgranates*—German stick grenades...used in both world wars. The Allies called them potato mashers."

Kane eyed the blurred images behind the soldier. "Baptiste, can you bring up the background, enhance and clean it up?"

"I'll try." Brigid enlarged the murky background. Not much could be done about the pixelation, but she reduced the bleaching-out effect of the sunlight and highlighted features. She manipulated the keys until a woman's face filled the screen. A visored military uniform cap cast a shadow over sculpted features.

Kane drew in a sharp breath. Brigid glanced at him quizzically. "What is it?"

Slowly, Kane said, "I guess you and Lakesh are right to be shaken up—these people time-jumped from the 1940s."

"How could that be?" Shizuka argued, gesturing in the direction of the temporal dilator. "Nothing has functioned in here for years!"

"Projekt Kronoscope," Brigid said quietly.

Kane threw her a fleeting look of surprise. "How did you know that?"

"From the files I brought back from Slovakia. That

was the purpose of the installation we found in the cave."

Kane nodded toward the image of the soldier on the screen. "The troopers are the military arm of an organization called the Brotherhood of the Black Sun."

"And who is the woman?" Shizuka demanded impatiently.

"The Scarlet Queen," Kane answered. "Otherwise known as Countess Paula von something."

"Schiksel," Brigid said helpfully. "And lurking somewhere close by, if we look hard enough, I'm sure we'll find the so-called wickedest man in the world."

Chapter 23

Between clenched teeth, Shizuka grated, "With all due respect, I ask you both to speak straight with me. I need to know *exactly* all that you know so I can get an idea of what is happening here. The safety and security of Thunder Isle is my responsibility."

Brigid exhaled wearily. "I'm still trying to make sense of it all, but judging by what I read in the files I salvaged from Slovakia, Nazi Germany built a precursor to the Operation Chronos temporal dilator at the tail end of World War II. They called it the Kronoscope, but it was never put it into military use."

"Why not?" Kane asked.

"They didn't have a reliable propagation medium," Brigid stated. "Not at the time, anyway."

"Which is what?" Shizuka inquired.

"Basically, anything that will serve as a conduit for energy. Obviously, it requires an astronomical amount of energy to travel through time. However, by working together, a group of occultists known as the Ordo Templi Orientis and the Brotherhood of the Black Sun found a way."

Kane angled an eyebrow at her. "The vortex point in the cave?"

"Exactly," Brigid replied. "The brotherhood had always known about it, since centuries before the cave had been their major place of pagan worship. An Englishman named Aleister Crowley claimed that by using channeled information from Lam, the brotherhood could activate the interdimensional energies and basi-cally jump-start a fusion reaction. They could then manipulate the force it would release into a massive big ball of Prima Materia."

Brigid paused and smiled wryly. "I know it sounds mad, but it's a historical fact that the Nazis and their inner occult circle were desperately trying to unleash a supernatural force upon the world, for which the brotherhood had apparently groomed Hitler.

"The Brotherhood of the Black Sun latched on to a very old archetype already in the minds of alchemists and magicians, which was only reinterpreted by Crowley, who believed in blending occult principles with scientific progress."

"Lakesh mentioned a bit of that," Kane said. "Crowley's ideas went beyond time travel."

Brigid nodded. "The idea of mutation and transformation into a higher form of a 'god-man' was envisioned, through the Prima Materia. Crowley himself was an initiate of all the arcane-esoteric philosophies and was aware of the greatest advances in the sciences of his day, since he was a consultant in the early stages of the Totality Concept. That's probably where he first learned of the Archon fusion generators.

"In his writings he expressed the conviction that there are beings endowed with superhuman powers. Crowley believed that the advanced beings would bring about a formidable mutation in the elect of the human race. Of course he and the membership of the Ordo Templi Orientis and the brotherhood were a part of this evolutionary jump. Obviously, he foresaw the hybridization program."

Kane snorted. "Or it was just the same old master-race horseshit that the Nazis and the barons practiced."

Irritably, Shizuka said, "You are really starting to confuse me."

"Get used to it with her," Kane said, indicating Brigid with a jerk of his head.

Not responding to his observation, Shizuka asked, "Are you claiming you found a parallax point in a cave?"

Brigid hesitated before saying, "Yes and no. I think at one time, it was *the* parallax point, the main manifestation in this dimension of the continuum."

"And that is…?" Shizuka eyed her expectantly.

"In essence, the continuum is the sum of all the interwoven world-lattices, all of the parallax points, space-time to quote Einstein. The continuum is so named because it fills superspace, forming a dense, continuous volume that even encompasses time."

Shizuka pursed her full lips. "It sounds more like the Heart of the World in China."

Brigid nodded. "Similar, but far more powerful."

Shizuka referred to the convergence of geomagnetic energies called the Heart of the World, buried deep with the Xian pyramid in central China. The Heart existed slightly out of phase with the third dimension, with the human concept of space-time. From its central core extended a web of electromagnetic and geophysical energy that covered the entire planet.

The mat-trans gateways functioned by tapping into these quantum streams, the invisible pathways that crisscrossed outside of perceived physical space and terminated in wormholes.

"According to the writings of physicists and even the German scientists themselves in the Kronoscope undertaking," Brigid stated, "the continuum's lattices are perpetually expanding or collapsing, pursuing localized cycles of evolution. For instance, just as say, a drill bit endures the oscillations of movement and friction, the continuum absorbs and compensates for the interdimensional exchanges of energy. A drill bit is forged with expansion gaps along its length to accommodate such movement, and so, too, does the continuum possess expansion gaps."

"So in other words," Shizuka intoned, "the parallax point you found in Slovakia is like a great hole, a core drilled through the strata of the universe?"

Brigid smiled, relieved that Shizuka followed her line of theory. "Pretty much, yes. And the Brotherhood of the Black Sun jumped into the hole in Slovakia over 260 years ago and hit bottom today, here on Thunder Isle."

"But how did their Kronoscope connect up with the temporal dilator?" Kane asked.

Brigid shook her head. "I really don't know. I can only speculate. Because the so-called Black Sun lay at an intersection point of all the lattices, the vortex gap became part of space-time curvature—it was the single point through which access to other dimensions is possible, like an elevator that runs among the floors of a building, yet belongs individually to none of them.

"Whatever mechanism is out there on the island acts as a corresponding point in the continuum's grid. I'm sure it uses Cerberus and Chronos technology, which is no surprise. I've got Nguyen searching the database for the specs for it…whatever 'it' really is."

During development of the mat-trans gateways, the Cerberus researchers observed a number of side effects. On occasion, traversing the quantum pathways resulted in minor temporal anomalies, such as arriving at a destination three seconds before the jump initiator was actually engaged.

Lakesh found that time could not be measured or accurately perceived in the quantum stream. Hypothetically, constant jumpers might find themselves physically rejuvenated, with the toll of time erased if enough "backward time" was accumulated in their metabolisms.

Conversely, jumpers might find themselves prematurely aged, if the quantum stream pushed them further into the future with each journey. By studying these temporal anomalies, Operation Chronos found its starting point, using the gateway technology, to develop time travel.

Brigid and Kane were aware that the first technicians of the Totality Concept researches were German scientists, brought over to America on the secret "rat lines" at the end of World War II.

"Like you said…it sounds mad," Shizuka remarked darkly.

"I'm getting a distress call," Sela Sinclair broke in tensely, pressing a hand against the earpiece of her headset.

Kane and Shizuka turned toward her, noting how her eyes narrowed. "It's Reynolds, on the north wall. He's exchanging fire with four of the intruders."

Without hesitation, Shizuka spun toward the door. Kane followed her, saying over his shoulder, "Baptiste, review the briefing jacket for anything useful."

She nodded. "Will do. Be careful."

"We're just going to take a closer look…right, Shizuka?"

The woman did not reply, breaking into a jog, the scabbarded swords crossed over her back bouncing. Kane rolled his eyes in exasperation and increased his pace, glad his Sin Eater was still holstered to his forearm. He had seen the anthracite-hard glint in Shizuka's eyes before and he didn't like it. Although not as reckless as Domi when her warrior's blood beat hot and fast, the samurai could be suicidally fearless if she perceived her home and those under her protection were threatened.

Shizuka ran swiftly and lithely along the catwalk and through the Cube, snapping out orders to the Tiger of Heaven standing guard, as well as to the men at the security station, commanding them to disable the lock on the outer door.

Once outside in the cloying heat, they heard the staccato roar of an MG-73 heavy machine gun firing on full-auto and they raced in the direction of the sound, cutting across the grounds at an angle. Absently, Kane realized it was a particularly lovely day with a flawlessly clear blue sky.

He and Shizuka reached a flight of wooden steps leading to the north wall guard post. Kane allowed the woman to climb to the top of the defensive palisade first, joining Reynolds at the MG-73. He swung it back and forth on the gimbel stanchion, depressing the trigger switches. The rounds thundered through the machine gun, the reports making the still air shiver. Smoking brass cartridges arced from the ejector and tinkled down into the wire catcher.

When the firing pin struck dry on the empty chamber, Reynolds straightened, glancing at Kane and Shizuka with frightened eyes. A middle-aged, blond-haired Manitius émigré, the man blurted, "They shot at me!"

"That's part of the job," Kane retorted, gazing out at the bare terrain below. Sprawled on the ground, lying as if they had been clubbed, were two bodies. Bloody patches showed through bullet-slashed black cloth.

Reynolds spoke quickly, his words tumbling over one another in their haste to leave his mouth. "There were four of them. I warned them to back off, but they kept coming, then they started shooting."

"Where are the other two?" Shizuka demanded.

Reynolds squinted, looking to the left and right. "They got away, I guess, but I ought to be able to see them. It's like they disappeared."

"Or hid themselves," Shizuka commented darkly.

"Could be," Kane agreed reluctantly. "If they had commando training."

"Or ninja," Shizuka stated. "Which means they could still be out there and we just can't see them."

Reynolds eyed her doubtfully. "That doesn't seem very likely."

Kane found himself in tacit agreement with the man's opinion, but at the same time he realized that Reynolds had not only emptied the MG-73, but made no effort to reload. Even as Kane opened his mouth to mention it to Reynolds, two black figures rose from the sandy ground directly below them.

Instantly Kane realized the Black Sun troopers had covered themselves with neutral-colored squares of fabric and their comrades had sprinkled sand over them before being shot down.

The pair of goggled men lifted their right arms and jerked them forward in perfect, machinelike unison, as if they were hurling spears. Reynolds cried out wordlessly and Kane glimpsed two small objects arcing overhead.

Pivoting on a heel, Kane took Shizuka in his arms and lunged with her toward the edge of the wall. He hoped to cushion her fall with his own body, but he toppled into a roaring whirlpool of blinding light, an earsplitting crack of thunder and an all-consuming pain.

Chapter 24

With Tshaya in his arms, Grant led Philboyd, Edwards and Nakai through the jungle. Nakai limped due to the bullet that had gouged the flesh of his right hip, just above his buttock. Although the wound had been bandaged and blood loss was minimal, the man moved slowly, refusing help from Edwards and Philboyd.

Although the samurai had not been able to retrieve either of his swords before he and his companions made their escape, Edwards managed to snatch up the M-14.

As he walked beside Grant, Philboyd spoke breathlessly, quickly, still trying to process all he had seen earlier and make sense of it. "Okay, so we know from Lakesh that a scientist named Silas Burr was in charge of the Chronos section of Overproject Whisper, which was the main division of the Totality Concept…he was the one who coined the term the 'Jamais vu Principle,' about a time-perception disorder. Maybe that's what we're dealing with here."

"How so?" Grant asked, flicking a fly that had landed on his mud-encrusted forearm and become stuck.

"Burr claimed that an event horizon dysfunction was brought into being when the temporal dilator was focused on the future instead of the past. By his reasoning, if the Totality Concept researches had been left to molder in old military intelligence files at the end of World War II, the dysfunction, the alternate future scenario, wouldn't have come into existence, right?"

"If you say so," Grant replied doubtfully.

Philboyd nodded. "So why didn't Burr or the Chronos techs use the dilator to fix the dysfunction and avert the whole nukecaust?"

"I thought they wanted the nukecaust to happen," Grant said.

"No, only a few people were hoping for it to happen. They'd been lied to by the Archons about the end-result of the whole thing. They bought into the bullshit that a better world would arise from the ashes of the old, with them in charge. But I think the main reason nobody tried to repair the temporal dysfunction was fear."

"Fear?"

"It's a given that when you try to alter or manipulate the flow of time, you're asking for a whole *universe* of headaches. Change the one major thing you're hoping to fix, then you overlook the effect on the thousands of tiny details that led up to it and you end up with a worse mess."

"Yeah," Grant muttered. "So I've been told. What's that got to do with those big-ass metal rings?"

Philboyd fell silent, pondering the question for a few seconds, then he shook his head dolefully. "I don't know. Maybe nothing. But—"

"But let's conserve our energy," Grant broke in.

Philboyd eyed him in confusion. "What do you mean?"

"He means," Edwards snapped from behind him, "let's have a little less backchat and a lot more legwork."

Philboyd pretended not to hear the remark. Addressing Grant, he asked, "What about your comm?"

Reaching up with his free hand, Grant touched the Commtact and heard nothing but static. "Interference still."

"Localized ionization in the atmosphere," Philboyd stated positively. "So whatever those rings are, they generate a hell of a lot electromagnetic radiation."

Grant grunted. "Let's have some quiet."

He wasn't worried about encountering the black-uniformed troopers so much as drawing the attention of predators crouching in the undergrowth, waiting for tasty morsels like themselves to pass by.

Wherever they looked, there were growing plants, most of them ferns. The size ranged from tiny seedlings to monstrous growths the size of oak trees. Tangles of creeper vines carpeted the jungle floor. The atmosphere was like that within a greenhouse—impregnated with the overwhelming odor of vegetation and nearly impenetrable with water vapor.

Despite the shade, all of them could feel the oppressive heat and the humidity of wet moss and creepers and could smell the mud and rotting vegetation. The sun became a palpitating brightness, a dazzling disk of white-hot energy that blazed with an unremitting force that demanded surrender or eventual death.

The child Tshaya suffered in utter silence, her face and limbs sheened with perspiration, her hair hanging limp and damp. Her small arms clung to Grant's neck, her head leaning against his shoulder. She breathed fitfully through an open mouth, her eyes closed.

Hearing a short cry from behind him, Grant glanced over his shoulder and saw Nakai struggling to get to his feet, his expression displaying more embarrassment than pain. He clutched at the blood-soaked bandage on his right hip.

Pretending he didn't know the man had fallen, Grant said quietly, "Five-minute rest break. Keep your triggers set."

Nakai inclined his head in an almost imperceptible nod of gratitude toward Grant and sank back to the ground. Edwards dropped where he had been standing, gusting out a sigh of relief and closing his eyes. Grant knew he should sit down, too, but he was too keyed-up, Mag conditioning notwithstanding.

After a short break, Grant eyed the position of the sun. "Time. Let's move out," he said brusquely.

Helped by Edwards and Philboyd, Nakai rose to his feet and the little procession began walking through the jungle again. Clouds of tiny gnats and midges swirled in the shafts of sunlight slanting down through roof formed by the fronds of the trees. Here and there fell blankets of leaf-edged shadow.

After another fifteen minutes, Grant called for a short halt to get his bearings. He couldn't hear the crash of breakers on the shoreline, but the gurgling of running water, either a river or a stream came to him faintly. Another sound reached their ears, a grunting, snuffling noise. The four people froze in place, rooted to the spot.

A humanoid figure, walking with a listing gait pushed through underbrush a dozen yards ahead of them. Grant caught only a glimpse of a thick torso covered by black hair and attached to that swung a pair of arms that were blunt-fingered and obviously powerful. The head was small, the top rising to a rounded cone, a bony brow bulging above the eyes. Still, the features were more human than simian. The silver-scaled tail of a fish flapped between its jaws.

Hastily, Edwards raised the rifle to his shoulder but Philboyd gestured to him to lower it.

"It's one of the primitives," he whispered tensely. "A male."

Grant guessed that for himself, but he had never seen one of the subhumans before. The creature did not seem aware of their presence, as it continued walking, water dripping from its limbs. He figured it was returning from the stream.

When the creature was out of sight, Grant said quietly, "Let's keep going."

Grant strode down the narrow path, shoving his wide shoulders through the vegetation on either side. They entered a clearing bisected by a small creek. They forded it in single file, the water shallow and tepid.

Setting Tshaya on the bank, Grant splashed water on his arms and chest, working loose the mud. He wasn't pleased with the result, but he decided being only half-caked with dried mud was an improvement. He picked up the girl and started walking again.

"Are you sure this is the right direction back to the Cube?" Philboyd asked, shading his eyes and examining the tree line.

Grant regarded him darkly. "You're welcome to walk point if you have no faith in my sense of direction."

Philboyd considered Grant's suggestion for a few seconds then shook his head. "No, thanks. Never mind me. I'm a natural-born worrywart."

Edwards uttered a scoffing laugh. "You're about half-right."

Philboyd cast the man an angry, over-the-shoulder

glare. "Shove it up your ass. I'm the only one who has any kind of theory about what's going on here."

A pleasant male voice floated from the shrubbery on the other side of the clearing. "In that case, perhaps you'll be good enough to share it with all of us, dear boy."

Tshaya's arms tightened reflexively around Grant's neck as he swept the bore of his Sin Eater in short back-and-forth arcs, questing for a target. Edwards brought the rifle to his shoulder, sighting down its length.

Philboyd barked, "Crowley!"

"Quite right," the voice declared. "Allow me to point out that you are outnumbered and most satisfactorily outgunned, so I suggest you all disarm."

Grant did not move, his eyes narrowed behind the lenses of sunglasses as he sought to pinpoint the location of the man behind the wall of vegetation. He said, "Show yourself."

"Must I make an example of one of you?" came Crowley's voice again.

When no one replied or made a move to drop their weapons, Crowley said petulantly, "Very well, then, but remember—you brought this upon yourselves."

The single gunshot sounded like the cracking of a tree limb. Without making an outcry, Nakai staggered, a neat blue-rimmed hole appearing in his forehead, barely half an inch above his right eyebrow. His head snapped back as blood misted at the rear of his skull.

He toppled backward limply as if every bone in his body had instantly become like molten wax. With a sickening wrench in his belly, Grant knew the man had been killed instantly.

"See?" Crowley taunted. "But I chose the most expendable of you this time around. If you force me to make another example, don't expect me to be so fair-minded in my judgment. Compassion is the vice of kings."

Chapter 25

Not allowing the fury that surged through him to show on his face or be heard in his voice, Grant said calmly, "On the other hand, if we open up with everything we have, we're bound to kill you."

"Me, perhaps," Crowley conceded. "But not my two companions who have you trapped between a cross fire."

"How do we know you're not running a bluff?" Philboyd demanded.

Within seconds of the scientist's question two gunshots cracked on opposite sides of the clearing, bullets kicking up divots of dirt very close to Grant's feet.

"I trust that demonstration is sufficient," Crowley stated. A wheedling note entered his voice. "Please, Mr. Philboyd…I enjoyed our brief talk earlier before the unfortunate event separated us. May we not continue our exchange of information? That's preferable to dying, isn't it?"

Grant's jaw muscles knotted but before he responded, Philboyd surprised him by declaring defiantly,

"Bullshit! You need the kid, Tshaya. You won't risk killing her."

Silence fell over the jungle glade, broken only by the cheep of a bird and the rustle of breeze-stirred foliage. Then, at length, Crowley said regretfully, "I will not argue with you about that. But may we speak at least? Perhaps we may come to an accord, an understanding."

Grant eyed Philboyd questioningly, who lifted a shoulder in shrug. "Why not?" he whispered.

"Come on out," Grant said loudly. "I don't discuss terms with a man who I can't see."

"And just who are you?" Crowley asked, his tone rich with haughty suspicion.

"My name is Grant."

"And," Philboyd interposed, "he can probably answer most of your questions better than I can."

After a moment, they heard a heavy, resigned sigh. "As you wish. I'm coming out. Please lower your weapons. I am unarmed."

Grant pretended to think over Crowley's request, then he nodded peremptorily. Edwards removed the rifle's stock from his shoulder and knelt beside Nakai, swiftly examining him. Grant let his Sin Eater dangle at the end of his arm, but he didn't holster it.

A faint, whispering conversation came to him from behind the screen of brush, then a bloated figure pushed his way through. The man's hairless head glistened with pebbles of sweat, and the colorful robe he wore was torn and stained. He dabbed at the perspiration on his face with a finger as disgustingly soft and white as a grub.

The fat man did not step more than two feet from the shrubbery. "My name is Aleister Crowley. Does it mean anything to you?"

Grant shook his head. "Any reason why it should?"

"It did to Mr. Philboyd."

"That's Dr. Philboyd," the scientist corrected. "And the only reason your name means something to me was because I was born in the midtwentieth century."

Crowley's lips curved in a fatuous smile. "So my fame did not fade."

"Infamy, more like it," Philboyd snapped. "By the time I was a grown man, you had a notorious reputation as a drug addict, a pervert, a con man, a black magician and a Satanist."

Crowley's eyes narrowed a trifle. "By the time you were a grown man, you said. Are you a time traveler as I and my companions are?"

"No, I came to be here through a completely different set of circumstances."

"And those are?"

"A form of suspended animation."

Crowley nodded. "Cryonics."

"Not of the kind you're familiar with," Philboyd replied diffidently. "I wasn't frozen. Instead, I was—"

"When and where are you from, Crowley?" Grant broke in impatiently. "What the hell are you doing here?"

Crowley intertwined his beringed fingers. "Let's stop this foolishness, shall we? I'll ask a question or two and you will answer, then you can ask a question or two and we will be about our business…after you return Tshaya to me. Dr. Philboyd claimed we are on an island off the coast of California, but I never heard of an island like this one off the coast of any place."

"It's pretty unique, all right," Philboyd said agreeably.

"Is it part of the United States of America?"

Grant's mind raced as he tried to formulate an appropriately evasive response. He countered with, "Why wouldn't it be?"

Crowley's eyes narrowed. "Who is the current President? What is his name? In what year was he elected? What is his political party affiliation? Who won the last World Series?"

When neither Grant nor Philboyd answered, Crowley disentangled his fingers from one another and raised a hand. A gunshot rang out and Edwards uttered a cry of pain. Clapping a hand to the right side of his face, he came to his feet in a rush, eyes wild with fear and anger. Blood trickled between his fingers.

"Just an ear that time," Crowley announced coldly. "As per my instructions."

As Tshaya's arms tightened around his neck, cringing against him, Grant's Sin Eater swung up, the bore centering on Crowley's torso.

"Your belly this time," he snarled. "As per *my* instructions."

"That won't do, Mr. Grant. That won't do at all. Lower your gun or the next shot from my companions will take off Dr. Philboyd's nose."

Automatically, Philboyd reached up to cover the lower half of his face. Slowly, Grant dropped the barrel of his autopistol.

"I am somewhat familiar with the American male psyche," Crowley stated. "Even if you did not know the name of the President you would know instantly the baseball team who won your coveted World Series pennant."

"What the fuck is baseball?" Edwards husked out, crimson streaming down the side of his neck.

Surprised, Crowley snapped his head toward him and linked his fingers together in agitation, making a musical chiming as the multitude of rings clinked together. "You don't know what baseball is?"

Philboyd said, almost apologetically, "A lot of things have changed. I don't think you'll like it here very much."

The bald man glared at Philboyd in sudden rage. The sheer homicidal fury in his staring eyes and face rocked Philboyd back like the blow of a fist.

"I'll be the one to decide that!" he shouted. "I was promised this world would be the one I wanted, the one built to suit me. It is supposed to be the world of my dreams."

"Who made that promise to you?" Grant asked.

Crowley didn't answer.

"I'll bet it was Lam," said Grant, voice heavy with undisguised contempt. "And you believed him."

The statement did not seem to surprise or upset Crowley. His expression became vague and preoccupied. "Why would I not? I sought him out during the Amalantrah Working and he found me."

"Who did?" a perplexed Philboyd inquired.

"Lam," Crowley answered, his voice soft and almost dreamy. "Lam, whose name derives from the Tibetan word for 'way' or 'true path.' He became the subject of a portrait by me drawn from life—did you know the original was first exhibited in a New York art gallery in 1919? It was often called a remarkable piece of work."

"What's that got to do with anything?" Grant demanded.

Crowley drew himself up haughtily. "It was Lam's instructions through me that the Ordo Templi Orientis came in contact with otherworldly intelligences…and through him I learned of another world, one in the future, where the law of Thelema would be in ascendance."

Grant scowled at him. "What the fuck are you jabbering about?"

"I don't expect you to understand—"

"Good, because if I *did* understand, that would mean I'm as fused-out as you are."

Crowley nodded in grudging agreement. "Fair to say. I don't expect you or anyone else to understand."

"What about that Teutonic bitch with the riding crop?" Philboyd asked. "Where is she now?"

"Ah, the countess." Crowley's face creased in a worshipful smile. "My Scarlet Queen…and during some rituals, my Scarlet Whore. She is off on her own mission at present. I volunteered to stay behind and find you."

Philboyd's eyebrows rose. "Why?"

Crowley shrugged. "You are the only source of information about this place, about this time that we have." He paused, his smile faltering. "As you have probably guessed, neither is what we expected."

"What were you expecting?" Grant inquired.

Crowley stared at him, and Grant received the impression he stared into the past. Musingly, as if he were talking to himself, the Englishman said, "A world where 'do what thou wilt shall be the whole of the law.' We were promised we would find our destiny."

Sounding mystified, Philboyd asked, "You believe in destiny?"

"Of course I do. You called me a black magician

earlier. Well, all magicians of any color know that destiny is an absolutely definite and inexorable ruler. Physical ability and moral determination count for nothing in the face of destiny."

"What destiny did you figure to find here?" Grant wanted to know.

A mirthless smile ghosted over Crowley's lips. "One where humanity has been reduced to its normal state…that of bacteria."

Philboyd stared at him in confusion. "Excuse me?"

"Think about the old gods, my dear boy. It is impossible to perform the simplest act when the gods say no. I have no idea how they bring pressure to bear on such occasions—I only know they are irresistible.

"To the eyes of a god, mankind must appear as a species of bacteria that multiply and become progressively virulent whenever they find themselves in a congenial culture, and whose activity diminishes until they disappear completely as soon as proper measures are taken to sterilize them."

Crowley paused, hooding his eyes. He laughed, a low, bitter sound. In a voice barely above a whisper, he said, "My companions and I have come here to take those proper measures and to plant the seeds for the new future of humanity."

Grant's brow furrowed. "That's the destiny you're hoping to reach?"

"Indeed."

"Or check into a psycho ward, whichever comes first, right?"

Crowley glanced up, staring intently at Grant as if seeing him for the first time. Rage flared in his eyes. "Have a care, Mr. Grant. All I have to do is raise a hand—"

"And you'll be killed at the same time we are." Grant lifted his Sin Eater and brayed a short, scornful laugh. "Raise *both* of your hands, porky."

In a voice pitched so low it was a sibilant hiss, Crowley intoned, "You are a very reckless, very foolish man, Mr. Grant."

"And you're a very crazy, very close to being dead man, Mr. Crowley. Do as I say."

Aleister Crowley maintained his pose, hands clasped at his stomach. "Do not presume that the child is so important that we will not put her safety at risk."

"I don't presume that at all," Grant retorted. "I think you're the important one whose safety won't be put at risk."

"Grant," Philboyd began in a warning whisper, "are you sure you're not being as reckless as that fat bastard says?"

A part of Grant's mind agreed with Crowley's assessment of his actions and that he was endangering the child, Philboyd, Edwards and possibly everyone in the

Cube. But the rage boiling within him over Nakai's casual murder made him deaf to reason.

"Brewster," Grant said, "go get Crowley. Edwards?"

"Yes, sir?"

"Cover him."

As Philboyd moved toward Crowley, the Englishman chuckled. "You think it will be that easy?"

Then Grant heard a crash of foliage from behind him. With astounding speed, a black-clad and masked man burst from the underbrush. Edwards whirled, ready to use the butt of his rifle to strike a disabling blow. The helmeted man darted to one side, spun and delivered an expert kick to the small of Edwards's exposed back.

With a gargling cry of pain, Edwards careened forward, flinging his arms wide. He dropped the rifle, tripped over it and fell facedown at Grant's feet.

Grant sidestepped, pivoted and realigned his pistol's aim, bringing Crowley back into target acquisition. The man was nowhere to be seen. Philboyd stared in openmouthed shock, rooted to the spot.

"Where the hell is he?" Grant roared in angry frustration.

Philboyd turned toward him, then his eyes widened, his mouth dropping open. Grant instantly realized that something was right behind him and whirled around, finger depressing the trigger stud of his Sin Eater.

A stuttering triburst flamed from the bore of the pistol and the 9 mm rounds cored through a black mask, exiting at the back, pelting the earth and leaves with a scattering of brains and bone.

Then a very hard, heavy object smashed down against his carotid artery and his surroundings winked out.

Chapter 26

Brigid Baptiste slid the compact disk into the tray and waited through the booting cycle. Glancing over at the monitor screens, she watched Kane and Shizuka sprinting along the catwalk, past the temporal dilator.

A screen displaying an exterior view of the Cube's compound showed no overt disturbance in the vicinity of the wall, but she didn't take comfort in that. Inhaling a deep, calming breath, she tried to force her mind away from speculation about Grant's present situation.

Although losing contact with him worried her greatly, both Grant and Kane had proved time and again their almost supernatural resourcefulness, their ability to turn the tables on death and snatch not just survival but victory from the Grim Reaper's skeletal fingers.

Brigid supposed that Kane and Grant had been through so many harrowing experiences as Magistrates, and after that life-threatening situations no longer upset their emotional equilibrium. But she knew her assessment was a false one, despite the fact that they were hardened veterans of dozens of violent incidents. They had been raised to be killers, after all—to kill anything or anyone that threatened the security of the baronies.

The computer beeped, signaling the file had been accessed. Brigid directed the cursor to the menu and made her selection: "Crowley, Edward Aleister"

ON THE FACE OF IT, Aleister Crowley had lived an exceptionally odd life. For a man born in 1875 in Britain, and judged by the standard of Victorian mores, his life was more than odd—it had been mad, twisted, even evil.

Of course, Crowley himself claimed that he was remarkable from the moment of his birth and therefore destined to flout society's hypocritical conventions. He bore the three most important distinguishing marks of a Buddha upon his body and at the center of his heart, four hairs curled from left to right in the exact form of a swastika.

Following the death of his pastor father, the young Aleister turned to a form of satanism in an effort to come to terms with his grief. Involved as a young adult in the Hermetic Order of the Golden Dawn, he first studied mysticism with and later made enemies of William Butler Yeats and Arthur Edward Waite.

Samuel Liddell MacGregor Mathers, the leader of the Golden Dawn organization, acted as his early mentor in western magic, but in the years to come, he became his most implacable adversary.

Crowley attributed a mystical experience in 1904 while in Egypt, to his founding of the religious philosophy known as Thelema. When his then-wife Rose started to behave in an odd way, he suspected an otherworldly entity had made contact with her.

Following her channeled instructions, he performed an invocation of the Egyptian god Horus, and according to Crowley, the god told him that a new magical age had begun and that he would serve as its prophet. Rose continued to give information, telling Crowley in detailed terms that he had been chosen as the conquering lord of the New Aeon, and would be known as "the prince-priest of the Beast."

In 1910 Crowley was contacted by Theodor Reuss, the head of an organization based in Germany called the Ordo Templi Orientis. This group of high-ranking Freemasons claimed to have discovered the supreme secret of practical magic, which was taught in its highest degrees.

Both Reuss and Crowley shared ambitions to reform society at large by the sexual reeducation of the masses, which would be the responsibility of priests and priestesses. Crowley referred to the priestesses as Scarlet Queens or Scarlet Whores.

That was only the first step in the restructure of human society. Crowley planned for the elimination of private property, the institution of a class of forced laborers and a program of eugenics to be introduced, wherein only physically perfect parents would be permitted to have children. The religion of the OTO would become that of the state. Crowley wrote that every nonmember of the OTO was to be treated like a savage.

He met opposition from other members of the organization when it became obvious he was using the OTO and its resources to advance Crowley's own apocalyptic sex-magic system, Thelema, throughout the world.

Over a relatively short period of time, Crowley altered the OTO into a cult ruled tyrannically by him as a mentor, prophet, antichrist and savior, its core membership being financially, emotionally and sexually dependent on him.

To combat the opposition from high-ranking members of the OTO, Crowley sought support from other like-minded, protofascist occult groups, entering into a covert partnership with Germany's Brotherhood of the Black Sun.

Do What Thou Wilt Shall Be The Whole Of The Law became the motto for the OTO. In practice, for Crowley this meant rejecting traditional morality in favor of the life of a drug addict and bisexual libertine. His first wife, Rose, went mad, and after divorcing her, he treated himself to a seemingly limitless supply of drugs and women.

In the course of his life, he married a second time and

she too went mad. Furthermore, five of his mistresses ended up committing suicide although he was suspected of murdering two of them during satanic rituals.

Brigid caught herself shaking her head in wonder. Crowley claimed to identify himself with the Great Beast 666 and enjoyed the appellation of "wickedest man in the world." He worked very, very hard at being strange. He was especially alluring to dysfunctional women, among whom, she assumed, Countess Paula von Schiksel was one.

Those women and few men who tried to show tenderness to Crowley, or even loved him, were usually destroyed, because he could only truly love what was unattainable—his ideal, impersonal Scarlet Whore, one of the major deities in the Thelemic pantheon.

However, as absurdly theatrical as the man seemed to her, Brigid could not deny he had a brilliant intellect, but it was warped to serve distorted ends. His mind and apparent psychic abilities were devoted to self-indulgence, to gaining control over others, his sensitivity consecrated to serve cruelty, his reason turned to egomaniacal psychosis.

But the historical record showed Aleister Crowley dying of a respiratory infection in a Hastings boarding-house on December 1, 1947, at the age of seventy-two. He was penniless and addicted to heroin, which had been prescribed many years earlier as a treatment for asthma.

Suddenly, Brigid felt a presence behind her and she turned in her chair, glancing up into Sela Sinclair's grave face.

"What is it, Colonel?" she asked, trying to tamp down a sudden surge of fear.

The rangy-limbed woman pressed a hand against the earpiece of her headset. "Our other security posts report that we're under full-scale assault. I've lost contact with Reynolds."

She paused, took a breath and added, "I can't reach Kane or Captain Shizuka, either. I'm putting together a squad—you interested in joining?"

Chapter 27

Shizuka's mind bobbed back to consciousness like a waterlogged timber rising to the surface of a pool. She became aware of sharp pains in a good many places she hadn't expected them. Vaguely, she wondered why she couldn't move and if she lay dying. A sharp pain bored deep into the middle of her back and her skull throbbed, as if hammers pounded away at its inner walls.

A heavy shadow, like an umbrella made of gray smoke, floated over her. Burning in her nostrils was the chemical stink of high explosives. She tasted blood and realized it slid from her nostrils. By turning her head slightly, she saw that the wall gaped open like a mouth, spewing flame and acrid smoke. A mangled, red-spattered body lay in the midst of the rubble and absently she wondered if it was Kane.

Shizuka's thoughts suddenly began moving in a wild rush, and her stunned eardrums registered the crackle of flames and a stridently shouting female voice. Several distant thumps came almost together, then the west and south walls spewed flame and smoke. Chunks of stone rained down.

Shizuka instantly realized the compound was under simultaneous assault by grenades. Kane lay beneath her, his face slack with unconsciousness, limp arms holding her in a half embrace. She struggled to free herself to rise to her feet, her mind replaying the fragmented glimpse of the two grenades dropping down atop the north wall.

Shizuka shook Kane by the shoulder, and his head wobbled loosely on his neck. She saw a scarlet seep spreading under his hair on his right temple. Quickly, she inserted her fingers between the man's head and the ground, discovering a sharp-edged rock protruding up from the earth. Kane's skull had crashed against it.

Setting her teeth on a groan of pain and despair, Shizuka stumbled to her feet. She heard more explosions from other areas and the rattle of machine-gun fire. Eddies of thick smoke swirled around her.

The woman's voice was louder now, much more urgent: *"Schnell! Sturm! Schnell!"*

Turning to face the breach in the wall, Shizuka braced her feet wide and reached up behind her. She grasped the hilts of her swords, then slid both the *katana* and *tanto* from the scabbards with lightning speed just as two men in black plunged out of the smoke, stumbling over the rubble and the body of Reynolds.

They came to shocked halts when they caught sight

of the small Japanese woman in armor who held swords crossed to form a glittering *X*. Shizuka raised the *tanto* and *katana,* spinning them, the flat blades cutting bright wheels in the air over her head.

The two men stared at her in silence, their glass-lensed eyes lending them aspects of startled insects. In the second before they regained their composure, Shizuka lunged forward. The *katana* in her right hand sliced through a trooper's neck, and blood splashed across the masked face of the man standing next to him.

As he reeled away, trying to raise his subgun and clean his goggles at the same time, Shizuka performed a half spin on the ball of one foot and drove the shorter *tanto* into the man's midsection. For a sliver of an instant, the point of the blade met resistance before sinking through fabric and into flesh.

She whipped the sword free and as he doubled over, the *katana* flashed in her hand. The trooper's helmeted head fell from his shoulders and rolled across the ground like a lumpy ball. The severed arteries spouted a crimson-foaming fountain.

As the man's headless body collapsed, five more black figures materialized out of the smoke, like shadows given substance and independent movement. All of them were armed with the wicked subguns Sela Sinclair called Schmeissers. Desperation jolted through Shizuka, but she bounded to the attack.

A trooper stroked a short snare-drum rattle from his weapon, and bullets thumped very rapidly just above Shizuka's head—then she was among the intruders. She thrust the *tanto* at the man who had fired at her but he danced aside, managing to block the sword with the frame of his Schmeisser. Blue sparks flared at the point of impact.

She slashed the edge of the *katana* across another man's wrist and with a faint wet sound, the blade sliced off the soldier's right hand. Whirling around him, back to his back, Shizuka executed a half turn, the *tanto* and the *katana* cutting arcs in the smoky air. The crossed blades sank into a trooper's neck, catching it between a long scissors of steel. The razor-keen metal grated against vertebrae, then she whipped the two swords free, leaving the man to clap his hands to both sides of his throat, trying to staunch the river of blood.

She realized distantly that the men did not cry out in pain or anger, and she wondered at their eerie silence even as her blades whirled, rose and fell. With each stroke, blood sprayed in a vermilion mist. More masked, helmeted soldiers came through the breach in the wall.

Shizuka constantly shifted position so none of the men could achieve a proper aim with their subguns. If they fired, they would kill their own. She whipped her *katana* toward the first of the newcomers. The edge of the sword chopped into the man's midsection with a sound like a melon splitting. The man's guts burst out from the long vertical gash in his belly.

Shizuka pivoted again, slashing backhanded with the *tanto*. The razored tip sliced through a trooper's neck. Then she received a jarring blow between her shoulder blades from the butt of a Schmeisser. She staggered, throwing her arms wide to avoid spitting herself on her own swords, and managed to execute a somersault like an acrobat, bouncing back to her feet.

When she regained her balance, she faced a blue-eyed blond woman who trained an autopistol with a blue satin finish directly at her heart. Shizuka recognized her as the woman Kane had identified as Countess Paula von Schiksel. Her name was slightly ridiculous, but there was nothing absurd about the ruthless kill light in her cobalt eyes. Shizuka set herself to leap and die.

A trooper charged through the plumes of smoke. His vision impaired, his shoulder struck the countess, knocking her arm awry. She uttered an aspirated screech of outrage as her finger constricted on the trigger of her pistol.

The bore spit a little tongue of fire, the report like the snapping of a wet twig. The round struck the blade of the *tanto* with a spurt of sparks and a sound like a sledge pounding against an anvil. White-hot agony exploded up and down Shizuka's left arm, a nova of pain flaring in her wrist and metacarpals. The sword was torn from her grasp and clattered end over end, disappearing into the veil of gray vapor.

Through her pain-blurred vision, Shizuka flicked out with the *katana,* meaning to amputate the woman's gun hand. Instead, the edge of the sword locked behind the pistol's blade sight and jerked it from her grasp.

The Countess cried out angrily, *"Hure!"*

A trooper clamped both arms around Shizuka from behind, pulling her small frame against him. Without hesitation, she butted him under the chin with the crown of her head, hearing his teeth clack together.

Sliding out of the prison of his arms, Shizuka closed in on the blond woman again, meaning to use her as a hostage. She managed to grab her by the right shoulder, but the material of her scarlet tunic felt almost as slick as Teflon-coated vinyl, and the countess twisted furiously, breaking Shizuka's grip.

Shizuka expected her to run, but instead Countess Paula von Schiksel expertly delivered a roundhouse kick into the pit of her stomach. Although her breastplate blunted the worst of the impact, she still careened backward, arms windmilling. A hard object crashed against the back of her skull, and her surroundings faded away in a haze of pain.

Hands clasped her tightly, trying to force her arms up behind her back. Reeling, Shizuka tore her right arm free and tried to swing a *katana* blow from the shoulder, but she couldn't force her mind and body to work in tandem. She felt another impact against her head and she stumbled, sick and dizzy. Then she collapsed face-first to the ground and lay there.

A thick-soled boot pressed against her right wrist, her fingers opened and she felt her sword being wrested away. She was kicked in the stomach and she doubled up around the foot, her mind hovering on the edge of oblivion.

Shizuka was only dimly aware of being picked up like a child and heaved over a shoulder. Then she heard a sharp, hand-clapping report and despite her pain, she felt a surge of triumph, recognizing the unmistakable report of a Sin Eater. The trooper holding her jerked as if struck by a blow and his legs folded beneath him. He fell heavily, Shizuka rolling away from him.

Raking her hair out of her eyes, she saw a blood-streaked Kane marching forward, arm extended straight out, the Sin Eater at the end of it continuing to spit fire and lead. Several of the black-clad troopers careened away from the 9 mm barrage, bodies twitching under the multiple impacts.

The countess dropped into a crouch and grabbed a handful of Shizuka's hair, yanking her head back and pressing the edge of the appropriated *katana* against her throat. She shouted, "*Halten!* Stop or she dies!"

Kane froze, index finger poised over the trigger stud of the Sin Eater but no longer depressing it. He and the blond woman locked stares. Neither of them spoke for a long moment.

Finally, Countess Paula von Schiksel's lips twitched. "This is what you Amerikanners would call a Mexican stand-off."

"Amerikanners of your day," Kane bit out, paying no attention to the blood sliding from his scalp wound and painting the side of his face crimson. "In my day all I see is a vicious Nazi bitch holding a sword to the throat of a friend of mine. And if that vicious Nazi bitch doesn't take the sword away in precisely ten seconds, I'll shoot a hole right through her fucking head."

The countess began to sneer at what seemed like bravado, then she looked directly into Kane's pale eyes and reconsidered her response. "If I take the sword away, you'll kill me anyway."

"Maybe," Kane replied negligently. "Maybe not. There's a fifty-fifty chance I won't. But if you don't let Shizuka go, there's a one-hundred-no-doubt-about-it-percent chance I'll shoot you dead."

The countess contemplated Kane's statement for a silent second. She appraised him and asked, "What is your name?"

"Kane."

"Kane what?"

"Just Kane."

"I am the Countess—"

"Paula von Schiksel," Kane broke in harshly.

Her meticulously plucked eyebrows rose beneath the visor of her cap. "Ah, at last someone in this time who recognizes me."

"I don't recognize you, lady…I was briefed about you." Kane took a slow half step forward. "One second left."

"*Warte nur!* Wait…another few seconds." The woman glanced around her at the troopers with their Schmeissers all trained on Kane. "If I release this Nipponese *schlampe,* then both of you will be dead within seconds."

Kane nodded. "I'm very aware of that. Make your choice."

The countess frowned thoughtfully, then she snatched the sword from Shizuka's neck and swiftly rose. Shizuka climbed unsteadily to her feet, fingering the thread of blood trickling from a shallow laceration on her throat.

Although her face remained impassive, Shizuka exuded utter loathing when she extended a hand. "My weapon."

The countess laughed shortly, contemptuously. "You must be joking. You are in no position to ask for anything, much less make demands. This stronghold—or whatever you call it—is being overrun by my men. Shortly they will occupy it. That will happen whether I or you are alive or not."

"If that's the case," Kane said, aligning the bore of his Sin Eater with the woman's head, "then I might as well just kill you. What difference will it make, right?"

The countess stared at him, then at Shizuka, who had not withdrawn her hand. Baring her teeth in a silent snarl, she thrust the pommel of the *katana* into Shizuka's palm. "Take it. A sword will do you no good against us."

As Shizuka's hand closed over it and she stepped toward Kane, he asked, "Who is 'us,' exactly?"

"Myself, the dedicated soldiers of the Black Sun and a man named Aleister Crowley."

Kane nodded. "Figures."

Countess Paula von Schiksel's eyes widened, blazing with outrage. "Don't tell me you've heard of him, too! This is ridiculous! How could you know anything about us?"

Putting a hand on Shizuka's arm, Kane stepped back. "I have my own resources and my own questions about you…but I don't think this is the time to ask them."

The countess snapped, "Stop moving! You're not going anywhere."

Kane smiled coldly. "I beg to differ."

The woman turned toward a trooper standing beside her, Schmeisser at his shoulder. *"Schissen der Amerikanner—"*

An explosion flamed orange, and turf rained down around Kane and Shizuka. Thick smoke swirled around them like poisonous fog. Countess von Schiksel began screaming orders, then the words clogged in her throat as she succumbed to a coughing fit.

Shizuka and Kane ran, half-blinded by the spurts of smoke boiling up all around them and half-deafened by the exploding concussion and smoke grenades. They sprinted in the direction of the Cube although their visibility was limited to barely a yard in all directions.

In a hoarse, strangulated voice, Shizuka asked, "What is happening here?"

"I don't know," Kane husked out, his throat feeling raw from inhaling the smoke. "Just keep going for as long and as far as you can."

Then they heard Sela Sinclair shouting through the billowing vapor, "Lay down covering fire!"

They sprinted toward the woman's voice. The explosion that broke through the western wall of the compound caught Kane and Shizuka off guard.

Chapter 28

The crashing seemed to come from inside his skull, a ladder of noise Grant had to climb to reach consciousness. His eyes opened and he took in his reality with one swift glance.

He lay on his back, looking up at a patch of blue sky between swaying treetops. The crashing came again, this time punctuated by shouts in German and English. It required a few seconds for his dazed mind to recognize the crashes as gunshots, fired very close to him.

Grant's thoughts cleared despite the pain flaring at the base of his neck. He got his arms under him and pushed himself to a sitting position, silently enduring a spasm of dizziness.

"Easy, sir," Edwards warned from behind him. "Don't make yourself a target again. Stay low."

Grimacing, Grant carefully massaged the juncture of his neck and shoulder. He saw Tshaya kneeling on the ground beside him, face completely composed.

"Who hit me?" he asked between gritted teeth.

"I don't know," Edwards replied. "But there's what did it."

Glancing up, Grant saw the shaved-headed man standing behind him, rifle stock at his shoulder, sighting down its length, sweeping the undergrowth with the barrel. Hitching around, Grant's eyes fastened on a wood-hafted cudgel about two feet long. A fist-sized chunk of volcanic rock was affixed to a notch at one end by many twistings of dried vines.

"One of the subhumans threw that at me?" Grant asked skeptically.

"Yes, sir," Edwards replied. "They've been chucking rocks and spears for the last couple of minutes."

"Is that how long I've been out?"

"Give or take twenty seconds. I've been too busy to look at my watch."

Grant regarded him sourly, then a short-handled spear flew over the foliage, its flint point burying itself in the soft ground a few inches from Edwards's right boot. Instantly he squeezed off a drumming fusillade, raking the underbrush with a storm of slugs. Twigs, leaves and stems rose in a swirling cloud.

Grant didn't want to fight the primitives, and he certainly didn't want to be forced into a position where he had to use guns on them. They were abductees, prisoners on Thunder Isle, and though they might be better off dead in the long run, Shizuka had long ago ordered no violence was to be employed against them, unless there was no other option.

"Knock it off," Grant barked. "I don't want any of them killed."

Edwards gave him a reproachful stare. "I'm just trying to scare them off."

"You're apparently doing a pretty piss-poor job of that since they're still here. Besides, isn't Philboyd out there?"

Edwards nodded. "Suppose so. He took off into the bush after that fat slagger."

Grant gazed at the body of the black-clad soldier, lying spread-eagled nearby. "Where's the other trooper?"

"Don't know…mebbe the savages got him and are chowing down on his liver right now."

Grant didn't respond, glimpsing furtive movements among the shrubs, flickering too quickly for him to identify their outlines. He started to push himself erect, but agony blazed down through his shoulder and stabbed into his neck tendons. He wasn't able to completely bite back a cry of pain.

Tshaya swung her face toward him, a sudden gleam in the depths of her moonstone eyes. She reached out her left hand confidently and laid it on his bruised and throbbing flesh. She smiled slightly, then Grant felt a pulsating warmth spreading out from beneath her fingertips, permeating flesh, muscle and sinew. The warmth was followed by a pleasant pins-and-needles sensation that seeped through his shoulder.

Tshaya withdrew her hand, and Grant gingerly probed the contused area with his fingers. The pain was virtually gone. Mystified, but not saying anything about it, Grant stood up, sweeping the girl into his arms. "Let's get the hell out of here, Edwards."

The former Mag nodded. "Good strategy, sir."

Grant plunged through a clump of brush, shielding Tshaya from the thorns as best he could. Edwards covered their back trail, squeezing off two shots meant to discourage pursuit, although Grant felt more inclined to thank the sub-humans for their intervention. He figured they viewed the stream and the immediate environs as a source of fishing and freshwater and meant to defend it from any trespassers.

Risking an over-the-shoulder glance, he saw several shaggy figures emerge from the underbrush, wielding stone and wood clubs. Their motions were animalistic and although they were comparatively small in stature, their hair-covered limbs rippled with knotted muscles. The creatures howled and stamped in a victory dance, triumphant that they had driven the interlopers away from their stream.

Grant, Tshaya and Edwards had not penetrated the foliage more than a score of yards before they saw the body of the second trooper. His arms and legs were twisted at unnatural angles. Although the corpse lay on its back, the man's masked face was pressed into the ground.

Uneasily, Edward muttered, "Wrung his neck like a chicken."

"And dislocated his arms and legs for good measure," Grant pointed out. Bending over, he picked up the Schmeisser subgun, checking it over quickly, testing the action, making sure it wasn't fouled.

"Now what?" Edwards asked, eyes darting back and forth.

"We find Brewster and get on back to the Cube as soon as possible."

Edwards frowned, mopping impatiently at the blood flowing from his bullet-chewed right ear. "There's no telling where he got off to. For all we know, he panicked and ran back into the quicksand he found you in."

Grant considered the man's words for a couple of seconds, then shook his head. "Negative. Brewster is high-strung, but he doesn't panic and he's not a coward, no matter what you might think. He has his share of bad luck, though."

"I noticed," Edwards grunted.

"If we don't get out of the vicinity of these bodies," Grant said, shifting Tshaya in his arms, "we might have the same kind of luck, particularly if the Monstrodamii get wind of the blood of that trooper I shot."

Edwards looked around fearfully, hands tightening on his rifle. "I thought they were occupied with other food."

"Yeah," Grant agreed, "but they like to hunt their meals...especially the ones that got away from them."

"You think those dinosaurs are pissed off they lost you?" Edwards's voice held a skeptical note.

Grant shrugged, stepping into a narrow animal path cutting through the overgrowth. "I don't really know... that's the problem. I'll take point—you cover our back-track."

"Yes, sir."

Grant repressed a smile as he tried to navigate the closed-canopy foliage as quietly as possible. *A Magistrate is virtuous in the performance of his duty.* The deeply ingrained phrase drifted through his mind. The duties and obligations that had come with Edwards's badge and Sin Eater had been drilled into him long before he received them.

Grant recalled how the oath was a part of his every action and reaction as a Magistrate—at once a justification and a reason to live, a psychological shield and sword.

He heard Edwards slap at either a bug or a vine but the man said nothing, not even a one-word curse. Living only for duty and service was all a matter of how the individual adjusted to it, Grant reflected.

The sweat on his body crawled across his skin like the prickling feet of insects. He flicked beads of it away from his eyes. Although the sun still shone bright in the sky, little of the direct light penetrated to the treacherous morass of foul water, giant ferns and creepers that formed the jungle floor. It was like a world of endless green twilight, holding the suffocating heat and humidity. Tshaya's breathing was labored even though she was not exerting herself.

As a Gypsy, the little girl and her people were probably as scorned in their country as the outlanders were in his. Sneered at by the elite of the villes, outlanders were possibly the last real human beings on the planet, and they were an endangered species. During his years as a Magistrate, Grant had chilled dozens of outlanders in the performance of his duty, but he had murdered more than their bodies. He had destroyed their spirits, as well.

Grant felt his throat thicken with guilt. He held Tshaya tighter, cradling her head against his shoulder. Guilt, that was the whole gimmick. For the past century, it was beaten into the descendants of the survivors of the nukecaust that Judgment Day arrived and humanity was rightly punished.

Therefore, people were encouraged to tolerate, even

welcome, a world of unremitting ordeals, conflict and death because humanity had ruined the world; therefore the punishment was deserved.

Love among humans was the hardest bond to break, so people were conditioned to believe that since all humans were intrinsically evil, to love another one was to love evil. That way, all human beings forever remained strangers to one another.

Slogging through a patch of mud, the stench of marsh gas filled Grant's nostrils and awoke nausea in his stomach. He tried to ignore it, straining his ears for a sound that he could attribute to either Philboyd or Aleister Crowley.

At the thought of the Englishman, Grant felt a sense of something ominous and repellent drawing closer, as if by even thinking of Crowley, he could attract him. But he did not visualize the man, but rather a collection of vile images—a strange, slimy substance oozing along the jungle floor as an amphorous, writhing slug with only a hole for a mouth and a pair of lidless, incessantly staring eyes.

Suddenly, from ahead of him, he heard a rustle, leaves clattering as if touched by the wind, but no breeze tickled his perspiration-filmed skin. Grant came to a halt, holding up his right hand in silent command for Edwards to do likewise. Slowly, he placed Tshaya on the narrow trail, but she clutched at his leg.

With hand signs, he ordered Edwards to come abreast of him and make ready to fire. Stealthily, Edwards sidled around him, lifting the rifle to his shoulder. Grant's finger curled around the trigger of the Schmeisser.

The rustling became louder. Then Brewster Philboyd pushed his way through the tangles of vegetation. Aleister Crowley's head was pinned in the crook of his left arm.

Chapter 29

Kane and Shizuka were sprinting through the chemical fog spewed by the smoke grenades, moving toward the looming edifice of the Cube, following Sela Sinclair's voice when the explosion broke through the western wall of the compound.

The blast filled the air with broken concrete and flying debris. Kane crouched as grit and gravel rained down around him and Shizuka like grapeshot fired from a cannon. Shizuka cursed, her words unrecognizable but her tone unmistakable.

Spitting out dirt, fanning dust away from his face, Kane looked back at the western wall. A hole had been blown through the bulwark and smoke swirled in the opening, obscuring it for a moment, but there was no mistaking the black-uniformed figures that suddenly streamed through the gap, nimbly leaping over chunks of stone and mortar.

Kane reacted instantly, lifting his Sin Eater and squeezing off a triburst. Two of the rounds smashed into a trooper's chest and drove him backward. The third bullet scored a hit against another invader's right shoulder, spinning him.

The other troopers went to ground, dropping flat and raking the immediate area with a concerted salvo from their Schmeissers. As more of the soldiers squirmed through the grenade-blown gap in the wall, Kane fired again, but his target staggered on loose stone underfoot. The bullet struck a stick grenade attached to the man's bandolier.

It instantly exploded and enveloped him in a ballooning ball of flame. The other grenades detonated. The concussion slammed Kane violently against Shizuka, and they both fell under the rolling shock wave. He caught only glimpses of the trooper's fragmented body hurtling in all directions. Arms and legs and chunks of bloody, ragged flesh thudded down all around. Scarlet sprinkled the ground in a thick drizzle.

As his stunned ears recovered from the concussion of the multiple explosions, Kane heard Brigid Baptiste calling his name. Shifting through the settling planes of dust and smoke, he fixed Brigid's position, then he and Shizuka rose and ran across the open ground. He prayed the haze wouldn't thin out until they reached the safety of the Cube.

By the time they reached the foot of the steps leading into the huge building, the smoke had only begun to disperse. Sela Sinclair and ten men, a combination of samurai and Cerberus personnel, were assembled before the door. All of them carried SA-80 "point and shoot" subguns, automatic weapons that even the most firearm-challenged person could become proficient with.

Brigid came down the steps, her expression strained and anxious. "Are you all right?"

Kane nodded curtly, evading her hand as she reached out to examine the laceration on his scalp. "What the hell is going on, Baptiste?"

Sinclair, holding a grenade-launching H&K XM-29 assault rifle in her arms, took it upon herself to answer. "What do you think? We're under full-scale assault from all four quarters."

"I figured that out for myself," Kane retorted.

Turning to Brigid, he said, "I want to know why. The countess wasn't very forthcoming about much of anything."

Brigid's eyes went emerald hard. "You saw her?"

"And exchanged words with the dirty *omanko*," Shizuka interjected angrily.

"What about Crowley?" Brigid asked.

"No sign of him," Kane replied. "What does the countess want?"

"It's not important," Sinclair announced. "We just have to stop her from getting whatever it is."

Brigid glanced toward her irritably. "Tactically, it would help us to find out what it is."

"How is a librarian qualified to talk about tactics?" Sinclair shot back.

"This librarian has been instrumental in saving the world at least four times," Kane declared, an icy edge in his voice. "That's four more times than you or any other pistol-packing freezie with an attitude, so that qualifies her as far as I'm concerned. Go ahead, Baptiste."

Brigid took a deep breath. "I can only speculate, but I think Countess Paula von Schiksel, Aleister Crowley and the Brotherhood of the Black Sun have come to the future to establish a military foothold."

"Why?" Kane demanded. "And for what?"

"To achieve what they and the Third Reich failed at over 260 years ago," Brigid stated. "A literal case of 'tomorrow the world.'"

Kane nodded. "But how did—?"

"Here they come!" Shizuka shouted.

Three stick grenades dropped through the veil of haze and landed barely ten yards away. They erupted in solid geysers of flame and smoke. The triple concussions crowded everyone back against the wall of the building.

"Fire at will!" Sela Sinclair yelled, raising her XM-29.

The people drew up in a skirmish line at the top of the steps and triggered their weapons. The Cube's defenders fired more accurately than Kane had expected or hoped. Staccato hammering of a dozen subguns sounded like the beat of crazed snare drums.

The Black Sun troopers returned the fire, rounds chewing stone splinters from the short flight of stairs. Kane heard screams of both fear and pain when the bullets found targets among the samurai and the Cerberus personnel.

For a long moment, the two forces exchanged volleys through the wall of smoke and dust. Then black-clad troopers of the Black Sun swept around from two sides in a horseshoe crescent, firing a concerted fusillade with their Schmeissers, catching the defenders in a cross fire.

Against the swiftly moving targets, the Cerberus people and samurai lay down their fire ahead of the on-rushing soldiers. Brigid swept her own SA-80's deadly, chattering swath over them. The bullets chopped into the black-helmeted men in the forefront. They clutched at themselves and staggered, but the attackers behind them kept coming, pushing the wounded headlong, driven by the strident shrieking of Countess Paula von Schiksel.

A series of eardrum-compressing detonations overwhelmed the cacophony of gunfire and screams. The barrel of the XM-29 in Sela Sinclair's arms gouted smoke and grenades.

Three high-explosive rounds impacted among the Black Sun troopers, flinging up dirt and knocking down men in billows of orange-red flame. The Schmeissers in the hands of the black-uniformed soldiers roared in a stuttering rhythm of deadly syncopation. Two of the defenders went down, slapping at wounds. Then Sinclair staggered, hair and flesh flying in a bloody eruption from the side of her head.

Shizuka tried to catch her, but the woman was too heavy. "Fall back!" she cried. "Fall back!"

Kane was loath to obey Shizuka's order, even though he knew she was right to command a withdrawal. He squeezed through the remainder of the Sin Eater's magazine, the bore lipping a steady tongue of fire, but then a bullet smashed into his left side with stunning force. Knocked off balance and the wind slammed out of him, Kane fell heavily to the concrete steps.

For a wild, gasping second, he wondered if the bullet had penetrated the shadow suit and found his heart, but he rolled over and fired the remaining round in his pistol. He took only a small, cold comfort when he glimpsed a helmeted trooper drop out of sight. Then he swore, alarmed by the number of men advancing from the line of smoke.

"Fall back!" he shouted, despite the pain in his ribs. "Get inside!"

He felt a hand slip under his armpit and he glanced

up to see Brigid hauling him to his feet, firing the SA-80 one-handed, keeping the trigger depressed. Spent cartridge cases tinkled down around him.

The defenders fought a brief rearguard action, firing behind them before they retreated through the metal-paneled door into the Cube. They carried the wounded with them, but were forced to leave the dead. Only five of the personnel were able to make it into the building's lobby under their own power.

Sela Sinclair was one of them. The bullet had laid the flesh of her scalp open to the bone. Liquid crimson flooded her face and neck, clotting in her hair.

Kane dropped the locking bar in place over the door and leaned his weight against it, panting and probing his rib cage. "This won't hold 'em."

Shizuka nodded. "We must retreat to the control center. We can seal ourselves in there behind the security bulkhead."

"We don't know how strong it is," Brigid said, green eyes dull with worry. "I don't think it's vanadium."

"I can't think of a better time to test it," Shizuka responded tersely.

Gun butts and fists hammered on the other side of the door. Gesturing with her *katana* toward the arch on the far side of the lobby, Shizuka said loudly, "Move! Quickly now! *Iko!*"

The people crossed the lobby and just as they entered

the long corridor adjacent to it, Kane hazarded a backward glance at the door. It vanished in a blooming fireball of orange and white. The detonation of the grenade echoed like a handclap magnified a thousandfold.

The defenders of Redoubt Yankee ran along the door-lined hallway. Kane hoped the turns would confuse the pursuing Black Sun troopers, at least for a few minutes. The corridor slanted downward, stretching through the open security door into the monitor station before the catwalk.

As Kane sprinted over the threshold, he shouted, "Button us up!"

Brigid threw a lever on the wall next to the metal molding. Gears clanked, pneumatics hissed and the slab of a door slid out from a baffled slot, meeting the jamb with a muffled thud.

As Shizuka supervised the retreat along the catwalk into the control center, Kane joined Brigid at the monitor station. They watched a quartet of black-helmeted troopers appear around a corner, moving very efficiently, Schmeissers at their shoulders.

"You never did tell me how those maniacs got here, Baptiste."

She ran her fingers through her sunset-colored tangle of hair. "That's because I'm not sure. But judging by what I read in the files we took from Slovakia, Lam gave Aleister Crowley the idea that he and the Black

Sun brotherhood could use the Nazi Kronoscope to come to the future, linking it with the parallax point in the cave."

"How in the hell did he ever contact Lam?" Kane demanded.

"Mainly through a form of channeling…Crowley's psychic abilities are formidable and more than likely, he became aware of the Archons when he acted as a consultant for the Totality Concept. That's how he learned about the German prototype of Operation Chronos. It's difficult to assess whether the claims made for Crowley's introduction to Lam have any basis in fact. However, Crowley thought he was using Lam when the situation was actually the opposite."

"How so?"

"Lam led Crowley to believe that he would finally find the kind of world he always wanted in the future."

Kane arched a dubious eyebrow. "A wasteland?"

Brigid nodded. "Crowley wasn't careful about what he wished for. I think Lam, during his contact with the man, realized just how dangerous and evil he was. He persuaded him that in a century Crowley's philosophy and Thelema doctrine would be preeminent and he would be worshiped as a god."

"Maybe so," Kane argued. "But he traveled two centuries—" He broke off, sudden comprehension shining in his eyes. "Lam deliberately set him up to overshoot the mark by a century. And Crowley talked the countess into going along with him?"

"Exactly. I'm sure Lam provided all the coordinates and the Kronoscope operating specs." She smiled slightly. "Sending someone on a snipe hunt through time is a pretty novel way of getting rid of undesirables."

"But how did they get here, though? The dilator is fried."

Brigid lifted a shoulder in a shrug. "The dilator, yes, but not the temporal conduit."

"What's that?"

"Remember how we first came here, the temporal dilator's chronon wave guide conformals were activating on wild, random cycles? They either reconstituted trawled subjects from the memory buffer matrix, or snatched new ones from all epochs in history. Didn't you ever wonder how creatures the size of a Daspletosaurus or the dinocelphians were trawled from the past and reconstituted here on the island?"

Kane shook his head. "Not really."

Brigid sighed in exasperation. "A temporal conduit is a fixed wormhole that links two points in space-time. One end of it moves backward in time. Both ends become portals, points in the continuum that are temporally active. Events or beings from other space-time coordinates can intrude on this point."

"So?"

"So, the portal points require some kind of resonant connection between two circuits, like a power line. Once the energy path is established under power between the source and the target, it remains open even though the energy source has been removed. It's like a remanence phenomenon similar to how a firefly will continue to glow after it comes to rest, like an energy bleed-off.

"If a temporal nexus point was established in any past or even future time, the connection between the two will always exist in some measure. But the temporal conduit that opens in the past isn't fixed like the one in the future, or rather our present. It opened randomly and trawled the First-Fourth Norfolk Battalion from Turkey."

"If you say so, Baptiste," Kane said dismissively.

Crossly, Brigid shot back, "*I* don't say so, the scientists who developed Operation Chronos—"

She broke off, following Kane's suddenly intent gaze. On the monitor screen she watched a blond woman join the four Black Sun troopers clustered at the door. Behind her, more of the midnight-colored soldiers crept down the hallway.

"In case you're wondering," Kane remarked, "that's the countess. I might be able to arrange formal introductions."

As they watched, the woman gazed up at the camera, a coquettish smile creasing her lips. She touched the brim of her cap with the tip of a riding crop held in her left hand. Gripped in her right was a Walther P-38 pistol. She raised it and squeezed off a single shot. The image of her smiling face on the screen instantly dissolved into a pattern of pixels and rippling snow.

"I'll pass, thanks," Brigid said flatly.

Chapter 30

Brewster Philboyd relaxed his headlock. Aleister Crowley sank to the jungle floor, wheezing and gasping, pallid face congested. Rubbing his neck, he speared Philboyd with a glare of pure venom.

"So," Edwards began. He fell silent, cleared his throat and said blandly, "You got him, I guess."

Philboyd nodded with smug satisfaction. "He's pretty spry for a fat old satanist, but that dress he's rigged out in tripped him up."

"You would not have caught me if my bodyguard hadn't been set upon by the savages," Crowley said defensively.

"Yeah," Grant rumbled. "Point out which of the savages did the deed, and I'll leave them a nice fruit basket."

Crowley's face glistened with sweat, but a trembling as if he were chilled shook his frame. Rolls of fat jiggled beneath his soiled and torn robe, and his teeth chattered. He coughed, hawked up from deep in his throat and spit a glob of phlegm in Grant's general direction. "You're an arrogant nig-nog, I'll say that for you, Yank."

Philboyd brandished a small, rectangular case. "I found this on him."

He popped open the lid with a thumbnail, revealing a small hypodermic, a glass ampoule filled with a cloudy fluid and a coiled length of rubber hose. "In the parlance of my day, this was known as 'works.'"

"Works?" a mystified Grant echoed.

"No self-respecting junkie went anywhere without one. See, it's got a little solution of heroin, a rubber tube to tie off a vein and a syringe—also known as a hype-stick—with which to inject said heroin into the afore-mentioned tied-off vein."

Edwards narrowed his eyes. "What the fuck are you talking about?"

"Our devil-worshiping friend is a drug addict," Philboyd explained.

Sullenly, Crowley said, "It's my medicine. I need it for a medical condition."

"You mean a medical condition like this?" Edwards growled, stepping forward and kicking Crowley hard in his swag belly.

The Englishman went over on his side, grasping his stomach, coughing and wailing. Philboyd shot Edwards a look and for a long moment, the two men locked un-blinking stares.

"You have an objection?" Edwards demanded.

Philboyd shook his head. "I can't think of a single one."

He closed the lid of the case and tossed it over his shoulder, into the underbrush. Crowley cried out in wordless, shrill desperation and hiked himself to his hands and knees, clawing out for it. His mouth opened and closed like a landed fish, but only a gurgling noise issued from it.

Grant glared at him, filled with disgust. He had stepped on a sea slug once, and the Englishman had the same effect on him. The back of his neck flushed cold with revulsion.

Shifting Tshaya in his arms, he said, "Get up, Crowley."

The bald man shook his head, squeezing his eyes shut. Tears leaked from the corners and ran down the deep lines on either side of his thick nose. He moaned, "I can't, I'm sick, I'm hurt—"

Edwards tapped him atop his bald pate with the barrel of his rifle. "I can get you up or put you down permanently. Your choice, slagger."

Whimpering and sniffling, Aleister Crowley shambled to his feet. He wiped his dripping nose with the belled sleeve of his robe and coughed rackingly. He lifted the torn and muddy hem so he wouldn't step on it.

"Wickedest man in the world," Philboyd intoned with cold sarcasm. "Tell us how you got here, Crowley, and how the kid Tshaya figures into it."

"Talk while we walk," Grant said, handing his appropriated Schmeisser to Philboyd. "We need to get back to the Cube while there's still daylight."

The path was too narrow for them to walk abreast of one another, so Edwards led the way, Crowley and Philboyd following behind. Philboyd encouraged the Englishman to step lively by repeated jabs of the Schmeisser's bore into the small of his back. Grant and Tshaya brought up the rear. He kept his Sin Eater unholstered and in hand.

"Start spilling, Crowley," Philboyd ordered. "And I don't want to hear any black-magic hocus-pocus about cutting a deal with Satan so he'd bring you here. We already know you were involved with some kind of time-travel business."

Haltingly, Crowley said, "Much of the scientific breakthroughs at the end of the war were due to the invention and perfection of the cyclotron."

"What's that?" Grant asked.

"A device that enabled twentieth-century scientists to study subatomic particles," Philboyd said diffidently. "It was the forerunner of a particle accelerator. It helped them discover properties not suspected before, like the antiproton and antineutron."

"Exactly," Crowley said, turning slightly toward him, only to turn around again when Philboyd prodded him with the subgun. "When the Allies appropriated the German research called the Totalitat Konzept, they found that the linchpin of the reich's experiments turned out to be the discovery of a primordial superatom...one that the physicists theorized existed at the dawn of our universe, five billion years ago. This atom was the fundamental building block of the stuff our universe is made of...Prima Materia."

Philboyd blurted incredulously, "Prima Materia, the philosopher's stone, primal matter...is that what you're talking about?"

Crowley nodded. "Precisely, dear boy. The source of creation, the so-called black sun worshiped by various ancient cults. The Totalitat Konzept scientists found a convergence of this material, a vortex composed of the superatom, in a cave in Slovakia. It couldn't, of course, exist normally in our universe, even though nature permitted such a thing to be conceived."

Philboyd frowned. "Are you talking antimatter?"

"Frankly, I don't know," Crowley said. "Probably not. But the idea arose in the minds of the physicists that they could possibly create something that did not exist in this universe by manipulating the Prima Materia.

"Calculations by a scientist named Janos Rukh showed that by surrounding the vortex with electromagnetic harmonic forces, by conducting the field under certain stresses, it would forge a quantum pathway, an egress through what Einstein called the space-time continuum."

"Rukh," Philboyd murmured. "Heard of him…he was probably *the* scientist of the Third Reich…the Nazi counterpart to Einstein."

Grant growled. "Get to the point, Crowley."

"The superatoms of the Prima Materia would encapsulate themselves and become its own energy source…for all intents and purposes, a black sun. And through the study of the black sun, the Kronoscope was constructed."

Philboyd snorted contemptuously. "That sounds like Nazi crackpot pseudo-science to me."

Crowley chuckled. "Does it now? Then how do you explain my presence here?"

Philboyd swallowed, but rather than address the question, he asked another one. "Even if any of that has foundation in fact, how could you exert any control over the Kronoscope? It wouldn't be a simple matter of moving things from place to place, would it?"

Crowley shook his head and coughed into his fist. "Not even Rukh fully understood the forces flowing through the black sun vortex."

"Without a control mechanism of some sort," Philboyd argued, "your Kronoscope would probably trigger temporal fractures…anomalies that would erupt throughout the chronon structure of our universe, imperiling both the future and the past. Last year and this week could coexist, or we would experience the same day over and over again, and not even know we were trapped in *Groundhog Day* temporal loop for eternity."

Crowley cast him a troubled glance. "I don't understand."

"Never mind." Philboyd looked behind him at Grant. "You know what I mean, right? Operation Chronos?"

Grant nodded. Operation Chronos dealt in the mechanics of time travel, forcing temporal breaches in the chronon structure. The purpose of Chronos was to find a way to enter "probability gaps" between one interval of time and another. Inasmuch as Cerberus utilized quantum events to reduce organic and inorganic material to digital information and transmit it through hyperdimensional space, Chronos built on that same principle to peep into other time lines and even "trawl" living matter from the past and the future.

Since the nature of time could not be measured or accurately perceived in the quantum stream, the brief temporal dilation was the primary reason Operation Chronos had used reconfigured gateway units in its time-traveling experiments.

"The only way your Kronoscope could possibly

work," Philboyd said musingly, "is if what you called a black sun is actually a singularity, a black hole."

"A what?" Crowley inquired petulantly.

"It's a term coined by physicist John Archibald Wheeler in 1968, after your time. Essentially, it's a star that has contracted to the point where no light is emitted due to its gravity. The center of a black hole is called a singularity point, because it is the spot where the star has reached infinite density. It curves infinitely in space-time and causes a hole to open in the fabric of the continuum."

Grant grunted. "Yeah, I've heard about those, too."

Philboyd gave him a dour smile. "I forget, you've been around. Anyway, it was theorized that if a black hole were rotating, the singularity formed would be in the shape of a doughnut instead of a fixed point. According to theory, it's possible for an object to pass beyond the event horizon of the singularity and into a wormhole and travel forward and backward in time."

Edwards turned around long enough to favor Philboyd with a scornful look. "Bullshit."

Philboyd smiled patronizingly. "There's nothing in the general theory of relativity that prevents time travel. But there's only one challenge—how do you create a wormhole, then stabilize it so you'll know when and where it leads, and how do you do it in a cave in Slovakia?"

"I'm betting," Grant commented, "that Tshaya had a lot to do with it."

"She *is* a Gypsy, after all," Crowley said.

"What's that got to do with anything?" Grant demanded, noting that the girl's arms tightened around his neck as if she had become aware that she was the topic of conversation.

"Gypsies, the Roma people, often are born with advanced psychic powers. Historians attribute the invention of the Tarot cards to them. This may reflect the belief that the Gypsies, being of alleged Egyptian origin, had knowledge of the lost arts and sciences of the ancient Egyptians."

"I ask again," Grant said impatiently, "what's that got to do with anything?"

"Tshaya and her twin brother, Heranda, were born with extrasensory capacities developed to a remarkable degree. They were found in the Esterwegen concentration camp and tested exhaustively by representatives of the Abnenurbe Foundation. The Brotherhood of the Black Sun hid them from the Allies. Between Tshaya and Heranda, the girl possessed the more extensive range of psychic powers. Perhaps her blindness heightened her cognitive abilities. However, they did not seem to work unless she was in close proximity with her twin. In any event, she acted as our mediator, so to speak. She stabilized the energies of the black sun's matrix."

"What happened to her brother?" Edwards asked.

Crowley wiped sweat from his forehead with a trembling hand, examined the drops glistening on his fingertips and brought them to his mouth. He coughed and Grant heard a liquid gurgle behind the sound. "It was such a long time ago, so I have no idea."

"I do," Grant grated.

Crowley swiveled his head on his squat neck to regard him with surprised eyes. "You do? How?"

"Go on with your story," Grant ordered. "How'd you come by an Archon generator?"

Crowley's surprise became astonishment, judging by the expression that twisted his features. Then a cold, shrewd light glinted in his eyes. "How could you know about that?"

"Answer the question."

"I found the generator in the Slovakian cave when I was led to it, following instructions conveyed to me by Lam. It had evidently been hidden there for many hundreds of years, if not thousands. How could you possibly have any knowledge of it? I am perplexed."

Grant prodded the Englishman with his pistol, indicating he should face front and keep walking. "I saw the generator in the cave about fourteen hours ago. I figured it had been used to activate the vortex point and there had been some sort of power overload or feedback. Whatever happened, the entire installation was completely destroyed and drained everything of energy."

He paused, allowing the implications of his words to sink in. "So if you and rest of your goose-stepping crew had plans to go back to your time the same way you came to this one, you'd better do some improvising."

Crowley uttered a tittering laugh, placing a pair of beringed fingers before his twitching lips.

Edwards swung his head around, eyes slitted. "What's so fuckin' funny, fat man?"

The titter became a cough and after Crowley regained his breath, he said, "We embarked on this trip knowing it was one-way. In fact, that was one reason I was so eager to undertake the journey. I left nothing of any worth behind."

"What was your objective in coming here?" Grant asked.

"I thought that would be obvious. To conquer." Crowley dropped his voice to a hoarse whisper, his eyes vacant. "To what purpose was my life? Why did it go on? The glory of the Third Reich was a lost dream…my own life was in ruins…all of my old friends were dead. All gone and I was left with nothing…penniless and despised. Then Lam called to me. My destiny lay in the future, a new world to conquer."

Philboyd forced a derisive chuckle. "You've got a long way to go yet—not to mention that you've got some heavy-duty competition."

"Indeed? Who might that be, pray tell?"

Before Philboyd could answer, a thundering roar of triumph blasted through the jungle. The sudden sound froze everyone in their tracks. Another bellow erupted from the foliage. Then something very large and very angry came barreling their way.

Chapter 31

Brigid Baptiste swept her arms around the control center. "There are offices and rooms off this one, but no exits."

"That's poor planning," Shizuka replied sourly.

"Not really. If anything went wrong with the dilator, the op center and the holding module could be isolated from the rest of the building. The security door looks more like it was designed to be a radiation shield."

Kane divided his attention between Shizuka and Brigid's conversation while attending to the wounded. With the exception of Sela Sinclair, none of the injuries appeared to be life-threatening, but they were messy. Techs ran back and forth, applying bandages and compresses.

"Even so," Shizuka said, "we don't have the resources to withstand a siege."

"No, but we can gate back to Cerberus if necessary."

Kane turned toward the two women, holding a square of gauze against his scalp wound. "I think it will be necessary, at least for Sinclair. The wounded can be transported there, and our away teams can come back armed with the proverbial overwhelming firepower."

Shizuka considered Kane's suggestion, absently nibbling her full underlip. "I hesitate to do that, without knowing about Grant."

"Taking the wounded to Cerberus won't make much difference," Kane said, a bit more harshly than he intended. "Whatever we're going to do, let's do it fast. I wouldn't be surprised to find out the countess has a demolition expert with shaped charges out there. They can huff and puff and blow the door down any second."

Shizuka inhaled a deep breath and slowly released it. "*Hai*. Let's do it."

As she issued the orders for the injured personnel to be taken to the mat-trans unit, Nguyen called to Brigid. "I'm picking up some odd readings here."

Brigid and Kane joined the woman at the console, eyeing the glowing gauges. "Radiation registration of an unusual frequency and wavelength," Brigid commented.

Nguyen nodded. "I've matched the signature…it's chronon radiation."

Brigid stiffened, brow furrowing in consternation. "How can that be? The dilator isn't functioning. Can you trace the radiation back to its source?"

Nguyen focused her attention on the instruments. "I can try."

"Baptiste, I think you should go back to Cerberus," Kane said quietly.

She cast him an irritated glance. "You can't sideline me on a whim anymore, Kane. I don't need your protection."

"I wasn't offering any," he countered. "But you're our best bet for organizing a rescue op."

"No, that's *you*," Brigid shot back, eyes glinting jade-hard. "You're the de facto commander of all the away teams. They'd obey you a lot faster than they would me. You'd also know exactly the kind of weapons to bring back here."

Kane opened his mouth to voice a retort, but Brigid continued in a softer tone, "If the Black Sun soldiers happen to break in, we still have enough weapons and people to make a fight of it. Worst-case scenario is that we retreat to the gateway unit and jump to Cerberus anyway."

She smiled wryly. "Besides, it's not like you'd be gone very long, right?"

He nodded reluctantly. "No, I guess not. But set up a skirmish line on the catwalk while I'm gone."

"Will do."

Without another word, Kane heeled around and strode toward the mat-trans chamber. He felt embarrassed that Brigid had seen so quickly through his ploy to get her out of harm's way. However, other than Grant, there was no other person he'd rather have at his side when hell broke loose than Brigid Baptiste.

Despite their many quarrels, he was at ease with her in a way that was similar to, yet markedly different than, his relationship with Grant. He found her intelligence, her iron resolve, her well-spring of compassion and the way she had always refused to be intimidated by him not just stimulating, but inspiring. She was a complete person, her heart, mind and spirit balanced and demanding of respect.

In the dark hours between midnight and dawn, Kane had often wondered if he lost Brigid, lost his credential, would he become a damned soul, cruel, merciless and without any purpose in life except to kill.

Inside the mat-trans unit, Kane found a place among the wounded people. Sela Sinclair's head had been swathed in so many bandages she looked like a mummy, but she showed no signs of regaining consciousness.

Kane stood by the door, making sure everyone had positioned themselves on the interlocking pattern of floor plates. "Ready?"

The people responded with affirmatives and Kane swung the door closed. He quickly crossed the chamber and sat down between two of the injured. He waited for the subsonic hum to begin, for the hexagonal disks to exude their familiar glow, but nothing happened.

Everyone's eyes darted back and forth, first in puzzlement, then in growing fear. Kane rose, returned to the armaglass door, opened it and pulled it firmly shut. Nothing happened—no whine, no glow, no spark-shot mist.

He pushed the door open again, carefully inspecting the circuitry actuator on the lock, making certain full contact was achieved. He slammed it closed and stood in baffled anger. Then he heaved up on the handle and shouldered the door open again, saying, "We're not going anywhere."

He stepped down from the platform and called to Brigid. She turned away from organizing a defensive perimeter, her face first showing annoyance, then puzzlement. She walked to the jump chamber.

"Something is inhibiting it," he explained as she examined the circuits, running her fingers over it. "Interfering with the operation."

Brigid tossed back her red-gold mane. "I don't know what could be causing it. The mat-trans has an independent power source. Otherwise it wouldn't be of much use if the rest of the redoubt's power went offline."

Kane cocked his head toward the elevated platform. "I hear something running in there."

"It's almost like some sort of field is inhibiting the transformation of energy," Brigid said.

"What could it be?"

"Hey!" Nguyen called, standing before the console. Her short frame exuded tension. "I've traced back the source of the chronon radiation."

"Where is it?" Brigid asked.

"Here." The woman pointed to a short flight of steps and a sealed door. "Thataway."

BRIGID AND KANE WALKED quickly down a broad hall lined on either side by niches inset into the walls. They strode past a niche containing two stone tablets engraved with ten sentences in Aramaic. Another niche contained a litter of ancient weaponry, swords, maces and battered shields. One shield bore likenesses of crouching lions.

Niche after niche was filled with objects more incredible than that which preceded it. Skulls, machines, even something that looked like a sheep's fleece dusted with gold, filled the compartments. They were a gathering of relics from fact, fable and even fantasy.

Up ahead a shimmering radiance drove away the shadows, like rays of sunlight as viewed through thick cloud cover. The passageway terminated at a railed gallery encircling and overlooking a thirty-foot-diameter, metal-walled shaft. The cavity was barely fifteen feet deep, but a borealis-like glow exuded from the walls in waves.

At first all they saw was the dancing veil of amber light. They felt subtle energies tingling their flesh, like a weak static-electricity discharge. Kane and Brigid looked through the pulsing glow, stared past it, focusing their eyes on the shapes that lay beyond the stasis field.

Down below, within a recessed niche behind the glimmer, they saw a man in a starched blue uniform with a yellow neckerchief and gauntlets. On the crown of his broad-brimmed blue hat they could just make out an insignia patch depicting a pair of crossed sabers. Although he was as immobile as a mannequin, he clutched at one of three arrows jutting from his torso. His right arm was bent at the elbow, his index finger crooked around empty air.

There were other figures frozen behind the stasis screen. They saw a bearded man wearing a dented metal breastplate and steel casque from the days of the conquistadors, and a slouching, heavy-jawed brute wearing only a pelt of shaggy hide.

Two large creatures crouched motionless in the shadows cloaking the far side of the chamber. Reptilian monsters, their crocodilian heads did not move, nor did their massive scaled bodies stir. Huge, ribbed fins resembling sails rose from their backs. They were like fragments of dreams, snatched from the imagination and encased in amber.

"This is where the chronon radiation is being generated," Brigid said. "I don't know how, though."

"I don't even know what a chronon is," Kane replied. "I've heard you and Lakesh talk about them enough, but I never really understood it."

"Basically, a chronon is a fundamental unit of time…think of chronons as links, parts of temporal energy-event networks."

"Event networks?"

"Linked intervals of time that span two different events. If an open event has links to two events, which differ only in that one of the two has a chronon and the other does not, then both of the two links are annihilated."

"Ah." Kane nodded as if a mystery that had long vexed him had at last been solved.

Brigid smiled at him wryly. "You didn't understand any of that, did you?"

"Not really, but if you do, that's all that matters."

"I'm not really sure if I understand it, either. I was never certain of the process by which trawled subjects were brought here, to this stasis module. Obviously, there's a mat-trans system in operation. The trawled object is rematerialized here and held in a form of suspended animation."

"What about that ring-thing Grant reported? That's got to have something to do with it."

"It's apparently the secondary temporal conduit port, designed for payloads of a specific mass limit. I'd judge that the dilator delays transmission of the matter stream so the subjects are shunted there, out in the middle of the island.

"We know the mat-trans network always transmits an organic subject through a biofilter scan before materialization. I presume a similar failsafe protocol is in place with the dilator."

Kane rubbed his chin reflectively. "Yeah, if the dilator were functional, which it isn't."

Brigid nodded. "No, but it's become patently obvious that most if not all of the dilator's secondary and support systems are still operating. They engaged when sensors detected the conduit opening up. Since the conduit works in tandem with the dilator—and vice versa—when Crowley and the countess came through, the system skipped the failsafe step, and so they weren't scanned and their matter-streams redirected here to the holding chamber. But in preparation for a payload materialization, the stasis system is pumping out chronon radiation. That's what's interfering with the gateway, dampening the energy necessary to open a wormhole."

Kane narrowed his eyes, studying the shimmer of the stasis field. "Is there any way we can use this to our advantage?"

Brigid cocked her head quizzically. "In what way?"

"It stands to reason that the countess and her crew are saturated with chronon radiation, doesn't it?"

Brigid's eyes shone with a sudden inspiration. "You're absolutely right. Pairs of identical chronon links coming out of active temporal events are annihilated, even if temporal event A and temporal event B exist within a common context."

"Is that good for us," Kane inquired dryly, "or bad for them?"

Brigid had no opportunity to answer his question—her voice was drowned out by the muffled echoes of an explosion.

Chapter 32

Grant pushed everyone back into the thicket, away from the noise that sounded like the thudding of pistons in a powerful machine. Crowley hugged himself, coughing, eyes feverish. "What is happening?"

"Shut up," Philboyd whispered. "Nobody move, nobody talk, but more importantly, *don't move*."

The fronds of the close-growing trees parted, leaves rustled, twigs cracked and the group heard the squelching of soft ground beneath an enormous weight.

"Something wicked this way comes," Crowley said hoarsely.

A shattering, trumpeting cry pressed against their eardrums and Crowley slapped his hands to both sides of his head. Less than fifty yards from them, a Monstrodamii bounded into view, head swivelling on the neck like a gun turret, tongue flickering, nostrils flaring. The double rows of glittering fangs gave the saurian face the aspect of a grinning skull.

Brewster Philboyd shrank deeper into the foliage, heedless of the thorns pricking him. Grant recognized the scars crisscrossing the creature's scaled hide and he said very softly, "It's the runty one."

"He doesn't look runty to me," Edwards said, eyes wide in fear.

"He's smaller than the other one," Grant replied, "but he makes up for it by being real nasty."

"We've to get out of here," Crowley said. "How can such a monster exist?"

"If we start running," Philboyd said, "then we might as well just jump into the goddamn thing's mouth. Its vision is keyed to movement, but its sense of smell appears to be pretty good, too."

"It's hunting me," Grant stated. "Following my scent."

"How can you be sure of that?" Philboyd asked doubtfully.

Grant hesitated before answering. "I can't be certain, but it's no coincidence the damn thing shows up here. It's following some sort of trail and it has to be scent."

Suddenly Edwards tensed. He motioned everyone to be quiet. "I thought I felt something, like a tremor."

In the distance came a rumble like thunder.

"A storm coming?" Crowley asked, looking up into the limpid blue sky.

The rumble came again.

"That's not thunder," Grant declared grimly. "Explosions, grenades most likely."

He fixed Aleister Crowley with a piercing glare. "Those soldiers of yours have grenades?"

Crowley nodded, his face sheened with oily sweat. He covered his mouth and coughed.

"We're pretty close to the Cube," Grant went on. "And it's a fair guess it's under attack right now."

Eyes still fixed on the Monstrodamii, Edwards whispered, "All the more reason for us to get out of here."

"Assuming the Monstrodamii has been tracking me," Grant murmured, "I can draw them away. It won't think to look for anyone but me."

Edwards swallowed hard. "How do you know it will follow you? Dinosaurs are just dumb animals, right?"

Philboyd said softly, "Actually, the school of theory among late twentieth-century paleontologists was that dinosaurs, particularly the raptors, were a lot brighter than scholars gave them credit for."

Grant grunted impatiently and pushed Tshaya into Philboyd's arms. The little girl resisted, hanging on to Grant for a long moment.

"Take her," Grant said. "Don't move until the Monstrodamii leaves the area."

"You're going to let that devil lizard chase you?" Philboyd demanded in angry incredulity.

Grant handed Edwards his Copperhead. "I'd prefer an alternative, but there's no guarantee that the thing will get bored or hungry enough to leave on his own…at least not for a couple of hours. By then, Crowley's pals could occupy the Cube and slaughter everybody there."

Philboyd and Edwards considered Grant's words. They responded with terse nods. Philboyd thrust out his right hand and Grant shook it. "You'll make it," the scientist said, forcing a note of assurance into his voice. "You're superfucking resourceful."

"At this point," Grant replied sourly, "I'd settle for being superfucking fast."

As he turned toward the thicket, Tshaya groped for him and Grant's heart lurched in his chest. He took the child's hand in his, squeezed it gently, then slid into the foliage.

Grant stooped beneath the lianas interlacing the trees, noting that the air felt considerably hotter. The sun was finding its way through the thinning branches and fronds and he realized he was closer to the dead zone surrounding the Cube's perimeter than he had guessed initially. The back of his throat felt like dirt-covered sandpaper. He couldn't remember the last time he had taken a drink of anything and his thirst was intense.

The jungle abruptly dropped away as if the foliage met an invisible boundary. Beyond it spread a flat, sandy plain at least a quarter of a mile in diameter. Rising from the center of the barren zone loomed the black edifice of the Cube. Columns of smoke curled into the sky, rising from the walled perimeter. Even at such a distance, Grant saw breaches in the barrier.

Taking a deep breath, Grant strode across the thin, brown grassy and sandy soil. When he guessed he had walked a hundred or so yards, he stopped, raised his Sin Eater over his head and fired three shots, the cracking reports reverberating over the treeline.

He waited. When he heard the bellow, he suffered one fierce, almost paralyzing instant of terror. The foliage shuddered into wild, convulsing rustling, overlaid with a series of pounding thuds.

Grant whirled and ran, feeling the ground begin to tremble underfoot. Hearing a snarl from behind him, he risked a quick, over-the-shoulder glance. Bent over so that its upper body was parallel to the ground, its legs a blurred image of scaled flesh, muscle and talon, the Monstrodamii looked like a fanged missile launched on its roaring trajectory by fury and the desire to kill. Clods of dirt, torn up by the clawed feet, flew in all directions.

Grant's own feet churned up the sand as he ran toward the Cube with a steady pace and long, distance-eating strides. His throat constricted with a tightness not born of thirst. The pain of a stitch stabbed along his left side, the muscles of his legs felt as if they were caught in a vise, and his vision was shot through with gray specks.

Over the rasp and gasp of his own labored breathing, Grant heard the thudding feet of the Daspletosaurus behind him, and a bawl of anger. The skin between his shoulder blades crawled in anticipation of one of the creature's long hind-talons flaying his flesh open to bare the spine. He felt like a fox being chased by a hound. If he had the time to dig a hole, he would have crawled into it.

The snarling of the carnosaur grew louder and more ferocious behind him. He was half-convinced he felt the monster's breath scalding the back of his neck. Grant was growing dizzy with the exertion of the run. Every time his feet smacked down against the sere earth and sparse grass, bursts of pain shot up into his skull and blurred his vision.

He breathed in huge, noisy gulps as he closed the distance between himself and the wall. Altering direction, he headed toward the nearest breach. Flames smoldered at the jagged edges and on the other side of the wall he glimpsed a number of black-helmeted bodies sprawled on the ground.

He realized that even if he made it to the gap, he would have to slow down in order to get through it, so he briefly considered and rejected the notion of using the Sin Eater still clutched in his right hand. The time required to turn and aim for a vital organ would be too long. Even if he managed to inflict a mortal wound, the momentum of the charging creature would still trample him into the ground.

The whole thought process took place in Grant's

mind in seconds while he sprinted onward. He reached the tumble of debris scattered around the breach and scrambled over it, his feet slipping. He banged his elbows and knees, but struggled through.

Eyes stinging from the smoke, he looked toward the Cube and saw that the door was missing completely from the frame. He glanced behind him just as the head of the snorting Monstrodamii thrust its head between the edges of the wall breach, the maw snapping open and shut. Its serpentine eyes gleamed with blood lust.

Grant started running again, directly toward the open door. A plan sprang full-blown into his mind, a plan very desperate and very ridiculous because it was such a long shot. Hearing the crash of the Monstrodamii bulling its body through the wall, Grant decided to trust his instincts and go ahead—mainly because he had no choice.

Chapter 33

Kane fired two rounds at the Black Sun trooper, pounding dents in the wall next to his head. The helmeted man pulled back out of sight. At the same time, Brigid Baptiste slapped a fresh magazine into her Copperhead, braced it against her hip and fired a short burst down the catwalk. Answering fire erupted from the smoke-shrouded doorway.

Only moments before the door leading into the control center had been blown askew, but a combination of samurai and Cube personnel prevented the soldiers from storming through. Shizuka placed a subgun's stock against her shoulder, opening up with a full-auto barrage. She ignored the bullets thudding through the air around her. A helmeted invader showed himself, a Schmeisser blazing in his right hand, an autopistol in his left.

The Copperhead's line of steel-jacketed death tore into the man's head, ripping chunks out of his masked face, shattering his goggles. Even as he fell, another soldier appeared behind him and then another.

Without hesitation, Brigid squeezed the trigger of her own subgun. The stream of 9 mm subsonic rounds caught the man in his chest, knocking him back into the corridor.

One of Shizuka's samurai suddenly stutter-stepped as a round cored into his belly, but he remained standing, bellowing in pain and rage, dropping his gun and drawing his *katana*. Another bullet punched a hole directly above his left eyebrow. He reeled backward.

Countess Paula von Schiksel shouted strident orders. The invaders surged out onto the catwalk, but they were hampered by the narrowness of the doorway. Only two of them could squeeze out at a time, but they fired their weapons in a wild frenzy as they did so. Bullets crashed and ricocheted all around the doorway leading into the center.

Several soldiers directed their fire upward, toward the big round light fixtures affixed to the high ceiling. One of them shattered with a sputter and shower of sparks and went out, plunging the area into semidarkness.

Kane held his Sin Eater in a two-fisted grip, left hand cupping the right, squeezing the trigger stud and unleashing 3-round bursts. Brigid and Shizuka stood on either side of him, shoulder-to-shoulder, firing with their own weapons. The triple full-auto cannonade hammered into the front line of the Black Sun troopers, knocking them off their feet.

Brigid picked off two men, placing shots through their bellies. They flailed and plummeted over the railing, plunging down to the vanadium floor twenty feet below. Other soldiers got their legs tangled with those casualties and dropped flat, firing as they did so.

Shizuka continued firing, keeping the trigger pressed down, not relaxing the pressure until the magazine cycled dry. A small object flew through the smoke, turning end over end. It clanged against the metal plates of the catwalk.

Kane had barely enough time to shout "Down!" before the grenade detonated with an eardrum-piercing bang and an eruption of dazzling white light.

Although the grenade had fallen short, the concussion still shook the control room and sent slivers of metal in all directions. A cloud of smoke hung in the air between the control center and the far end of the catwalk, like a veil of soiled chiffon. A barrage of gunfire erupted from the Black Sun troopers, tearing through the haze.

The fusillade was not aimed at anyone in particular, but meant only to prevent any of the Cube's personnel from organizing a concerted counterassault. Kane, Shizuka and Brigid ducked back inside. They could barely see the flames wreathing the stuttering muzzles through the smoke as bullets peppered the walls and the desks behind them and ricocheted off metal.

A spray of bullets tore gouges in the surface of a desk very close to Kane, splinters stinging his backside. He jumped, biting back swear words. Brigid looked toward him with raised eyebrows and smiled crookedly.

"How much longer do we have to do this?" she asked.

"Until the Scarlet Queen is too angry to think straight," Kane retorted, firing another burst down the catwalk. "I don't want her getting wise and calling a retreat at the last second."

The rounds fired by the Black Sun troopers smashed into the computer stations, chips of plastic and shards of glass flying in all directions. Slugs bounced from the walls, beating a drum roll on the alloy sheathing.

The countess began another shrieking tirade in German, followed by a grenade flying toward them, spinning end over end. It landed just before the threshold. Everyone in the area wheeled away. A giant fist punched Kane in the small of the back, and a storm of flame and smoke swirled around him, accompanied by a painfully loud blast of sound.

A battering ram of hot, almost solid air sent him cartwheeling over the top of a desk and he slammed down hard on the floor. Dizzy, rib cage throbbing, Kane fought his way to his feet. Brigid came to his side, helping to steady him.

"I think the countess is now officially too angry to think straight," Brigid announced, wiping at the blood trickling from a cut on her right cheek.

"Good," he croaked. "We have her just where she wants us."

Raising his voice, he shouted hoarsely, "Everybody fall back! Fall back!"

The defenders began a swift retreat to the far side of the control center, firing sporadically through the doorway toward the catwalk. A quartet of Black Sun troopers came through the door in a head-on rush, Schmeissers rattling in unison, the flaming bores sweeping in left-to-right arcs.

The personnel took refuge in adjacent offices, while Brigid, Kane and Shizuka backed away to the mat-trans unit, stepping into it but keeping the heavy door partially ajar. Bullets splatted harmlessly against the armaglass.

Turning to Nguyen, who had joined the wounded within the chamber, Kane extended a hand. Wordlessly, she placed a RG-34 grenade into it. He unpinned it and lobbed the little canister with an underhanded toss toward the Black Sun troopers, then ducked back behind the impenetrable cover of the armaglass.

The soldiers dived for cover, but only a few of them were quick enough to get out of range of the explosive charge and the effect radius of the shrapnel. The grenade detonated with a brutal thunderclap. A hell-flower bloomed, petals of flame curving and spreading outward. Spewing from the end of every petal was a rain of shrapnel, ripping into bodies, walls, equipment. Fragments rattled violently against the armaglass walls of the mat-trans, ricocheting way. The rolling echoes of the explosion faded, punctuated by the furious screaming of the countess.

Kane eased out of the chamber, squinting through the haze of eye-stinging, throat-closing smoke. He stroked a single shot from his Sin Eater, saw a wounded trooper jerk, lurch and fall.

Brigid joined him, subgun at her shoulder. "The countess is still hanging back."

"I'm not too worried about her," Kane replied. "It's the troopers. We don't know how many she has. I hope your chronon-radiation-temporal-event theory is right."

"It's a theory," she said curtly. "And there's only one way to test it."

"Yeah," he drawled, stepping farther into the room. "So let's do that very thing."

He triggered his Sin Eater, bullets pounding through a black coverall he glimpsed through the smoke. The trooper vaulted backward, blood spurting from three holes neatly grouped over his heart.

The floor was awash with looping liquid ribbons of vermilion. Five Black Sun troopers sprawled across it, coveralls wet with fluids, the flesh beneath flayed to the bone by shrapnel.

Hefting her Copperhead, Brigid sidestepped toward the short flight of stairs leading to the stasis module. She exchanged a quick, grim nod with Shizuka, who double-fisted her *katana*. She intended to stand guard over the wounded people within the mattrans unit.

A quintet of troopers raced through the doorway, firing in the direction of Brigid and Kane, their weapons chattering, muzzles flashing with little twinkles of dancing flame. Behind them on the catwalk stood Countess Paula von Schiksel, shrieking and striking the soldiers with her quirt.

Racing to the foot of the stairs, Brigid framed a trooper in her sights and fired a two-second burst that opened up his chest, propelling him backward in a crimson mist. Then she and Kane heeled around and bounded up the risers. Shouldering open the door, Kane cast a quick glance behind him to make sure the full complement of Black Sun troopers were in full pursuit.

As he and Brigid jogged side-by-side down the corridor, he panted, "So far so good."

"You realize that if my theory is wrong," she said breathlessly, "then we'll be trapped in the module."

He had no breath to reply. The two people sprinted down the passageway, not turning even when they heard the tramp of multiple boots on the floor. They ran past the niches containing the artifacts trawled from past

ages, hoping the troopers were too single-mindedly intent on killing them to be distracted by the treasures.

When they reached the stasis module gallery, Brigid
and Kane darted to opposite sides of the broad doorway,
trying to soften the harshness of their respiration. The
first three Black Sun troopers rushed onto the railed gallery and stumbled to clumsy halts, staring around
through their goggles in confusion.

For the briefest fragment of an instant, a blue dazzle
flashed from the amber stasis field like a blade of light.
It stabbed through the chamber. Brigid and Kane heard
a faint crackle and the three soldiers vanished.

A ripple of blue-white force spread out from the
module in a flat circle of energy that bisected the room,
flowing upward and outward as ripples in a body of
water. The ripples blazed with intolerable glares, sparks
spattering. Kane and Brigid shielded their eyes from the
flares that carpeted the floor of the corridor with burst
after burst of pale energy.

They heard no outcries, no thuds of falling bodies or
clatter of dropped weapons, only faint, repeated crack-
les and sizzles, then even those sounds faded away. A
sharp odor of ozone spread upon the air.

Cautiously, Kane removed his hands from his eyes
and peered around the edge of the door frame. He saw
only eddies of white smoke and scorch marks on the
floor in the shape of boot soles. Man-sized and -shaped

outlines were etched into the walls, black silhouettes of men, as if the bodies of the troopers had been flattened and merged with the alloy.

It took Kane two attempts before he was able to say, "Temporal event A annihilating temporal event B... pretty novel way of killing your enemies."

Brigid stepped out into the corridor, eyes flicking back and forth. "They may not be dead at all."

"After all that trouble," Kane snapped, "they had better be."

"The chronon radiation blowback might have just blasted them back to their own time period. The temporal events canceled each other out."

A line of confusion appeared between Kane's eyes. "So this never happened?"

Brigid shrugged, removing the magazine from her Copperhead and checking the remaining rounds. "Let's go find out."

THE SALIVA-WET FANGS crashed shut within inches of Grant's heels as he shoulder rolled through the door and over the slick floor of the lobby. Dragging himself by his elbows, he scrambled away from the snout of the Monstrodamii.

The Daspletosaurus had managed to wedge its entire head through the doorway. It squeezed the upper part of its body through, snapping viciously at the air, growling and snarling. Its small arms strained to reach him, talon-tipped fingers twitching.

Powered by its massively muscled hind legs, the Monstrodamii pushed more of its body through the frame. A network of cracks spread through the wall, pieces of plaster popping loose.

Grant climbed to his feet, raised his Sin Eater and took careful aim, bracing his feet wide apart. He squeezed the trigger and the bullet struck the carnosaur in the right eye. The glaring orb disappeared in a splash of gelid red. The Monstrodamii roared deafeningly, lunging forward, pushing most of its body into the lobby. The wide hips and pelvic girdle caught in the frame.

Taking aim again, Grant began to depress the firing stud of his pistol. Then a heavy weight collided with him from behind, knocking him off balance. He staggered forward, trying to recover his footing.

He caught only a glimpse of a blond woman in a formfitting scarlet tunic stumbling across the floor, arms windmilling, flailing at the air with a riding crop.

When she caught sight of the Monstrodamii she had time to scream once, then the jaws of the creature closed over her head. Her legs kicked in a futile spasm and she slapped weakly at the carnosaur's snout with the quirt. Then the fangs sheared through flesh, crunched through bone and the woman's headless body flopped to the floor.

Grant backed away as the Monstrodamii opened its jaws and allowed the blond-haired head to thud to the floor, where it rolled like an awkward ball. He lifted his Sin Eater again, but knew he would not be able to inflict lethal wounds before the saurian crashed through the wall.

The familiar rattle of a Copperhead drowned out the sound of the Monstrodamii's snarls. The beast jerked as steel-jacketed slugs cut through its scales. Whirling, Grant saw Kane, Brigid and Shizuka march out of the passageway. The subgun at Brigid's shoulder hammered on full-auto.

Kane tossed a grenade at the Monstrodamii, and the giant saurian snapped at it as if it were a morsel of food. The head and upper body of the carnosaur disintegrated in a blast of smoke and red, wet flesh. Swearing, Grant ducked as blood and viscera splattered all around him.

As the echoes of the explosion faded, Grant walked over to his three friends. All of them looked weary, blood-streaked and disheveled. They stared fixedly at the corpses of the Monstrodamii and the woman.

Taking a deep breath, Grant pushed his Sin Eater back into its holster. Kane arched an eyebrow at him and asked, "Well, what have you been up to today?"

Epilogue

In the immediate aftermath of the attack, there was very little to do. A way to dispose of the corpses of the Monstrodamii and Countess Paula von Schiksel would come later.

Brewster Philboyd, Edwards, Aleister Crowley and Tshaya emerged from the jungle when the immediate crisis appeared over. After everyone had told their stories, Brigid cautioned that bringing the child into close proximity with the chronon stream, even as it depleted as it seemed now, might be dangerous to her.

Aleister Crowley, of course, was another matter entirely. Grant, Kane and Brigid escorted him to the stasis module, where he stared in wide-eyed awe at the amber shimmer.

"Your turn, Crowley," Kane said.

The man coughed and asked, "Why are you so sure it will work on me?"

Brigid smiled coldly. "The historical record shows Aleister Crowley dying of a respiratory infection in 1947. Therefore, it *must* work on you."

Crowley shrank away from the gallery. "It could kill me!"

Grant stared at him stonily. "And that's a problem for us why?"

"No," Crowley bleated, shaking his head. "I won't. There's nothing for me to—"

A hand pushed him into the shimmer of light and he could no longer speak. His head became a roaring maelstrom of agony that sucked him in, although he fought to hold on to the world around him.

Lights of a thousand colors and a thousand combinations of shapes swirled before his eyes. Then he looked out at the snowcapped mountains and inhaled the icy air. His chest hurt as if white-hot bands of iron were tightening around his lungs and he coughed, feeling the phlegm work its way up his throat. He shuddered, turned his head and spit into the snow.

Aleister Crowley waited for the end of his last day in the twentieth century. He hoped he would not live to see the sun set behind the Carpathians again.

TAKE 'EM FREE

2 action-packed novels plus a mystery bonus

NO RISK

NO OBLIGATION TO BUY